Caffeine Nights Publishing

COLD DEATH

The second novel in the

DS Hunter Kerr series.

Michael Fowler

Fiction aimed at the heart
and the head...

D1078509

Published by Caffeine Nights Publishing 2012

Copyright © Michael Fowler 2012

Michael Fowler has asserted his right under the Copyright, Designs and Patents
Act 1998 to be identified as the author of this work

Published in Great Britain by Caffeine Nights Publishing

www.caffeine-nights.com

British Library Cataloguing in Publication Data.

A CIP catalogue record for this book is available from the British Library

ISBN: 978-1-907565-28-1

PREFACE

Cold Death is the second novel featuring the central characters Detective Sergeant Hunter Kerr, and his working partner DC Grace Marshall.

MICHAEL FOWLER

Michael was born and grew up in the once industrial heartland of South Yorkshire and still lives there with his wife and two sons.

He served as a police officer for thirty-two years, both in uniform and in plain clothes, working in CID, Vice Squad and Drug Squad, and retired as an Inspector in charge of a busy CID Department in 2006.

Aside from writing, his other passion is painting and as a professional artist he has achieved numerous accolades. His work can be found in numerous galleries throughout the UK.

He is a member of the Crime Writers Association.

Michael can be contacted via his website at:
www.mjfowler.co.uk

Acknowledgements

My grateful thanks go out to my relations up in bonnie Scotland – John, June, Iain and Sharon - the Watson clan – who between them over the years have introduced me to all the places which feature in this story. Especially to Iain, who spent one evening cruising Glasgow city centre to find me, and then photograph, an ideal murder scene: God knows what he would have said if he had been stopped by the police.

Also to Inspector Dawn Watson, Strathclyde Police, who placed my characters in the right 'nicks' and who increased my policing knowledge as to the procedures back 'in her neck of the woods.'

To Stuart Sosnowski, Crime Scene Investigator Supervisor, South Yorkshire Police, for his technical expertise after I had 'transported' him to all of my crime scenes.

A special thank you to Margaret Ardron who read the original manuscript and pointed me in the right direction to make it stronger.

Finally, to Caffeine Nights Publishing for making this possible.

This is for Chris and Kyle.

'I've found in life you don't just teach your children, you learn from them too.'

Cold Death

PROLOGUE

Glasgow's East End, Scotland; November 1971

Winding down his window, and switching off the headlights of the black Mercedes, Iain Campbell swung the car into Fielden Street and straddled along the centre white lines for a few yards until his eyes adapted to the dimness. Then following the direction of the pointing finger of his front seat passenger he switched off its three litre, throaty, engine and coasted quietly towards the nearside kerb.

For a few seconds the three occupants of the Mercedes sat motionless, watching, and listening.

Deathly silence.

* * * * *

Staring out through the windscreen Billy Wallace's slate grey eyes darted from side to side scanning the high tenement buildings each side of the street. Billy knew the area well. He used to live here as a child; that was until his family went up in the world.

He couldn't help but notice how the area had deteriorated over the last few years. It now had the stigma of being one of the hardest, poorest places in Britain. Most of the people he had grown up with here had moved out, leaving behind the unfortunates who had fallen to the hands of the drug dealers and money lenders.

This was his turf.

Easing open the passenger door and gripping the frame, he used it as a springboard to launch himself upright onto the pavement, rocking for a second on the balls of his feet. Arching his back and pulling at the lapels of his signature black Crombie overcoat he uncoiled his six foot, four inch, muscular frame. Looking around he noticed that the old overhead street lights still hadn't been replaced and their dim glow resulted in more of the street being obscured than illuminated.

He knew that a lot of people had a fear of the dark, but he loved the dark, and this was perfect cover for what he had to do.

Billy flicked a comb of fingers through his crown of chestnut coloured collar length hair and surveyed the street again, searching for activity, narrowing his eyes to search within the shadows.

A light wind brushed around dead leaves cluttering the gutter. Other than that there was no other sound or movement along the road.

Good, he thought, he had a score to settle and he needed the element of surprise on his side.

He beckoned the back seat passenger to join him. Rab Geddes was his most trusted henchman, chosen for his pertinacity and penchant towards violence.

Billy stuck his head back into the warmth of the car's interior.

"Just keep the engine running Iain, we shouldn't be long," he whispered to the driver in his gravelly tones.

Using their hips Billy and Rab nudged closed the car's doors.

Somewhere nearby a dog started barking; its sudden bawl fracturing the stillness of the surroundings.

Setting off at a jog they dodged into one of the stairwell passages leading to the rear of the tenement blocks.

Billy screwed up his nose as he was greeted by the strong whiff of bleach and disinfectant, which was doing its best to disguise the stench of stale urine and animal faeces which had stained the bare cement floor.

Not stopping, he mounted the concrete steps two at a time with Rab matching his pace, and despite the rubber soles of their shoes, Billy couldn't help but notice that every footfall echoed in the stairwell.

At the first floor they slackened their pace and slunk back against the wall. Their dark overcoats helped them melt like phantoms into the shadows. They slipped onto the walkway. For a brief few seconds Billy checked his bearings, then he nudged Rab and they moved on. At number thirty-four Billy paused, signalling to Rab. Satisfying himself that he had the correct address he placed an ear to the panelling. He listened. Straightening, he looked around to ensure that there were no witnesses and then he stepped back two paces and launched himself. The flimsy lock was no match for Billy's fourteen stone of muscle and the door flew inwards smashing and bouncing against the interior wall.

The pair sprinted towards the well-lit room at the end of the corridor and were only a few yards from the doorway when a slim dark shape appeared as a silhouette in the opening.

Its scream of protest was silenced when Billy snapped out a fist and smacked the unknown individual square on the nose. There was a sickening crunch of bone and gristle as the slender form sank to the ground.

Morag McCredie lay motionless for several seconds.

Billy could see that she was straining to focus her vision through the film of tears that now covered her eyes. He listened to her moaning and saw her close her eyes for a split-second, squeezing her eyelids to force out the teardrops, before snapping them open again.

He took pleasure in watching as the colour drained from her face, smiling, guessing from her reaction that she now recognised him. He edged forward, leaning over her, pushing his face within inches of hers.

"Where's Davie, Morag" Billy growled.

"He's," she broke off, her voice trembling as she suppressed a sob.

"Nobody fucking rips me or my family off Morag. Davie knows what's coming to him." Billy moved within an inch of her face giving her his hardest stare then slowly delivered in his harshest tone "now - where - is - he?"

She craned her head away from his.

"He's not here," she managed to spit out, and then cupped a hand over her nose that had already swollen to twice its size. She pulled it away slowly staring at the bright red globules of blood dripping through her fingers.

"You've broken my fucking nose." She groaned in her broad Glaswegian accent.

"That's not all I'm going to break if you don't tell me where fucking Davie is," Billy menacingly snapped back. He reached down and grabbed a handful of her bottle blonde dyed hair and yanked hard, hoisting her upwards.

She swung up an arm to protect herself and a handful of hair ripped from her scalp. She yelped and bit her lip: Tears welled up again.

Billy fixed her with a penetrating, hate-filled stare. "I'm going to ask you one more time Morag. Where's Davie?"

She started to quiver and grabbed hold of a nearby armchair for support.

Billy snared his hands around her chin and jaw, seizing her in a vice-like grip. He dug his fingers into her skin until he was squeezing bone.

Morag let out a piercing scream and Billy raised a hand to silence her. In that same instant, in a defensive act, she shot out her hand and grabbed the handle of one of her kitchen knives lying on the nearby coffee table. In one swift movement she had snatched up the blade and lashed out. It slashed across Billy's cheek, opening up his flesh to the bone.

He released her immediately, stumbling backwards, slapping both hands over the gash. Blood was pouring from the wound, seeping through the gaps in his gloved hands and onto the front of his coat. Rab Geddes had spotted Morag's actions too late to stop the damage to Billy's face, but he reacted to prevent a second attempt, smashing his clenched fist into the side of her head. She reeled back against the armchair and flipped over it backwards.

Billy stared at the amount of blood staining his gloves. His face contorted taking on a demonic appearance. The pupils of his eyes became so dilated that they appeared almost black.

"You fucking bitch." He snarled. Kicking aside the armchair he towered above Morag, now sprawling in her own blood, a badly swelling face disguising once pretty features. She was groggy, trying to raise herself.

Billy reached into his Crombie, pulling the handgun from the waistband of his trousers. It became an extension of his hand as he aimed down at her.

Morag tried to swallow, her Adam's apple cavorting stubbornly. Her eyes pleaded, and instinctively she again swung up an arm to protect herself.

The bullet passed through her hand and into her right eye. She was dead even before her head smashed against the tiled hearth of the fireplace.

The reek from the cordite drifted quickly, catching the back of Billy's throat. It caused him to swallow hard, jerking his head backwards and it was then that he spotted movement to his left; a small shapeless form at the periphery of his vision. Immediately he spun around.

The sharpness of his turn caused Rab to follow and they caught sight of the petite form just outside the room.

Shuffling into the doorway was a young girl, dressed in pink striped pyjamas, plaited dark hair hanging over one shoulder. Under one arm she clutched a teddy bear to her chest and with other hand she rubbed at her sleepy eyes. She glanced at both of them with wide exploring eyes and then saw Morag lying prostrate in a growing pool of blood.

"Mummy," she whimpered.

Billy raised the gun again and fired off another shot. It smacked into the frontal lobe of the young girl's head, and instantaneously blood, brain and bone splattered the wallpaper behind her. She hit the ground almost the same time as her teddy bear.

A halo of blood crept slowly around the girl's head and Rab flashed a shocked glare at his boss.

"Jesus Christ Billy, she was just a kid."

Billy stared back, but it was as if his gaze was passing through Rab.

"She was a fucking witness," he mouthed brusquely. Then Billy dropped his eyes, spotting the stains on his overcoat deposited there from his wounded cheek. He tugged at the front of his Crombie, pulling the wide lapels in Rab's direction.

"Look what the bitch's done to my fucking coat," he growled. He raised the Smith and Wesson again, spun around and fired the remaining four rounds into Morag. Her body never moved. The first shot had taken her life. Billy continued clicking the trigger even after the gun had emptied and Rab had to grab hold of his forearm. He fixed Billy's wild stare.

"We need to get out of here Billy, before someone calls the cops," he urged.

Slotting the handgun back into the waistband Billy surveyed the carnage around him. Bending down he raised the hem of Morag's dress and wiped the blood from his leather gloves.

"We need to set fire to the place Rab," he paused for breath, getting back his composure. "Get rid of any incriminating evidence. Know what I mean?" he finished, easing himself back up.

Rab nodded and began scanning the room for suitable material to ignite.

* * * * *

Iain Campbell fidgeted in his seat. He had the driver's window down and was looking nervously around - and not for the first time. He had been like this ever since Billy and Rab had disappeared.

He brought up his watch closer to his face, picking out the position of the luminous hands on the dial and wondering how much longer they were going to be; they had already been gone ten minutes.

This had not been the job he had been asked to do. 'Look after my son's back!' that is what Billy's father had asked him to do and paid him for, but all he had done over the last three hours had been chauffeuring around these two thugs whilst they picked up their drug debts. He had already watched them give one guy a good kicking, and he knew from their conversation that they were chasing up another who owed Billy the best part of two hundred pounds.

They could stuff the job after tonight.

He scoured the streets again.

Suddenly he felt cold and yet he knew from the damp patches under his arms that he was sweating. Fight or flight! It had been a long time since he'd had these feelings. He felt sick.

He was just about to wind up the window when he heard a loud crack. He thought that it sounded like gunfire.

No it couldn't be!

He strained his ears. There was another! His heart leapt against his chest and he felt his stomach empty.

Four more shots followed in quick succession. He stiffened and clamped a firm hold on the steering wheel.

Less than a minute later both nearside doors were yanked open. It made Iain jump.

Billy threw himself into the front seat.

Iain saw that his face was covered in blood. Then he spotted the gun Billy was holding. Suddenly his head was in turmoil.

"Billy, your face." Iain could see that he had lost a lot of blood. Billy's shirt collar and the front of his coat were drenched and more was still oozing from a deep gash that snaked from the bridge of his nose and across his right cheek.

"Never mind that just get us the fuck out of here." He threw the gun into the footwell. "Come on, hurry the fuck up."

Iain Campbell, sharply engaged first gear and gunned the accelerator, spraying up loose road chippings beneath the spinning wheels, hurtling into the darkness, just as the front second floor window of Morag's flat exploded.

- ooOoo –

CHAPTER ONE

DAY ONE OF THE INVESTIGATION:
24th August 2008.
North Yorkshire:

Tentatively Hunter Kerr stepped towards the edge of the Cowbar cliff top. Only yards below seagulls screeched and swooped, their fleeting shapes silhouetted white against the village of Staithes below, which was still cloaked in early morning shadow. Glancing across the harbour he could see that the bright yellow sun was just beginning to appear above the grey rock face of the Nab opposite; an orange glow blurred the top of the hill.

Raising his digital camera he clicked off a couple of frames and then stepped back over the gorse to where his painting easel had been set up some twenty minutes beforehand. Screwing his steel blue eyes to slits he picked out the shapes in front of him and with brush in hand he began to mix the tones in the oil paint spread out over his palette. He knew from his many previous painting ventures to this tiny ancient fishing village that he would only have about another thirty minutes to capture the intensely bright first light punching its way through the cobbled streets and bouncing across the haphazard pantile roofs of the crop of old white-washed cottages, before the effect disappeared and the blueness of the day took over.

As he settled into his painting, occasionally looking out over the tranquil scene of old fisherman's cottages sloping towards to the beck that fed the North Sea, Hunter swore he could feel the stress and tension of the last few weeks easing from his body.

Scrubbing in the large blocks of colour onto his canvas board and feeling the breeze brushing across his unshaven face at that moment he realised how glad he was at having been persuaded by his wife Beth, to take time off this weekend to spend some rare quality time with her and their two sons: At the last moment they had asked his mum and dad to join them in their rented cottage. When they had left home the day before yesterday he had selfishly double-checked he had packed his painting gear because he very rarely got the opportunity to paint these days, what with juggling his career and the needs of his family.

When he had seen the weather forecast last night he knew that this morning would be an ideal opportunity to fire off a small oil sketch.

He had managed to sneak out at dawn without disturbing them and as he now worked his brushes across the stained canvas the vision of them all still tucked up in their beds, entered his head causing him to smile to himself.

He thought about work as well. He had left his team with a list of tasks, though he knew deep down they didn't need them; the squad were more than capable of finishing off the case they had just been working on so intensely over the past five weeks.

He had left his partner DC Grace Marshall in charge, and he could visualise her now, mothering the team in her own inimitable way; organising the clearing of the incident room: stacking the house-to-house documentation, categorising witness statement papers, sealing the hundreds of exhibits, and storing all the gory photographs into box files ready for the Coroner's Court inquest.

That last case had been the most intense and testing investigation he had ever been involved in. Not just since his appointment as Detective Sergeant into Barnwell Major Investigation Team but throughout his fourteen years as a detective.

When he had left the office two days ago, for this well earned break, they had just removed the forensic tent from the back of the serial killer's home after excavating the body of his fourth victim found in the garden.

The week previous to that the remains of two more of his teenage girl victims had been unearthed from shallow graves at an old colliery site.

They had known the names and ages of all of the girls who had suffered at his hands even before they had exhumed their remains; he had left behind such detailed accounts of every murder.

The killing spree of the now infamous 'Dearne Vally Demon,' as the press had so candidly dubbed him, had shocked them all and he knew would have lasting repercussions.

More so because so many revelations had come to light during the enquiry, some of which had not only involved colleagues, but unwittingly himself as well, and had caused him much personal angst over the last few weeks.

The phrase 'tangled web' came to mind as he fought once again to push the thoughts of the case out of his consciousness. He felt a chill shoot down his spine and shuddered.

Hunter returned his gaze to the view across the beck, spinning away from his daydream, noticing that the morning light had suddenly become less sharp over the landscape. He realised that in another ten minutes the artistic quality of the atmosphere would be gone. He returned to his sketch.

A few more brush strokes, and I'll call it a day and get back for breakfast.

Ten minutes later, setting down his brushes, he smoothed his hands into the base of his spine and eased himself upright, teasing the tension out from his vertebrae and stretching himself up to his full six-foot-one. He took another look at his subject, raising his camera to capture one last image to use as reference; to enable him to finish the painting when he got another suitable moment back home, and that was when he spotted his father leaning against the railings, overlooking the beach.

Dad's up early as well.

He clicked off a frame. As he did so he couldn't help but notice a fleeting movement to one side of the Cod and Lobster pub. He was sure he'd seen a figure dart into the shadows. He zoomed in his lens as far as it would go forcing the focus of the camera towards the side entrance of the pub where he had last seen motion.

He'd been right. There was someone, slinking against the wall, craning his head around, staring in the direction of his father. His policeman's sixth sense was telling him that something wasn't right. He snapped off another frame but the zoom was at its maximum and the image was blurred. He could just make out it was a guy with a bald or shaven head who appeared to be both squat and stocky.

He returned his gaze back to his father, still leaning on the metal railings, one foot resting on the bottom bar, staring out across the harbour. He could tell from his relaxed posture that he was totally unaware of the man hiding behind the wall only ten yards away. Hunter dug out his mobile from his jeans pocket and flipped up the screen.

Damn, he cursed to himself, *no signal.* He'd forgotten, the times he had been here he had never been able to get a signal.

He moved further to the edge of the Cowbar deciding to shout, hoping his father would be able to hear, and then he saw his dad spin around; the bald headed man had emerged from the shadows and was striding purposefully in his direction. The stranger halted just feet away and thrust out a hand, jabbing a finger inches from his dad's face. Although Hunter couldn't hear their body language was telling him that there was some kind of altercation. He raised his camera again; shot off a succession of quick frames, not checking if the images were good or not. That was when he caught the quick movement of his father, slapping away the prodding hand and slamming his palm into the chest of the uninvited guest. He dumped the man onto his backside and then leaned over him, spearing his own finger, only a foot from the man's face. Without doubt Hunter could see there was a frank exchange of words, and then as quickly as it started it was all over. His father spun back around and marched off in the direction of their rented cottage.

The bald headed man picked himself up and dusted down his knees, reached into his pocket and took out his mobile phone. Seconds later in obvious disgust he pushed it away again.

"He can't get a signal either," Hunter muttered to himself.

Then as the man turned Hunter raised his camera again, quickly adjusted the zoom and rattled off several more frames, just before the stranger disappeared from view.

Hands on hips, poised at the edge of the cliff, Hunter spent several more minutes scouring the cobbled High Street, straining his eyes into the narrow alleyways of the thrown together houses but he couldn't pick up the sight of either his father or the incomer.

I need to get back and make sure everything's OK.

With a sense of urgency he threw together his things.

* * * * *

Half-jogging, half-marching, breathing heavily, Hunter mounted the steep incline out of the old village and up towards the newer part of Staithes where their rented cottage was.

All the while he'd been keeping a watch for the bald headed man but the only people he had come across were the fishermen preparing their boats as he strode across the bridge overlooking the beck, and as he neared the top of the hill he could just make out his father approximately a hundred yards ahead. He was ambling along, hands thrust deep in pockets, as if nothing had happened.

Hunter took a deep breath and shouted him. His dad stopped, turned around and waited for him to catch up.

By the time Hunter had reached him he was gulping for air and beads of sweat were trickling from his hairline down the sides of his face, tickling his neck.

"I thought you were supposed to be fit son," his father said sarcastically in his strong Glaswegian accent, pointing to the glistening sweat on his son's brow.

Hunter set down his box easel and wiped his forehead with the back of his hand, flicking the residue onto the footpath.

"I am. It's that bloody hill, it's a killer." He took in several deep breaths. "I've been trying to catch you up to see what that was all about."

"What was all about?" replied his father, blandly.

"You know what I'm on about. Don't give me the all innocent. That argument you've just had with that bald-headed guy."

"That wasn't an argument. Just a case of mistaken identity. He thought I was someone else."

"You don't dump someone on their arse because of a case of mistaken identity."

His father's face flushed. "Leave it son, it's nothing to do with you."

"What do you mean it's nothing to do with me? My dad smacking someone is nothing to do with me? I think so."

His father held up a hand giving him the stop signal. "No you don't think so at all. That was my business down there. I said leave it and I mean leave it." He spun on his heels and marched away.

* * * * *

The mild August evening was giving way to a sheet of fine drizzle. It peppered the windscreen of Hunter's Audi, diminishing the view of the main road through Sleights village. Hunter flicked on the wipers and the blades swished across, clearing the screen. As he began the steep incline up towards Blue Bank he could already see that his father's car in front was almost at the top.

Hunter dropped down a gear, squeezed the accelerator and sped towards the steep summit.

Since they had set off from the cottage Hunter had been at odds with himself and Beth had sensed it, even checking to see if anything was wrong. He'd shrugged it off, telling her he was back to thinking about work. The fact was he couldn't get out of his mind the episode he had seen earlier involving his dad and the bald headed stranger. What had made it worse was that his father had initially lied to him about the matter and then dismissed him when he had tried to probe deeper. He'd tried to catch his attention for the most part of the day but his dad had deliberately avoided eye-contact.

Something was not right, but he couldn't think what. He thought he knew his father, but it felt recently as though he didn't know him at all. All these years and the only time he had seen him lose his temper was several weeks ago when his dad had come to his aid when he was getting a good hiding from three family members of someone he had just put into prison. In fact on that occasion he remembered having to drag his dad away before he did one of the guys some really serious injury such was the viciousness of his onslaught.

This recent incident had brought all that flashing back and was unsettling him again. He clutched the steering wheel tighter willing his Audi faster up the hill, and then upon cresting the brow of Blue Bank eased off and began the smooth journey on the long stretch of moorland road that passed through 'Heartbeat' country. Thirty yards in front it looked from the movement of nodding heads as though his parents were chatting happily. He wondered if his mum, like Beth, had sensed something was not quite right.

Because his concentration had been elsewhere he never saw the silver BMW until it shot past, so close that it rocked his car, almost catching the wing mirror.

For a split-second he lost control of the car, veering towards the grass verge, which he quickly corrected by braking sharply and swinging back into a straight line.

"The bloody idiot!" Hunter shouted and then halted his tirade, remembering Jonathan and Daniel, his two young sons, in the back.

He saw that the recklessly speeding BMW appeared to be almost taking on a collision course towards the rear of his father's car. He dropped into third gear and put down his foot, squeezing the accelerator further, trying to make ground so that he could take note of the car's registration number.

Hunter watched the BMW swing onto the opposite carriageway and pull alongside his father and mother's car and it was at that moment that he realised the silver car was not going to overtake. The BMW snaked quickly smashing its front end against the side of his parent's car.

Their brake lights flashed on and Hunter could see blue smoke burning from beneath the wheels as the tyres protested on the wet glistening road. Chippings flew up from the surface as their car lurched sideways and began to bounce crab-like. Then it hit the damp moorland grasses at the road edge, throwing up huge tufts, before sliding out of control. Their car bounced into a ditch, then back out, and flipped over into an uncontrollable spin, roof and chassis rebounding into the moorland heather, only finally coming to a halt when it thumped into a peat bog.

Hunter stamped the brake pedal and the Audi slewed sideways onto the grassed verge.

He flung open his door ready for the sprint towards his parent's crashed car. Suddenly it felt as everything had gone into slow motion.

He was conscious of Beth fishing around in her handbag trying to find her mobile, whilst on the back seat he caught a quick glimpse of the boys, straining against their seat belts, both pale-faced and displaying looks of horror. Switching his gaze he saw fifty yards ahead the BMW's brake-lights flash on and it skewed to a halt.

He stopped mid-pace as the driver's door flew open.

Hunter heaved a sigh of relief. He had initially thought this was going to be a hit-and-run; that this had been a deliberate act. Now that the car had stopped he guessed it was just bad driving and the driver was coming to help.

That was until he recognised the man who emerged. It was the bald headed man he had seen earlier back in Staithes arguing with his father.

The man took a long hard stare at Hunter, and then with outstretched hand he reached across the roof of the car and pointed towards his parents upturned car. He fashioned two fingers together and cocked his thumb into a makeshift pistol, and then jolting his hand he mimicked a firing action. He never took his eyes off Hunter, fixing him with a malicious grin before mouthing the words 'POW!'

Then the bald headed man was leaping back into the car, and it squealed away throwing up a film of spray in its wake.

Hunter just managed to clock the car's registration before it disappeared over the brow.

Snatching his thoughts back into focus he shouted to Beth to dial 999 and then he sprinted across the front of his Audi and bounded across the moorland heather to his parents crashed vehicle, a plume of steam now masking its predicament.

* * * * *

Barnwell:

'I just know this is going to be cold' Katie Williamson said to herself as she stepped ungainly into the murky waters of Barnwell lake, disturbing the stillness of its surface with her

26

finned feet as she sought out the security of the shale bottom; and she just knew that once she became fully submerged it would be even colder. From a previous dive here she knew that in a few minutes the pain inside her head was going to be as intense and sharp as if she had just eaten chilled ice cream.

"I'll be only a couple of feet behind you - remember the signals?" her dive instructor and buddy Craig Palmer said.

Katie watched her dive-buddies eyes roaming around her body, though she knew he wasn't eyeing her up – he was double-checking that all her diving equipment was in place.

Katie formed an 'O' shape with her thumb and forefinger. She could feel the resistance in the neoprene gloves as she forced them together.

"Good. And if you need to come up quickly?"

She stuck a thumb in the air and jabbed it skywards several times.

"Okay, final checks. This is your last dive and then we can sign your logbook up for your first qualification. Looking forward to it?"

"In these freezing waters, you're joking"

She watched a smile crease her instructor's face.

"You are such a wimp. Twenty minutes and the ordeal will all be over and this time next year you'll be able to take a novice out yourself. Now check your air pressure and that your hoses are not tangled."

Katie slotted the mouthpiece of her breathing regulator into her mouth, adjusting it slightly so that it fitted snugly between her teeth and lips. She purged the demand valve and a blast of concentrated air shot into her mouth, plumping out her cheeks. She swallowed, tasting the freshness and purity of the compressed air and formed another 'O' with her fingers.

"Okay, mask on and let's make our way to the centre of the lake."

Katie lifted her bright pink facemask over her eyes, waited a second to ensure that it wasn't going to fog over and then began to walk penguin-fashion over the loose stones and moss, edging slowly into the waters.

As she reached chest height she felt her stab jacket taking over her buoyancy, keeping her afloat and enabling her to flip her finned feet and push towards the middle of the lake. She could hear Craig splashing closely behind. After five minutes swimming Katie felt a tap on her shoulder.

"Okay this is it. Let the air out of your jacket and let's drop to the bottom. We're going to swing left and circle the lake, okay?"

She reached above the water and formed another 'O' with her gloved hand and then began slowly releasing the air out of her life jacket, feeling herself sink, aided by additional lead weights fastened around her waist. From her last dive she knew that it wouldn't be long before she hit bottom; the depth was only five metres.

Katie felt the slippery fronds of the reeds brush against her as she evened herself out and began sweeping through the gloomy depths, trying to acclimatise herself to her surroundings, pushing her hands forward to feel because it was so hard to see. Kicking hard she began her turn heading left. Her breathing was becoming less rapid and she was actually surprised that the water wasn't as cold as she had expected.

This is not going to be too bad after all, she said to herself, dragging one hand along the silt bottom and beginning to take in her immediate surroundings now that her eyes had adjusted in the dimness.

Katie felt a sudden tap on her calf and guessed Craig wanted her to take in another turn. She pulled her wrist towards her face and checked her watch. They had been diving for just over ten minutes.

Half way there already, time has flown.

With a kick she propelled herself left again and then adjusted her movement with a graceful flip of fins.

Then her knee hit something, taking her by surprise. Something that was soft and pliable. Something that cushioned her blow and which she knew was alien to the environment. Katie stopped in her tracks almost falling onto the object. She spun around and began seeking for her dive-buddies attention. She focussed on his facemask, waving a hand in front of him and then began jabbing her thumb downwards.

Katie dropped to her knees almost astride the entity and began rubbing her gloved hand over it. Enmeshed in the weeds she could make out the pattern of what appeared to be a rolled up carpet. Puzzled by this bundle she felt for an edge to unfurl, and finding a corner she tugged hard. For a split-second her mind wouldn't take in what was peeking out from one end of the rug. Then it hit her. The bloated green grey distorted blob had a face – a human face. Katie realised she was looking at a dead body. Gasping she almost released her regulator mouth-piece and in that same instance the opening of her mouth allowed water to rush in, hitting the back of her throat, causing her to gag. There was no time to signal to her dive-buddy. Blind panic took over and Katie kicked frantically towards the surface.

* * * * *

Ever increasing their pace, Major Investigation Team Detective's, Grace Marshall and Mike Sampson scrunched along the limestone footpath towards the entrance of Barnwell Country Park.

Grace had gone less than a hundred yards from where they had parked their unmarked car when her breathing became laboured and she began to feel uncomfortable. The warm effects of the sun, beating down through a cloudless blue sky were making her hot and sticky. She slackened her pace, unbuttoned her jacket and slipped off the elastic scrunchy from around her wrist and corralled her tight black, blonde highlighted, corkscrew curls back from the sides of her face and fastened them into a tidy bunch.

That was better.

Threading her way between the laurel bushes, which lined the route towards the lake, Graces thoughts momentarily drifted. Being here brought back happy memories; all those times of strolling around the lakeside path and then munching through a homemade picnic and watching the world go by with her two daughters and husband. Times she still treasured in her memory especially now that the girls were growing up fast and no longer wanted to do those things.

The two detectives nodded their greetings to the uniformed male officer who had been given the job of guarding the entranceway to the crime scene. He returned their acknowledgement and scribbled down their arrival on his log. Then ducking beneath the blue and white police tape and pushing through another set of laurel bushes Grace and Mike finally found themselves' staring out over a very busy, yet organised setting.

Three Scenes of Crime Officers were already evident, dressed in their white forensic suits. Two were in the process of cordoning off a small wooden jetty which led out into the lake whilst another was snapping off a number of photographs; adjusting his tripod as he took in the panorama. Grace recognised the cameraman as Duncan Wroe the Force's very experienced civilian SOCO manager.

Just a few feet from the edge of the quay two wet suited police frogman controlled their rubber dinghy whilst another was just slipping beneath the water; a burst of air bubbles from his breathing apparatus frothed the surface signifying his descent. Grace guessed that directly beneath there was where the body had been discovered and the Underwater Search Unit was now trying to haul it up safely from its silted grave.

At the lake's edge a uniform sergeant was briefing her team instructing them before they carried out an initial search of the area. By the picnic benches next to the country park reception centre Grace spotted two other divers. The female of the two was seated on one of the benches doubled-up, her fair-haired head being supported in her hands. The male, with tanned complexion and short crew cut hair, stood over her, resting a hand on her shoulder. From the earlier phone call Grace had picked up back at the office just over an hour ago she guessed that these were the two divers who had found the corpse. She reached inside her jacket, excavated her warrant card and slipped it into her breast pocket.

Let them know girl that you're in charge.

Hunter had handed her the mantle of Acting Sergeant whilst he was away and she was going to show she could handle it. She took in a deep breath at the same time taking in all the details of the scene; determining inside her head who was doing what and what remained to be done. Gathering her thoughts, slowly she exhaled and then turned to Mike. "I'm guessing those two are the ones who've found the body," she said pointing in the direction of the man and woman occupying the benches. "You go and have a word with them and I'll go and have a word with uniform and also see what SOCO have got for us."

Grace watched Mike Sampson scrutinising the slim, faired haired girl, now kneading her eyes.

"Now that's how I like my women – dressed head to toe in black rubber." He winked at Grace

"Mike!" Grace fixed him with her warm burnt umber eyes.

"What?"

"What is it with you men? A bloody murder scene and you're still thinking of sex."

"That's just my way of dealing with a crisis ma'am," he quipped mockingly and cracked a grin.

"Go on, bugger off and see what they have to say."

Mike spun on his heels tugging the sleeves of his oversized jacket away from his pudgy fingers.

She knew it was a perpetual habit of his. From her time working with him she had become aware that Mike had bought his jackets several sizes larger than his chest measurement, in order to fit over his barrel shaped paunch. This meant that the sleeves were longer and therefore partly covered his hands.

"Oh, and Mike," she shouted towards him.

He spun around.

"Don't start playing pocket billiards whilst you're interviewing her."

"I shall ensure my afflictions are kept under control at all times Acting Sergeant Marshall," he retorted in an exaggerated tone, then set off towards the witnesses.

Grace smiled to herself. Despite Mike being the joker in the pack she knew that when he was given a task he always approached it as the consummate professional.

By the time Grace had reached Duncan Wroe, the SOCO manager had removed his camera from its tripod and was manually aiming its wide lens in the direction of the frogmen.

There was still no sign of the body being brought to the surface.

"What have you got for me Duncan?" asked Grace striding towards him.

The SOCO manager spun around, taking his eyes away from the viewfinder. "Oh hi Grace, I saw you arrive but I was busy."

With his sharp features, unruly hair and regular unshaven face, Duncan Wroe's outward image depicted anything but the sharp minded and experienced forensic specialist that he was. Fortunately for Grace any prejudices she had about his appearance had been blown away early doors in her career. He had been called out to the scene of her first rape case; a teenage girl attacked whilst out walking her dog. A good quarter of a mile from the scene Duncan had found some trainer marks amongst bushes and a discarded cigarette butt and acting on a hunch had recovered them. Within a week they had DNA of the perpetrator, and whilst carrying out a search of the young man's home Duncan had discovered his trainers secreted amongst the rubbish of a wheelie bin. It transpired the rapist had carried out two other similar crimes, and at court he was given a life sentence. Since then she had worked with him on many cases and knew that his technical craft and knowledge of forensics was second to none. Such was his ability and standing that he was one of the very few civilian scenes of crimes officer's in the country to be promoted to the position of manager; most supervisors being police officers of rank.

Grace nodded towards the lake. She watched air bubbles rising to the surface, plopping and then rippling away. "No sign of the body being brought up yet?"

"Apparently it's in a bit of a mess. I think they're trying to secure it tightly so it doesn't lose any of its limbs when they bring it up."

"What do we know then Duncan?"

"Well we don't know anything about the body yet. I've been told that it's bound inside a carpet or rug of some kind so I don't think we'll be able to get anything at all even when it's brought to the surface. We don't know how long it's been in the water so we'll need to get it into a body bag and down to the mortuary as soon as possible because once its exposed to the air there will be a rapid acceleration to the decomposition."

"Have you got anything in the forensics line?"

"Too early yet, Grace. What I can say is that I'm pretty confident the body was thrown off the edge of the jetty there," he replied, pointing to the wooden platform leading from the shale banking out into the lake. "You can see where the Search Units dinghy is, well that's roughly above where the body is. That's about six feet from the edge of the jetty and that's why I say thrown. Because of that I would say at least two people were involved in dumping it."

Grace returned a puzzled look. "Two?"

"Yep two – at least. If one person had carried that body they would only have been able to drop it or roll it off the edge. It's virtually impossible for one person to sling a dead weight body any distance. With two people they would have been able to get enough swing to heave it that far into the water." He tapped his nose. "Simple when you've dealt with as many bodies as I have." A smile crept across his wizened features.

"Couldn't they have used a boat?"

"And only gone out a few feet?" He dismissed her suggestion with a curt nod. "No it was thrown, trust me." He paused and continued, "Because the body's wrapped inside a carpet or rug of some type I'm running on the assumption that the person was more than likely killed elsewhere and bought here to be dumped. Nevertheless we're taping off the jetty and checking it for bloodstains, hairs and fibres. Then we'll be searching it for footwear marks. I'm also setting up a search grid and looking for tyre tracks. The underwater search unit will be bringing the body up to another landing stage and then I'll body bag it to be transported to the morgue. I understand Miss Marple is already making her way there and will be performing the post mortem later this afternoon."

Grace knew that he was referring to the forensic pathologist Professor Lizzie McCormack, who had acquired her nickname not only because of her ability to catch killers through her forensic skills but also because of her uncanny likeness to the actress Geraldine McEwan.

She thanked Duncan with a nod, smile and wave of her hand and spun back in the direction of Mike Sampson. She could see he was still heavily engaged in conversation with the two divers. As she was running through everything again inside her head, marrying what the homicide investigation manual recommended together with her experience of attending murder scenes, her mobile rang. She delved into her jacket pocket and pulled it out. The screen displayed the name and mobile number of her work partner – Sergeant Hunter Kerr. She knew that Hunter was somewhere up in the Whitby area in a rented cottage with his family.

I bet someone back in the office has rung him and told him about this and now he's phoning to check up that I can cope.

And even though she knew he would be enquiring in that nice, caring and unobtrusive way of his nevertheless it was still checking on her. She needed to do this without someone holding her hand – to prove to herself more than anything that she was capable.

"Well Sergeant Kerr I am coping very well thank you," she muttered beneath her breath. "And I don't need you checking up on me."

As she was about to disconnect the call she heard a shout come from the centre of the lake. She spun around just in time to see the police frogman break the surface raising a hand in the air. It looked as though they were about to bring the body up.

Her phone stopped in mid-tone; Hunter would be transferred across to her voicemail. She switched off her mobile and plunged it back into her jacket pocket telling herself she'd ring him later in the evening - once she had got everything up and running.

* * * * *

Screeching to a halt in the rear car park of the Medico Legal Centre Grace again checked her watch for the umpteenth time that hour. She inwardly cursed; she was running late and she was now regretting not having followed the body carrier from the Country Park when she knew she should have done. Instead she'd sat in her car, on her mobile, updating her Detective Inspector – Gerald Scaife, who was setting up the incident room back in the MIT department. She had given him as much information as she could from her scribbled notes, but because the post mortem had yet to be done she found herself unable to answer the majority of the questions he had bombarded her with. Once again she realised she should have gone with the body. To cap it all and cause further delay the DI had then passed her across to DC Isobel Stevens, the HOLMES supervisor, who had begun logging in the information onto the National (Home Office Large Major Enquiry System) network, and she had found herself listening to another round of questions which she had been unable to answer. Fortunately she was of the same rank as Isobel and was able to politely fend her off, promising to get back to her the minute the post mortem had concluded.

Grace pushed through the rear entrance doors of the Medico Legal Centre, pulling off her elastic scrunchy and running her hands through her thick mane of hair, shaking out her corkscrew curls, as she hurried along the corridor to the post mortem suite. Quickly she slipped into her protective body suit and in her haste, as she slotted the white shoe coverings over her flat ballet pumps she stumbled forward shouldering the wall. Beneath her breath she cursed again, rubbing the top of her arm as she barged through the double set of doors, which gave access into the Medico Legal Centre mortuary. Her actions caused the occupants in the cutting room to all snap their heads in her direction.

"Quite a dramatic entrance – Miss?" Professor Lizzie McCormack, the forensic pathologist said glancing over the thin gold rims of her spectacles.

Grace felt that the way the pathologist had paused and then added 'Miss' felt as if she being chided like a schollgirl.

She smiled apologetically. "DC Marshall," she responded, feeling herself blush. "Grace," she finished and quickly scanned the faces of Detective Superintendent Michael Robshaw and Scenes of Crime Manager Duncan Wroe who had not surprisingly beaten her there. She could see the disconcerting scowl on the Superintendent's face.

That's it make an arse of yourself Acting Sergeant Marshall.

"Ah yes, of course – Grace. You have to forgive me I'm terrible with names these days. We met several weeks ago at the old farm near Harlington, a fourteen year old girl badly mutilated, by our infamous serial killer, if my memory serves me right."

Grace nodded.

"Terrible business that. You finally got him though. What did the papers nickname him?"

"The Dearne Vally Demon." She shuddered. The mere mention of that monster's nickname sent shivers down her spine.

"Yes that was it. And he certainly was a demon wasn't he. I remember the injuries to that poor girl." She shook her head. "It always amazes me how cruel humankind can be. Wasn't it six girls he murdered?"

The professor's rhetorical question provoked a flashback. Grace could feel her chest tighten as images burst inside her head. And even though twelve days had gone by since that fateful evening, the memory was still as sharp as if it had all happened yesterday.

That last investigation had caused her so much mental pain, and had physically exhausted her. She had only just got back to work after taking a week off sick in order to pull herself back together. As she reflected, not for the first time, she thought about how catastrophically things could have ended for her that night, after they had finally tracked down their crazed serial killer. She knew that the mental pictures and feelings from that night were going to live inside her for quite some time to come; the Force's counsellor had told her that.

She took in a deep breath, held it, let it out slowly; exactly the way Beth, Hunter's wife, had advised her to handle the onset of a panic attack.

"Any way that's all in the past now. Back to the present eh! Well Grace you're not a moment too soon we are just about to start." Lizzie McCormack's voice snapped her out of her daydream.

The petite grey haired Professor peeled on her latex gloves and pulled a metal trolley to her side. Upon it, laid out in pristine condition, glinting beneath the bright artificial lighting was every conceivable surgical tool and evidence collection container imaginable.

The body, fished from the lake, was laid out on one of the central steel mortuary tables. It had been removed from its body bag but was still wrapped up in its bundle. Despite being soiled by a substantial amount of silt and broken reeds Grace could now see that the body had been shrouded inside a rug, which had an Asian style design.

Professor McCormack reached up and switched on a microphone suspended above her. In her soft Scottish accent she began her PM preamble, opening with the time and date. Then instructing her technician to cut away the bindings she took a step back and slid her green scrub mask up over her mouth and nose.

He began to snip at the cord securing the rug. The binding appeared to be white plastic coated washing line.

"Careful as you unwrap it," Duncan Wroe said to the technician, moving in closer with his camera. "I've known in the past that the murder weapon has been thrown in when the killer has wrapped up the body." He seesawed his gaze between Detective Superintendent Robshaw and Grace. "By dumping the body in the lake the murderer was obviously hoping it would never be found and therefore they might just have thrown in any weapon they used."

The second the technician carefully peeled the sides of the rug away from the cadaver the stench hit Grace and she reacted by quickly slapping on her own paper facemask, which had been hanging around her neck.

The mephitis seemed to be stronger because of the sterile antiseptic smell that permeated inside the brightly lit room, the very same odour that was supposed to cover the rot and decay of the dead.

The body was grotesque; dark, bluish, purple and swollen beyond recognition, though there was no mistaking it was female; long black matted hair covered most of her face and neck, and she was naked.

The technician moved aside and Professor McCormack took over, exploring inches of the cadaver at a time, pausing from time to time to scrutinise certain marks before moving on. She cleared her throat and continued with her exordium.

"The clothing has been removed to reveal the body of a woman of Asian appearance in a state of advanced decomposition. This is manifested by skin slippage, discolouration, bloating and the presence of a foul odour." With thumb and forefinger she began sliding the long strands of black hair away from the deceased's face. "Well, well." she exclaimed, "I think I've more than likely found this young lady's cause of death."

Angling one of her slender fingers over the corpse's neck she leaned back to allow the SOCO manager in and snap-off more photographs. Grace and the Detective Superintendent took a step forward, adjusting their posture to get a look at what the pathologist was pointing to.

Lizzie McCormack continued in her soft Scottish lilt. "On the left hand side of the neck approximately two and a half centimetres below the jaw line is an incision which is approximately fifteen centimetres in length. The large vessels either side of the neck have been severed. The larynx has been severed below the vocal chord through to the intervertebral cartilages. The arteries and other vessels contained in the sheath have all been cut through. The cut is very clean, very precise." The Forensic Pathologist raised her eyes catching Grace's gaze. "Her death would have been immediate."

She returned to the corpse, picking up limbs, examining the hands and fingers. Then she began to turn the body. As she rolled the cadaver onto one hip she suddenly gave off a surprised "hmm," and beckoned to the SOCO Manager. "Mr Wroe, I take my hat off to you." She supported the bloated carcass whilst he shot-off a series of frames. Then picking up that he had finished she pulled out an object which had been hidden beneath the body.

Grace could see that Duncan was doing his best to suppress a grin. It was one of his triumphant grins that she had witnessed so many times before when he had uncovered a vital piece of evidence.

"In all my years as a pathologist I have never seen anything like this before," she said holding up something which closely resembled a knife.

Grace looked at the object and then exchanged glances with her colleagues. It was quite apparent from the looks each of them displayed that like her not one of them had quite seen anything like it before.

Lizzie McCormack dropped it into an exhibit bag and handed it to Grace.

She eyed it again, this time studiously, through the clear plastic, turning it over repeatedly.

"A real vicious looking thing," said Detective Superintendent Robshaw looking over Grace's shoulder.

The weapon was twenty centimetres long and had a curved blade. Half of it consisted of a black metal handle or grip with two small metal hoops at either end.

"These loops look like where your fingers should go - you know like a knuckle-duster type of grip." Grace said out loud. Her response was as much as a question as that of an answer. She searched for agreement in the face of her boss but he merely shrugged his shoulders. She scrutinised it one further time before handing it over to the SOCO manager just as the pathologist was about to start her internal examination of the body. Picking up a scalpel Professor McCormack began the Y shaped incision at the front of the torso, cutting from the breastbone down to the pubis.

A rancid gas suddenly filled the room and Grace caught herself gagging. She pressed her head down into her chest and tried to fill her nasal passages with the floral perfume she was wearing. She had always hated this part of the post mortem.

An hour later after careful removal and examination of the corpse's internal organs the forensic pathologist rounded off her head-to-toe examination, reported on her findings and wrapped things up. She reached up, switched off the microphone, snapped off her latex gloves and faced Grace and Detective Superintendent Robshaw. "The girl has taken a severe beating prior to her death. I've found at least thirty blunt trauma wounds to her head, upper torso, buttocks and legs, caused by clenched fist and boot. Three of her ribs are broken - she would have been in a great deal of pain before she died." Lizzie shook her head in disgust. "Duncan should be able to get one good sample of a shoe print from the girl's thigh area. She also has defence wounds to her hands and arms. Several of her nails have been chipped and broken and I have managed to swab them for perpetrator DNA. There is also bruising to the inside of her thighs and genitalia. In other words she was raped prior to death as well." She shook her head again. "I have examined the girl's trachea and lungs and there is no airway froth or sediment indicative of drowning. And there is no fluid in the paranasal sinuses or stomach. Therefore she was already dead before she went into the water. In conclusion death was the result of the severe haemorrhaging of the carotid artery in the neck caused by a sharp edged instrument. Forensics will no doubt match the wound to that knife found with the girl." She paused dropping her latex gloves into a biohazard bin and then continued. "The incision across the throat is left to right and the penetration angle of the cut suggests that the killer was above or on top of her to carry out this action. That leaves me to believe your killer is left handed."

"What about identification of the girl?" enquired Grace.

"Other than what I have already said, height weight, of Asian appearance etc, that's all I am able to give. The bloating and decomposition has put paid to physical identification. She has also lost a number of teeth from the blows she received but dental records might be still of use, and of course I have taken a blood sample for DNA purposes, but that of course is if she or her family are on the database."

"I will sort out the dental impressions and fingerprints," interjected Duncan Wroe. "I've had a look at the ridges and they are in a bit of a mess. There is a lot of skin slippage because of the length of time the body has been submerged. What I can do however is cut around the top section of each finger and peel off the flesh and then put them over my gloved fingers and roll an impression. I have done that once before and it worked."

Grace felt her skin suddenly go all goosey.

"I can show you how to do it and then let you have a go if you want."

"Duncan that is gross."

"Needs must Grace, needs must!"

* * * * *

Feeling mentally and physically drained it was well after seven pm before Grace eventually got home.

She had spent the last two hours updating DC Isobel Stevens so that she could input the HOLMES system ready for the following day. She had also begun the timeline sequence on the incident boards, finishing the task by blue-tacking photo images of the crime scene, which included a sequence of mortuary shots; rug wrapped body, unwrapped body and the unusual looking weapon which had been used to slay the Asian woman. She'd then had to sit down with DI Scaife so that he could fill in the gaps in his journal ready for the next morning's eight am briefing. It was only when she had finished all that did it hit home to her just what the responsibility of acting Detective Sergeant really meant. Never before had she ever given it any thought just how much Hunter put in after they had all called it a day and headed off home or down to the pub. She made herself a mental note that from now on she would always ask him at the end of a busy day if he needed any help.

Unlocking the front door she called out. There was no reply. She made her way through to the kitchen. On the table she found a note. She picked it up and headed back into the hallway. Climbing the stairs slowly Grace read the note. It was a mixture of scribbles made by David, her husband, and Robyn and Jade her daughters. They had gone to a fast-food restaurant and then onto the cinema; to see a 'chick-flick – she recognised Robyn's handwriting. The note ended with 'love u lots' and a smiley face. She mouthed the end text without making a sound and smiled to herself.

Grace stripped off her things as soon as she entered the bathroom, dumping her clothes in a pile by the door on the landing. She could still smell the stench of rotting flesh clinging to them and she made the decision to wash them straightaway and not put them in the dirty clothes basket for fear of contaminating the rest of the washing.

Turning the thermostat hotter than usual she jumped in the shower and scrubbed herself with perfumed soap foam, lingering longer than she normally did under the powerful jet of hot water.

Ten minutes later, feeling totally cleansed, she towelled herself off in front of the bathroom mirror. As she dabbed the moisture away from her tawny coloured skin she found herself lingering over her reflected image. She turned sideways and clenched her stomach muscles and continued to admire her shape. Although she maintained her fitness through regular swimming sessions Grace knew she owed her lithe well-toned figure and height to her Yorkshire born mum, whilst her hair, skin colour and burnt umber eyes were the product of her Jamaican father's genes.

You've still got it girl.

She patted the final droplets from her shoulders and then slung the towel through onto the landing, adding to her pile of washing. Finally she picked out her tub of aromatic body butter from the mix of bathroom products on the shelf and began to moisturise her skin.

Half an hour later dressed in a T-shirt and jogging bottoms and clutching a glass of chilled Chardonnay Grace flopped onto the sofa. Tucking her legs beneath her she began to run the day's events through inside her head. Graphic images began to kaleidoscope around and she couldn't avoid reflecting on the post mortem. Especially thinking how indifferently Professor Lizzie McCormack had treated the corpse. First how she had been so brutal slicing open the young Asian woman, almost defiling her and then mirroring that with just how gentle she had been when it had come to washing and combing the hair and washing out the nasal passages for evidence. Watching Professor McCormack during the latter sequence she had remembered what the forensic pathologist had said to her, "the body gives up so much of where it has been before it has had its life ended. Pollen or fibre samples can be matched to the place where it met its death." She would store those words for the future.

Suddenly she jumped out of her reverie, remembering the early phone call which she had cut-off. She had completely forgotten to return Hunter's call.

Reaching across the coffee table she scooped up her mobile. She couldn't wait to tell him how she had coped whilst being in charge of her first murder.

* * * * *

North Yorkshire:

Jock Kerr stirred. He let out a low moan as he shuffled uneasily in the bed. The groaning snapped Hunter out of his doze and he drew himself up in the high backed bedside chair just in time to catch sight of his father's face twisting in pain; he'd been in and out of a restless sleep since his admittance to the hospital side ward that afternoon, despite being heavily dosed with a strong painkiller and sedative.

"Okay dad?" Hunter enquired. "Do you need me to call a nurse?"

His father eased opened his eyes. "I'd rather have a dram son." He started to laugh, chest shaking, then winced. "Jeez son, I feel like I've gone ten rounds with Mohammed Ali." He licked his dry lips. "What's the doc's verdict? What's the damage?"

Hunter noticed that his father's Scottish accent was brittle and more laboured than normal.

He leaned forward and rested an elbow on the edge of the bed, cupped his chin in his hand and stroked growing bristles; he was in need of a shave.

"Four broken ribs, more than a few cuts and bruises, and a couple of stitches above your right eye. You'll live."

"How's your Ma?"

"She's on Ward Two." He saw his father's face change. It was a look of anguish as well as concern. "Don't worry she's only there for observation. She's had a nasty bang to her head. And she actually looks like she's done ten rounds with Mohammed Ali." He cracked a wry smile. "Beth and the boys are with her, keeping her company."

"I'm glad she's okay son. I wouldn't know what I'd do if anything happened to your ma." He made an attempt to clear his throat and that sent him into a paroxysm of coughing. His

43

chest shook fitfully and a rasping sound broke from his mouth.

Hunter watched on helpless as tears welled up in his father's eyes.

"Bloody hell that hurt," he cried out as he clutched his upper torso and pushed himself back into the bed. "What happened son?"

Hunter recounted the incident, the silver BMW ramming the car and how they somersaulted across the moorland. "You're lucky to be alive."

"Some accident, eh?"

"That was no accident dad. The BMW deliberately rammed you." Hunter pushed himself back upright. "Was this to do with that guy you were arguing with this morning?"

He saw his father tense. "I've already told you what that was about. Leave it," he snapped.

"Look you and mum were nearly killed today, if that guy was involved then I'll find out."

"And I said just leave it. I'll sort this once I get out of here."

"Dad you're in no state to sort anything out. Leave me to deal with it. That's what I get paid to do. That's my job."

"Just leave it son."

"I can't. Now why don't you tell me what that was all about this morning? It's too much of a coincidence that what happened to you was only a couple of hours after you've dumped a guy on his backside. What are you hiding dad?"

"Nothing," he snapped again. "Just leave it I said."

Hunter saw his dad suddenly pale. He dropped back onto his pillow. His face glistened with sweat.

Hunter raised himself from the chair. "Do you need me to get a nurse?"

"I could do with a couple of painkillers. I hurt all over." He closed his eyes.

In that instance Hunter saw that his father's face looked tired and drawn; there was almost a look of frailty about him.

He left the room and made for the nurse's station. As he was speaking with a staff nurse, asking for extra painkillers, his mobile rang. He'd switched it to silent because of the hospital rules and now it vibrated in his pocket.

He quickly fished it out and viewed the screen; it was his work partner Grace Marshall calling. He'd been trying on and off for most of the afternoon to get hold of her. Slotting the mobile to his ear and opening up the call he used facial expressions and his hands to signal to the nurse that he needed to get the call and he shot away from the nurse's work station and bounded along the corridor.

"Hi Grace," he answered pushing through the double doors and exiting the ward. He came to a halt in the corridor. "I've been ringing you most of the day and all I've been getting is your voicemail." He didn't wait for her to reply. "Listen I need a favour."

Hunter narrated what had happened. How he had seen his father arguing with the bald headed man that morning and then the lunchtime incident when his parents car had been deliberately run off the road. "We only managed to get a part index and I've given that to North Yorks police, but I could do with someone following it up." He paused for breath. "Grace, do you remember a few weeks ago when we dealt with Steve Paynton?"

He was trying to visualise the reaction on her face. It had been Grace who had found the photographs, hidden behind a bath panel, during the search of Paynton's home; undraped images of pre-pubescent children. He had seen how it had disgusted her.

"Well do you remember I had a run in with his two brothers and a cousin shortly after we got him remanded. Well I think they might have something to do with this. I think the Paynton's might be trying to get back at me through my parents, but my dad won't tell me anything. Could you do me a favour and just find out where the Payntons were today and see if they have access to a silver BMW. It'll have some nearside damage to it."

"Hunter I can't."

He listened as she excitedly related over the line what she was currently occupied with. Suddenly he caught his ghost-like image in the glass panel of one of the doors he had just come through. His facial expression was one of disappointment and he was glad she couldn't see him. As she finished he composed himself.

"A real baptism of fire eh? Good for you. Okay Grace, don't worry. I can see you're going to have your hands full and it sounds as though you've got it all well under control. Listen I'm going to be up here for another couple of days until they release my parents. You crack on and I'll ring you daily so that you can update me." He ended the call sounding bright but deep down he was agitated. He needed someone to do some discreet and maybe underhand digging for him. Someone whom he knew he could trust and Grace had been his best hope. Then at that moment someone else sprang to mind; someone whom he knew always got a result. Hunter checked his mobile contacts, selected the name he wanted and began to make the call.

- ooOoo –

CHAPTER TWO

Coruscating light forced its way through the thin fabric of the closed blinds and the smell of fresh furniture polish greeted Grace as she breezed into the MIT office. Judging by its freshness she must have just missed Angie the cleaner she thought to herself as she swished open the blinds. That was a pity because she loved having girlie chats with Angie; she knew all the building's gossip, especially the real juicy stuff; who was having an affair with whom.

Shrugging off her jacket and draping it over the back of her swivel seat she pulled a large file from the top of her tray and opened it up on her desk blotter. She fired-up her computer and dropped into her chair.

She had got into work early; in the absence of Hunter she had the responsibility of pulling together the inquest file of 'The Dearne Valley Demon,' and she wanted to make in-roads into its completion before things got manic when the new investigation got underway that morning.

For a few seconds whilst waiting for the programme to load, her mind wandered - mulling once more over the events of the 12th August, and she felt her chest beginning to tighten. As the blood pounded somewhere inside her head, causing a rushing sensation in her ears, she took several deep breaths in an attempt to retake control. Suddenly she felt sick in the pit of her stomach. She hated the sensation these attacks brought and wondered if they would ever go away.

'This isn't fair. I want my life back.'

After just a couple of deep breaths she could feel the tight band across her chest slacken. She steadied herself and left-clicked the computer mouse, opening up the document folder titled 'Inquest doc.' She'd already drafted most of it and she speed-read back over the summary to the point where she had ended the report the previous day. Closing her eyes she thought about the final points she needed to add. Less than a minute later she snapped open her eyes, scanned the screen again, flicked the curser to the point where she needed to pick up, clicked her mouse and began typing.

* * * * *

Footfalls along the corridor outside the department broke into her deep concentration. She glanced at her watch; the last hour had flown. The first detectives were beginning to filter into the office. With the opening of the doors a new aroma assaulted her nostrils; the greasy smell of bacon sandwiches from the canteen. Her stomach rumbled, suddenly she realised how hungry she was; she had given breakfast a miss at home that morning.

Mike Sampson and Tony Bullars, her team members, were amongst the first in. She acknowledged them with a smile and a nod. Mike was making for the office kettle. He stopped in mid-stride catching Grace's gaze and mimed the act of pouring a cup into his mouth, silently mouthing the words 'want one?' She nodded gratefully and began bundling up her papers. Less than a minute later Mike was clonking down a mug of freshly brewed coffee in front of her just as she was closing down her computer. She caught sight of his cheery well-rounded face. "Right let's get ready for briefing" she announced more to herself than to Mike and saved the file before closing down the computer.

Detective Superintendent Michael Robshaw had the role of SIO again. He stood in front of the incident boards flicking through the notes belonging to DI Scaife. He peered over the top of his spectacles and swelled his muscular chest straining his crisp white shirt. Grace knew that the Superintendent was a man who regularly maintained his fitness; she knew that like Hunter he worked out regularly despite his workload. Snapping the journal shut he cleared his throat.

"Good morning ladies and gents," he began. "In the words of the old adage it never rains but it pours, we have just cleared up one set of nasty murders and now we have another particularly grisly one turn up." Pausing, he added, "This is playing havoc with my budget."

There was a ripple of laughter around the room.

He started tapping the incident board behind him over the photograph of the bloated grotesque face from the mortuary shots. "Okay on a serious note, our job is to find out who murdered this young Asian woman. As you can see from the decomposition she is unrecognisable. She was found stripped naked and with no marks of identification. We have her DNA and we have her fingerprints but at this moment in time we do not know who she is or anything about her life." He tapped another photo. "But what we do know is that three to four weeks ago she was badly beaten, raped, had her throat cut, was bundled inside a rug and then dumped in the bottom of Barnwell lake where she lay until yesterday afternoon when two divers on a training schedule found her."

'Succinctly put' thought Grace to herself. She realised that in just those few words he had made short shrift of the forensic Pathologist's two hour post mortem.

"Our main priority is to find out who this young lady was. We also have quite a wide time frame between the murder and the body being found and as yet we don't know where she was killed, only where she was dumped. We are up against it, but we have all been here before and I know you lot will fill in the gaps." He tapped the incident board again, glancing behind him before resetting his gaze on the faces of the detectives. "What we do have is the rug she was found wrapped up in and the weapon that was used to slit her throat. We can all see that these appear to be foreign and these are our leads at the moment so if no one has any questions DI Scaife will give you your tasks so you can get out there and clear this up."

There were no questions; the briefing broke up and the MIT detectives picked up their assignments for the day.

Grace was still acting DS; the DI told her that Hunter had been in touch and he wouldn't be back for at least another three days. She collared Mike and Tony.

"Right you two we've got the job of checking missing persons because of our experience with the last set of murders and also finding out about the murder weapon, especially to see if there are any local outlets who sell it." She snatched her jacket from the back of her chair, picked up the car keys and slung them towards Tony. "Bully you're driving," she said and strode purposefully towards the doors.

* * * * *

North Yorkshire:

Hunter paced the hospital corridors. He was frustrated and tired. He had slept very little the previous night; they had managed to book a family room in a motel not too far from the hospital and he had spent a restless night going over the events in his head. The more he had mulled over the incident the more he made connections with yesterday morning's clash between his father and that stranger and this aftermath.

Now he had another long day before him at the hospital unable to do anything regarding who was responsible for doing this to his parents.

Beth and the boy's were flitting between Ward Two, where his mum was 'comfortable and stable,' and the side ward where his dad was resting. He was having trouble being in the same room as his father; he wouldn't say anything. He had tried to be patient in his approach but he knew his dad was holding back on some secret and was refusing to give it up. It had got to the stage where his father refused to answer any of his questions and he just lay with his eyes closed.

Several times he had tried to call the number he had rung last night but it was now switched off, and on divert and his head was swimming around in circles.

He strolled down to the drinks machine on the floor below even though he hated drinking out of plastic cups and dropped his loose change into the slot. They were out of tea, milk one sugar. He kicked the bottom panel and growled. Then his mobile rang. He viewed the screen; 'withheld' flashed up; he guessed who this was – he would be ringing from one of the office phones.

"Hello – Hunter" he answered.

"Hunter it's me."

He recognised the broad South Yorkshire dialect immediately. "Have you got anything for me?"

"Afraid not. I've made quite a few phone calls but there's not a whisper down here. I also went round to all of the Paynton's houses, and the locks-ups they have access to, but there's no sign of a silver BM. And everyone I spoke with yesterday have never seen any of the family in one. I've checked with Intelligence and nothing with that part registration features on our system. It's a complete blank at the moment but I've put a few feelers out so if I turn up anything I'll bell you. Okay?"

Despondently Hunter thanked him and rang off; though he knew shouldn't feel down. If any villains from his 'back yard' had carried this out then he knew his source would get to hear. He would have to rely on that for the moment - well until he could get back to base and then he would shake some trees himself.

- ooOoo –

CHAPTER THREE

DAY FOUR: 27th August.
Glasgow.

Fraser Cullen kept in the shadows, pressing himself back against the crumbling brickwork of the high walls at the entranceway to the derelict car park. He lit up another cigarette; he'd only just finished the last one – but then he was more nervous than normal.

He pulled up the collar of his jacket. Was it his imagination or had the temperature dropped since his arrival half an hour ago? It had to be the dampness of his surroundings he told himself.

Every time he heard the sound of a car's engine he stuck his head out from his hiding place and scoured the partly cobbled street of Sauchiehall Lane. Fraser glanced at his stolen designer watch; he'd give them another ten minutes then he was off.

He almost missed the silver BMW; it was coasting slowly past hardly making a sound. He took a final drag on his cigarette, dropped the burning remnant, and scrunched it underfoot, before he stepped out into the lane.

The car reversed and pulled alongside, its wheels scrunching over loose chippings, the rubber walls of the nearside tyres squealing as they scraped against the kerb. Fraser bent down dispersing the smoke from his lungs just as the passenger window slid down.

The front passenger wafted a hand in front of his mouth and nose. "Fucking hell do you have to do that?" he exclaimed.

The deep gravelly tones in the voice of the man had not changed, not even after all this time thought Fraser: Though his appearance had. The hair had been ravaged by grey and he couldn't help but notice the flash of the scar that ran from the bridge of his nose down towards his jaw. The occupant of the front seat had been a hard bastard when he known him thirty odd years ago now he looked even harder.

"What have you got for me then Fraser?"

Fraser lowered himself, resting a hand on the car door, levelling his with the front passenger. "I found him Billy. It wasn't easy mind," he replied in his broad Glaswegian dialect. "You'll find him drinking regularly in Lauders on Sauchiehall Street. He's there most days. Goes in about four in the afternoon, and usually leaves about half seven. He comes down this way to get to the subway off Bath Street. I've followed him three times now without him knowing. And there's nae CCTV," he said darting his eyes around the high buildings which lined both sides of the narrow lane.

Billy smiled, reached inside his coat pocket and brought out a handful of Scottish notes. "There's a ton Fraser. Now piss off and don't tell anyone we've met."

Before Fraser could even reply the smoke glass window was sliding up and the rear wheels were spinning and chewing up the loose gravel as the BMW lurched towards the main road.

* * * * *

Alistair McPherson stood at the front steps of Lauders bar tapping the filter of his cigarette on its packet before popping it into his mouth. He lit it in cupped hands; it was an old habit from his army days. He inhaled deeply and his chest shook sending out a spluttering cough. It lasted several seconds before he banged his chest and brought it under control.

Jesus these things are going to kill me one day.

He stood for a good minute taking in the sights and sounds of Sauchiehall Street; how it had changed over the years. It had gone upmarket since his time of working here. It was now a busy thoroughfare full of high-class shops and many of the gracious houses had been converted into offices. He stepped onto the pavement and began his steady meander home. He would pick up his fish supper on the way back he told himself. He turned the corner into Sauchiehall Lane, heading for the subway which would take him towards his home. As he did so he heard the car pulling up behind him; guessed it would be someone wanting directions; lots of tourists got confused by the traffic system. He stepped to one side and waited whilst it drew level and then removed the cigarette from his mouth; held it in one cupped hand as the electric window coasted down. Alistair turned sideways to talk to the driver but could only see his chest and shoulders. He slowly bent down to get a better view only to be met by the piercing stare of the scar-faced passenger leaning across the shaven-headed driver. There was something about that face that registered.

"Remember me Mr McPherson?" said scar-face.

The voice was deep and menacing and a wave of panic shot through Alistair.

* * * * *

The DOA – 'dead on arrival' call was logged at seven-fifty pm; discovered by a young waiter who had slipped out through the back emergency doors of the restaurant into the derelict car park for a 'smoke-break.' He'd had the shock of his life when he had tripped over the crumpled mess. He thought at first it had just been a pile of rags; people were always dumping their rubbish here, but then he'd spotted the thick congealed blood beneath his feet. The sight of the mush, which had once been a head, had almost made him sick.

He had immediately dialled 999 on his mobile and asked for the ambulance service; because the body was close to the fire stairwell he had assumed that the dead guy had accidently fallen. Then he'd fled back inside the restaurant and dragged out his boss to bear witness to what he had found.

The ambulance crew who turned up, knew, from a brief examination of the deceased, that the horrific injuries inflicted upon the man's head had not been the result of an accident, and they radioed in an immediate request to their control for police attendance.

The first officers on scene were there in a matter of minutes; Pitt Street police station was only three hundred yards away.

The uniform Sergeant stooped over the prostrate body trying to make out the facial features. There was little doubt the man had taken a severe hammering, his head and face was one mass of blood and his forehead had been caved in; he was barely recognisable.

"Looks like somebody's tap-danced on his head," he said, glancing at his colleague, whilst slipping on a pair of latex gloves.

He began to search through the dead man's pockets. He had already determined that if they could get some form of ID it would be a start. He found the man's wallet in an inside jacket pocket and began rummaging through the cards. In the back section he found a laminated National Association of Retired Police Officers membership card. It had immediately grabbed his attention. He stared at the name and then at the photograph. He shot a glance back at his team-mate, his face taking on a sudden look of disbelief.

"Bloody hell I know this guy," the sergeant exclaimed. "He was in CID at Shettlestone nick."

By eight-fifteen pm, the full length of Sauchiehall Lane had been cordoned off; a major enquiry was underway.

- ooOoo -

CHAPTER FOUR
DAY SIX: 29th August.
Barnwell:

Grace took a final look over her notes and then scanned the faces of her colleagues seated around the room. MIT detectives were waiting for her input. She had been given centre stage this morning; Detective Superintendent Robshaw had been called into headquarters to liase with the press office; he had a meeting booked with the local press and regional TV news teams to give an overview of the murder investigation and make an appeal for witnesses.

Grace's stomach turned. Pangs of nervousness drifted from her gut up into her throat. This was her first up-in-front briefing and she was outside her comfort zone. Her brown eyes jumped between Mike Sampson and Tony Bullars; her team mates. They were giving her their thumbs up, a 'you-can-do-it-girl' signal. She smiled nervously back. She suddenly contemplated on how much support her two team mates had given her during her spell of acting Sergeant. The three of them had not stopped over the past two days in their attempts to identify the murder weapon. She'd carved up the jobs between them. They had searched the Internet, made dozens of phone calls, and finally they had teamed up to trawl the many and varied Asian artefact and martial arts shops in both South and West Yorkshire. Their efforts had paid off. Late the previous morning they had found their answer in Bradford, in a small warehouse that sold Asian ceremonial weapons; more for show than for use. Along with a brief history of its use she had watched in amazement as one of the young male storekeepers had given them a demonstration in its application. However, there it had ended. Grace had requested a list of people who had purchased such a weapon, but the owner had explained that they only dealt in cash and kept no till receipts. Even with Mike's veiled threats of letting the tax man know of their accounting methods, it still hadn't take them any further forward, other than to provide the stores distribution outlet over in Pakistan. Grace and her team settled on a *free gratis* replica of the murder knife and left.

One light moment in their exhaustive pursuit had been when they ran into DCs Andy France and Paula Clarke from the other MIT team who were also in Bradford making enquiries into the Asian rug into which the girl's body had been bundled. Their bumping into one another resulted in a pub lunch in Holmfirth before driving back to the office. It had given them all a well-needed break from the stresses of the investigation. The conversation over lunch got around to Hunter and the hit and run involving his parents. As she had left the pub Grace had made a mental note to ring him later in the afternoon to check how his parents were getting on and to update him on the murder enquiry.

Now as she perched herself on the corner of her desk ready to feed her information into the morning's briefing she suddenly remembered she still hadn't made that call; it had completely slipped her mind because of her workload.

I'll text him straight after briefing, she reminded herself.

She cleared her throat, picked up the replica murder weapon that had been lying on the desk beside her and began her input.

"A bagh nakh." She held up the knife with its curved angled blade and two brass knuckles fixed into the hilt. Behind her pinned to the incident board were the scenes of crime photo of the weapon, which had been recovered with the girl's body. Her replica was an identical match to the killing instrument on the photograph.

"An Indian hand-to-hand weapon designed to fit over the knuckles or concealed under and against the palm. This is a variant of the traditional weapon that consisted of four or five curved blades and is designed to slash through skin and muscle, mimicking wounds inflicted by a wild animal. As a matter of interest the bagh nakh features in many of the kid's video games they play these days. It was originally developed primarily for self-defence, but in this case, as we know, it was used to attack and slit the throat of our young murder victim." She explained how they had got hold of the replica. "Unfortunately even though this is a strange knife to our eyes amongst the Asian population it is not. There are a number of outlets for this weapon both in this country and abroad and at this moment in time we are unable to find out who purchased one. However the detective superintendent in his TV appeal will be showing this to see if it will jog any memories." Grace placed the knife beside her on the table and then went on to explain that they still had no positive identification of the body. She told them how she had gone back into the National Missing Persons database but such was the putrefied state of their victim that it was hampering the search parameters, and despite the DNA database having some six million indexes and the National Fingerprint Database having eight million individuals they still had no trace. "We can only hope that the Super's TV broadcast will give us a lead," she finished and dropped down off the edge of the desk and returned to her seat so that DS Gamble from the other team could finish off the mornings briefing.

Mark Gamble took over Grace's place in front of the incident boards. Clutched in his right hand was his rolled up bundle of notes from the previous day's actions though he never opened them as he addressed the detectives. Tapping them on the side of his thigh he picked up where Grace left off, running through yesterday's day long footslogging visits to the traditional Asian carpet stores in Bradford. He explained that two members of his team had eventually tracked down rugs of a similar make and design to a warehouse store on an industrial unit on the outskirts of the city. Shipping receipts held by the owner identified they were part of a large consignment from the Punjab Province of Pakistan. They had pressed the owner to narrow down the location where they had been made but he had been unable to give a precise area. He had told them that many of the rugs were crafted in small factories and even family homes to an ordered design which would be picked up on a weekly basis and delivered to a warehouse by the docks. Dozens of villages would be involved in one single design; it was impossible to pinpoint where the rug their body had been bound in had been made. Detective Sergeant Gamble paused, but only momentarily as though gathering his thoughts. He swapped his bundle of notes to his left hand and continued.

"We also had the task of gathering any CCTV evidence at the country park. There is some and it does have night vision software but unfortunately it only covers the Lakeside Café, reception area and storeroom, which is all of the main building, and is a good hundred metres from the jetty where the body was thrown from. Having said that there is some coverage to the outside of the building for security and so anyone passing close by would be picked up by the system. They do store discs for a month before they are re-used so we have got our civilian investigators currently going through days and weeks of footage. If whoever killed this girl carried the body past the main building before dumping it off the jetty they will have been picked up by the cameras." Mark paused again and stroked a comb of fingers through his thick fair hair, resting his hand at the back of his neck. "It's a long shot but fingers crossed."

The briefing broke up again with the DI handing out fresh enquiries for the day. Grace scanned her eyes over the half-dozen sheets generated by the HOLMES team. She had been given the task of tracing and interview the Countryside Rangers employed at the park. She handed them over to Mike Sampson and Tony Bullars to complete; she still had to put the finishing touches to the Coroners Inquest file.

As her two colleagues wandered out of the office, chatting about last night's televised football game, Grace picked up the folder from the top of her tray and dropped it onto her blotter. Then she slipped off her jacket, cloaked it around the back of her seat and pulled the chair away from the desk. At the last moment before settling down she checked herself. She spun round and strode towards the office kettle, she needed a coffee; an extra caffeine hit before she started her laborious chore.

* * * * *

Hunter drove the hour and a half back from Scarborough District Hospital only making small talk. His head was thumping. His father beside him had been virtually silent and only Beth and his mum had struck up any long drawn-out conversation, and that had been idle chit-chat lifted from their soap magazines.

It had been a very strained journey and one he was glad was over as he pulled up outside his parent's home. He followed his dad in through the front door carrying in their overnight bag and set it down in the hallway. He checked that Beth was helping his mum and then strode after his father who had made for the kitchen. His dad had just filled the electric kettle and was settling it into its base to switch it on. "Tea son?" he asked rhetorically, flicking down the switch and then reached up into a wall cupboard for cups.

Hunter saw him grimace, setting his teeth against one another and biting down, doing his best to disguise the pain. He edged forward. "Let me do that dad."

"Nae I'm fine son, it's only a twinge." He took out four cups, set them down and spooned in sugar for himself and Hunter.

"Look dad I don't want us to fall out over this," Hunter said quietly. He could hear Beth fussing over his mother through in the next room.

"And neither do I son."

"I know something's not right, maybe it's the policeman in me, I don't know. I know you haven't wanted to talk about it, but just think about what happened up on those moors. If I hadn't been following you could have been there for hours. You and mum could have been killed. I don't know what you're covering up but it seems to me to be too dangerous not to share it."

Hunter's father turned and touched his arm, looked him square on. A film of tears washed over his dad's bright and intense blue eyes; eyes that he had inherited. "Give me some space son. I won't promise you anything but I need some time to think it through."

* * * * *

Grace ducked beneath the police crime scene tape and stepped towards the edge of the lake. She rested near to the jetty and fixed her eyes on the spot, where six days earlier, she had watched on as the Underwater Search Unit had hauled up their so-far unnamed body.

She listened to the sounds around her; the lapping of the water and the regular thunk of the moored rowing boats against the damp wooden pilings of the quay. Behind her she could also hear instructions being shouted out to the line of boiler-suited officers who were on their hands and knees carrying out a finger-tip search in one of the grid areas marked out by the forensics team. Most of Barnwell Country Park was still off limits; cordoned off as they searched for any evidence which would trap the killers of their unknown victim. She lifted her eyes and scanned the park; a place she had been so many times and which she normally associated with peace and tranquillity.

She had come here for some fresh air having finished the Coroner's Inquest file half an hour ago; it had taken longer than she had anticipated. All that was required now was for Hunter to read it through before it was submitted. She wondered when he would be back.

Damn; she remembered she still hadn't rung him. She took out her mobile, flicked up the screen and speed dialled his number. As she listened to the ringing tone she stared out again across the lake. The sky suddenly looked angry, threatened rain. Last night's forecast had said early sunshine with heavy bursts of showers later in the day. It looked like being accurate for once.

- ooOoo -

CHAPTER FIVE
DAY SEVEN: 30th August.
Barnwell:

Hunter sat at his desk stroking the sides of his still damp hair from the shower he had taken twenty minutes previously. He had awoken just after six that morning and decided to run into work to clear the past week's cobwebs from inside his head.

He booted up his desk-top computer - he knew there would be an abundance of e-mails waiting for him – and leaned back in his chair. As he waited for the programme to go through its firewall security checks he set his eyes on his desk calendar. He picked up his pen and crossed off several of the previous dates; he had been away from the office for eight days.

Another day and they would be in September; the beginning of Autumn.

The first of September, he reminded himself – the date pricked his conscience. It had been that date twenty years ago when he had been given the news that had momentarily tore his world apart. His first serious girlfriend - Polly Hayes – had been found murdered. She had been walking her dog in woodland close to her home when she had been attacked. The dog had returned home without her sparking off a search. Police found her body three hours later.

She had been the reason why he had joined the job seventeen years ago.

Her killer had never been caught and he always hoped that one day he would get justice – not just for himself, but for her parents as well, who were still around, and who he still called on from time to time – though those times were becoming less frequent with the passing of years. He made a mental note to call in the next couple of days – especially with the anniversary of her death.

He broke himself out of his reverie, pulled his eyes away from the calendar, lifted the handset of his desk phone and began dialling the number of the forces voicemail system. Upon hearing the mechanical voice beginning its preamble he switched to speaker phone and punched in his six-digit password to retrieve his personal messages.

"Hi, its Zita," the first communication greeted him. "It's three-thirty pm on Friday afternoon. Just wanting a quick chat about the country park murder. I think I might have something for you! I'm in the office tomorrow from eight am. Can you give me a call? You've got my number."

A wry smile played across his mouth. He knew a quick chat is what she did not mean. He had met Zita six months ago at the Barnwell Museum and Art Gallery where he had won the Open Art Exhibition and was attending the award ceremony. She had introduced herself as the reporter for the Barnwell Chronicle and wanted to do a piece on him. Once she had discovered he was a DS with the MIT team she had rung him on almost a weekly basis. Deep down, he didn't mind. He never gave anything away which would compromise an enquiry, though he privileged her with the first phone call whenever they had broken the back of an investigation. And it had worked in his favour. On a few occasions she had helped him out with background details on individuals he had been interested in. He guessed that by using the form of words she had done – that she may have something relating to their investigation – was her way of guaranteeing a call-back.

He noted her request in his head and then hit the next message button, simultaneously he pushed himself up from his seat and made for the office kettle; he was in need of a strong, sweet, cup of tea. He switched on the kettle and listened to the next recorded call as he dropped a tea bag into his mug. It was the voice of an ex-colleague who was now the safety officer at his beloved football club, Sheffield United. He was letting him know that he had got him a couple of tickets in the Directors box for next Saturday's home game and to give him a call. That was too good an offer to miss. He checked the time on his watch – he would make that his priority call straight after the morning briefing.

The day's starting well.

He took his hot drink back to his desk and returned to the task of dealing with his e-mails – he saw from the list that most of them appeared to be in-force spam. He was relieved because he had gone into work early with the intention of clearing up as much of the accumulation of paperwork as he could, before the start of the days play. He spotted that Grace's Coroner's inquest file was at the top of his pile. He picked it off and opened it up across his jotter.

Twenty-five minutes of reading, whilst slowly supping lukewarm tea, in between chewing on his pen top, saw him making headway with the inquest report and as he finished the last paragraph of Grace's dossier he became conscious of the clamour of voices further along the corridor. He checked his watch and cursed. The team were already beginning to filter in for briefing and he'd not even made a dent in his 'to do' tray. He knew he was in for a long day.

He picked up the bundle of papers and jostled them together into a semblance of neatness, and then added a post-it note reminding Grace to have all the exhibits ready, including photographs and video evidence for the inquest proceedings.

He signed it off with 'good job' and 'thanks,' dropping it across onto her desk opposite, and then he snapped the well-chewed plastic top back onto his biro. He glanced at the damaged pen as he laid it across his blotter and shook his head. Terrible habit he knew, but better than biting his nails like he used to.

Scraping back his chair he stretched his arms up over his head and straightened his back and then made for the office kettle again; he'd let the last cuppa go cold before he had finished it. As he listened to the water boil he updated himself with the timeline sequence on the incident board. He also studied the mortuary shots. It was the first time he had seen them; they were horrific; such appalling violence had been meted out prior to her death. And she still had no name despite the detective superintendent's TV appeal. He had managed to catch it twice last night, first on the early evening local news slot and then after the ten o'clock news. He double-checked the log to ensure nothing significant had happened overnight; he knew that the HOLMES team would have been covering a late shift yesterday evening to take any calls following the news plea.

Grace was the first in and Hunter watched her following a similar ritual to his; making a beeline for the kettle; but in her case he knew it would be coffee.

Hugging her steaming cup he followed her movement as she sunk gently into her chair opposite whilst reading the note on the front of the inquest file. She looked up and met his eyes and then responded with a thumbs up and "cheers" before slotting the file into her out tray.

The morning's briefing was a low-key affair. The HOLMES team were still checking through all last night's calls but there appeared to be nothing new to add to what had already been uncovered. DI Scaife issued some fresh priorities but Hunter's team still had to track down and speak with all of the park's rangers. He checked with Grace to see if she, Mike and Tony would mind finishing off the actions without him. He made the excuse that he wanted to clear his tray, but in reality he had more personally pressing things to sort out.

"Fine Hunter, no problem. We should be able to clear them all by late this afternoon, but do you fancy working a bit over tonight?"

"Not really," he hesitated. "Why is there something urgent to follow up?"

"Not urgent as such. One of the park rangers we tracked down yesterday let something out which could lead somewhere."

"What's that then?" Hunter asked leaning across his desk, resting his elbows and interweaving his fingers.

"Apparently after the park closes the ranger told Mike that some parts which are covered by trees and bushes are used by couples in cars. They have been told by their boss that whichever one of them covers a late shift should try and discourage it because there had been complaints by a few walkers out for an evening stroll. One of them let fall in conversation that one girl in particular turns up quite regular but with different guys. They know her as Tanya and it seems she has spun them some yarn about being a Russian dancer who has fled her brutal husband and is trying to make ends meet." Grace rolled her eyes and clucked her tongue against the roof of her mouth dismissively. "It's obvious she's a prostitute who has found a decent spot for her clients." She pursed her mouth. "I just thought that if she is a regular visitor that there might be a chance she might have seen something suspicious, might even have clocked who dumped the body and won't have come forward because of what she does. I thought we could stake-out the lake for a couple of evenings, and see if she turns up."

Hunter unlocked his fingers and pushed himself back into his seat. "I'd love to say yes Grace but I've got something else planned tonight."

"Oh okay, sorting out your parents - I understand."

"In a way - just something I need to follow up that's all."

Grace's eye-brows knitted together. "That all sounds rather mysterious Hunter."

"That's because it is." He pushed himself up. "It's top secret and if I tell you I might have to kill you." He exaggerated his smile, tapped his nose and turned towards the door.

* * * * *

Hunter tracked MIT's civilian investigator Barry Newstead to the ground floor CCTV room; the back room editing suite to be precise, where he found him going through footage from Barnwell country parks security system. He crept into the semi-darkened room silently and he could see that Barry was intensely scrutinising speeded up images, which were floating across one of the small viewing screens set into a desk console. Barry looked sharply over his shoulder, acknowledged Hunter with a nod and then returned to the TV monitor.

Hunter fondly ruffled a hand through Barry's rumple of dark dyed hair. "How's it going big guy? Found anything?"

The thickset, large bellied investigator grunted and shuffled to one side in his swivel chair, shaking his head away from Hunter's rifling fingers. Hunter pulled up a chair and slotted himself beside his old friend and colleague.

Hunter had a real fondness for Barry Newstead. He had first met him shortly after his girlfriend's body had been found. Barry had been one of the investigating detectives'. Early on in the enquiry he had been interviewed by him on several occasions and such had been the probing nature of the questions that he had felt like a suspect. He had been so glad he had been able to offer up a solid alibi for the relevant times between her going missing and her body being found.

Later he had deliberately sought Barry out in the pub he regularly used, to talk through the case, and it became apparent to him, from their discussions, that Barry was working slavishly to catch the killer. Unfortunately that had never happened. Barry had been the officer who had broken the bad news to him that the enquiry was being wound down because of lack of further evidence. That had been twelve months after her murder – he had been almost eighteen years old. And that had been when he had made his decision to join the police.

He had bumped into Barry four years later, as a young twenty-two year-old detective, on the very first day of his being appointed to District Headquarters CID; fourteen years ago. Barry had been at the peak of his career then and had taken him under his wing, showing him all the tricks of the trade. They had formed a formidable team until his promotion to Detective Sergeant eight years ago.

"Not a damn thing so far," Barry replied without taking his eyes off the screen. "I've been here looking at this lot for the best part of a day and a half and I'm getting square eyes. The most exciting moment was watching a female mallard and her seven chicks waddle across the front of reception. This is almost as boring as going through all the missing from home files from the last job."

Despite Barry's bemoaning the tediousness of the task Hunter knew it would be done thoroughly. He edged his seat closer. "Glad I've caught up with you. Sorry to have put you on the spot with those enquiries, but I was stuck up in North Yorks and there was only Grace and you I could trust with something so sensitive, and Grace was in charge of this murder."

"No problem, that's what buddies are for."

"Anything new cropped up?"

Barry pressed the pause button on the system and turned to face Hunter. He smoothed a thumb and forefinger across his dark bushy moustache and then stroked his chin. "I followed up a few calls late yesterday for you but there's nothing on the grapevine at all about what happened. I've only given my snouts half a story, they've no idea it's your parents, just told them it's a hit-and-run near the east coast. That way if someone does come back with something I'll know if they're telling me the truth."

Hunter patted Barry's shoulder. "Cheers for this – I owe you one."

"No problem Hunter. You getting me this job has more than paid a debt. I was getting bored stiff at home. It's great to be back in the thick of it especially after being thrown on the scrapheap."

Hunter knew what that meant. He recalled how Barry had been forced to retire six years ago by a newly promoted Chief Inspector who had specifically targeted him because of his unorthodox methods. He remembered how on several occasions the man had threatened to discipline Barry for 'bringing the force into disrepute,' before finally side-lining him to a desk job, which he knew would hurt him the most. He could still recollect Barry's virtual last words to him whilst they were out celebrating a result from a job one night. "I'm going to call it a day before I smack that bastard," he'd said to him with a slur. It had been the first time he had ever seen Barry so morose. Then six weeks ago his ex-buddy had come back into his life again. Barry had rung him right out of the blue with vital information on the serial-killer case, which they had just put to bed, and Hunter had managed to persuade the boss to take him on as a civilian investigator at a time when their backs were against the wall and the team needed more experienced staff.

"Fancy doing some night-fishing?"

Hunter caught the smile creeping across Barry's mouth – he had grasped what Hunter was alluding to. Between them they had used this term so many times over the years. It had been their coded phrase whenever one of them had decided to engage in underhand activities and required back up.

"I've nothing much else on - what do you have in mind?" Barry returned in a low voice.

* * * * *

The Masons Arms on Barnwell High Street was a drab Victorian pub that had not changed in character for years. It was a place with a reputation. Local decent folk and anyone with an ounce of sense gave it a wide berth. Such was the clientele who frequented it that a simple brawl always turned into a wild-west saloon fight.

It was the first time Hunter had ever entered the pub, and under normal circumstances would have avoided the place, but tonight he was on a mission.

He pushed through the lounge doors with Barry following up behind – watching his back. They were met by an interior that belonged somewhere in the past - dingy, low-lit, and with the smell of stale tobacco hanging heavily in the air. Because of the smoking ban Hunter guessed it was emanating from the pores and clothing of the dozen or so customers who hugged the bar. But then taking one look at them and recognising some of the faces, he wasn't too sure. He knew that some of the people in here didn't like to be governed by society's rules and laws.

There was an instant silence as the small sea of faces 'clocked them,' but as he and Barry strode past it appeared that the punters had returned to their drinks and hushed conversation, though he guessed in reality that eyes would be slyly fixed on them right until they left.

Hunter quickly scanned the room and spotted his quarry, now sporting a Mohican style haircut since their last meeting, tucked into a corner, nursing what looked like a half drunk pint of lager.

He and Barry had already snuck-up and pulled up chairs before David Paynton realised they were there.

"Mind if we join you?" Hunter said rhetorically, squatting down on his seat, slotting his legs under the small round table that separated him from his foe. Barry took up a position at the side leaving David Paynton well and truly boxed in.

David's hazel eyes burned into the pair of them. "What the fuck do you two want?"

"Now that's not a very nice greeting for two old friends of yours David, is it?" Hunter couldn't help but notice Paynton's disfigured nose. It now gave him the look of a boxer who had lost more fights than he had won. For a split-second it gave him a pang of self-satisfaction. He knew that had been his handiwork – but it had been well deserved. A month ago David, his brother Terry and his cousin Lee had ambushed him coming out of his father's gym. Thankfully Barry and his father had been on hand to come to his aid and between them all three of the Paynton clan had been hospitalised.

"How's your Steven? Heard from him?" asked Hunter.

David's face suddenly took on a keen and menacing look. "You fucking know how he is. You and that bitch are the ones who got him banged up. He's on the nonce's wing for his own protection thanks to you."

"Now, now David don't get yourself worked up," interjected Barry. "Steve has only himself to thank for being banged up. He was the one who raped those women and abused those children. He admitted it remember?"

"So you say, so you say." He pushed his six-foot wiry frame back into the high-backed seat. "Anyway what do you two fuckers want?"

"A little chat that's all" answered Hunter.

"A little chat my arse." He leaned forward and took a sip from his pint, never taking his eyes off them. As he set it down he said, "Just piss off and leave me alone."

"Look David we can do this the easy way or the hard way," Barry snapped one of his shovel-like hands across David's knee, then squeezed, digging his fingers into the joint.

David twitched.

"The easy way is we ask you some questions to which you give some honest answers. The hard way is I walk over to that bar, buy a fresh pint of lager, set it down in front of you, drop a tenner on the table and then we walk out of here. I'm sure those at the bar will not be too impressed, especially if they think you're a grass." Barry released his grip. "Now which is it to be?"

David pushed away Barry's hand. "What do you want?" he snapped back.

"That's better," said Hunter, "you know it makes sense." He leaned in towards David Paynton. "First question – what car do you own?"

He saw the puzzled look on his face. Paynton raised his eyebrows seemed to think about the question for a good ten seconds then said, "Mondeo, blue, O five plate, you'll have it on your computer,"

"Second question; which one of you or your mates owns a silver BMW?"

He returned an even more puzzled look; shook his head. "None of us."

"Sure about that?"

Paynton swelled his chest. He stroked at uneven tufts of bristle, which peppered his jaw-line. "Sure I'm sure. We've never owned a BMW; German crap."

"Who do you know then that owns a silver BMW?"

"No one. BMs are for pimps." He swung his gaze back and forth between Hunter and Barry. "Look, where is this going? All these questions about a silver BMW. Was it used in a robbery or something?"

"A hit and run," Hunter replied. He watched for a reaction; there was none.

"Look I'll say this once more and only once more. None of us – that's my family, have ever owned a BMW – never mind a silver one. It's not our style. If I were going for flashy it would be a Porsche. And as far as being involved in a hit and run I have absolutely no idea what you are on about. When was this? Was it in Barnwell?"

"On the North Yorkshire moors six days ago. Ring any bells?"

"I can't even remember the last time I was anywhere near the moors." He paused and began stroking his chin, then blurted out, "Six days ago! Ha! It can't have been me! I was with our Terry. We had to go to the job centre for an interview - they were going to stop our benefits. A bloody waste of time that was as well." His face creased into a smile. "Check it if you want?"

"Don't worry we will," replied Hunter sharply pushing away his chair. He tried to hide his disappointment.

David Paynton's look suddenly took on an air of confidence. "Now wind your neck in and get off my case."

Barry pushed a finger within an inch of David's face. "Watch your mouth. We can still do the dirty on you."

Paynton stared back defiantly. He picked up his pint and took a long swallow.

Hunter and Barry kicked back their chairs and retreated the way they had come.

Hunter paused outside on the footpath looking along the quiet High Street. It was just turning dusk; an orange glow low on the horizon poked between a bank of grey cloud.

"Think he's telling the truth?"

"It wouldn't be hard to check out would it? I hate to say this Hunter - because he's a Paynton, but I think he is."

- ooOoo -

CHAPTER SIX

DAY EIGHT: 31st August.
Barnwell:

The sky had been full of leaden grey clouds all afternoon but somehow the rain had held off and now all that was left of the northerly weather front was a gentle breeze. Grace and Hunter paused at the lakeside edge of Barnwell Country Park listening to the water lap against the shale close to where they were standing and watching the surface undulate as a warm evening wind whipped across the murky lake.

Hunter turned his gaze skywards. He watched as tufts of pink cloud scooted quickly across a blue-green sky. The sun was beginning to drop low. He glanced at his watch. 9.25pm. He reflected that the summer was drawing to a close. Another month and autumn would be here.

It had been a day of mixed fortunes so far. Hunter had listened to the briefing earlier that day with a greater degree of enthusiasm than previously. It had been a mixture of bad and good news. He'd learned that although the team had been working flat out for just over a week the enquiry now appeared to be stalling. None of the detectives were bringing anything new back to briefing. Michael Robshaw, the Detective Superintendent, reiterated that they were still no nearer to identifying who the victim was. He had confirmed that there had been no luck with dental records, fingerprints or DNA and were no nearer to matching the rug she had been found wrapped up in to a crime scene. However he did end the session on a high. He finished by stating that he was excited by a phone call he had received from Professor Lizzie McCormack. It appeared that the pathologist's niece was a forensic medical artist whose skills lay in facial reconstruction and that she had agreed to rebuild the victims face so that a fresh appeal could be made on TV. The detective superintendent ended with an announcement that work to build up the victim's facial features was going to start within the next few days and should be done in just over a week.

Hunter had spent the remainder of the day getting to grips with his overdue paperwork. Then he'd caught up with Grace and arranged to stake-out the country park to see if they could track down Tanya. To that end an hour earlier the pair had left their unmarked car near the reception centre, and aided by a park ranger carried out a reconnaissance of the location where the young woman had been frequently spotted.

Now free from their escort and dressed in their outdoor fleeces the pair looked like any other couple who strolled the lakeside of an evening. And thanks to the ranger's guidance they were able keep themselves in a position at all times where they had a clear view of where the prostitute parked up with her clients. It was now a waiting game.

From out of the corner of his eye Hunter stared at his partner, watching as the gentle breeze lifted her tight curls away from her face, revealing the dark summer freckles which peppered her high cheekbones. He reflected on how he'd cracked on more than one occasion how they made her look like a cute little schoolgirl and she'd responded by slapping his arm.

He broke into a grin. Because although he knew that she'd been acutely embarrassed by his comments he knew that at times she had used her pasted on naive schoolgirl look to good advantage. Many was the time he had watched on with amusement as villain upon villain, as well as the odd Alpha male colleague, had been thrown completely off guard by her innocent childlike-look and demeanour.

At times it had been like watching a python hypnotise its prey.

She turned her head slowly to meet his gaze and it snapped him out of his thoughts.

"Grace now we're out of the office I want to say you've made a cracking job of leading your first murder case. You've made it so easy for me to pick up. I've been conscious about taking it back from you, especially as you've put in so much hard work. And you've managed to fit in the inquest file as well, that's no mean feat." He tried to catch her reaction without making it so obvious he was observing her. He himself had been a similar position so many times as a young detective; putting in all the hours and the enthusiasm only to have it taken away.

"To be honest Hunter I'm glad you did come back when you did. Don't get me wrong I loved it and the team have been stars but I was feeling the pressure. In fact I've not being able to switch off when I've got home and at this moment in time I need to." She took her eyes from the lake and latched onto his gaze. "Anyway did you get done what needed to be done last night? You don't have to tell me if you don't want."

"No I don't mind. I just didn't want to say anything yesterday. Not that I don't trust you but I needed to check things out." He went on to outline the previous night's event with David Paynton, all the time rotating his eyes between his partner and the spot across the lake.

"So you're no nearer to finding out who ran your mum and dad off the road?" she said as he finished the account.

"No and it's doing my head in. My dad's refusing to talk about it and I know he's hiding something. I thought it might have been that bother we had with the Paynton's after you and I locked up Steve; you know them trying to get back at me through my dad. But after our chat last night with David I think I need to be looking elsewhere."

"What about the photos you got of the bald headed guy who you saw your dad arguing with. Has that thrown up anything?"

Hunter shook his head. "Unfortunately they're not that good. I've tried messing about with them on the computer but the light wasn't that brilliant because it was early morning and also the shots were right at the end of my zoom." He diverted his gaze down to the waters edge where a line of ripples suddenly broke across its surface. "Anyway enough about my family's problems, how are you coping?"

"Oh so, so. It's Dave I feel sorry for. It can't be easy being married to a copper, especially as this cop's burdened him with so much just lately. I've promised to make it up to him.

I'm going to take him away for a long weekend. Paris or something - once this job's wrapped up."

"We're worse than teenage kids aren't we?"

Just then their attention was grabbed by the continuous sound of gravel crunching and churning somewhere across the lake, and after a few seconds of straining their eyes in the noise's direction a dark blue saloon swung into view and headed towards a screen of laurel bushes. It disappeared, and after waiting to see if it would re-appear further along the track – which it didn't, the pair swung into action. They kicked into a jog; they already knew from earlier that they could be at the location in just under three minutes; more than enough time to catch the woman if she was with a punter.

Two hundred yards from their destination they decreased their pace and took in a few deep breaths. They could just make out the front grill and a set of headlights through a gap in the bushes. Crouching low Hunter and Grace took a slight diversion slipping across to a dirt path which they knew would bring them behind the car, and it would give them enough time to completely get their breaths back.

The blue Rover was rocking from side to side on its suspension as they approached. Hunter and Grace smiled at one another as they moved in at either side from the rear.

Hunter banged on the roof, at the same time he yanked open the driver's door. "Police" he shouted.

In a simultaneous swoop Grace had the front passenger door open.

Two very surprised faces, a man and a much younger woman both in a state of undress faced them.

"Okay," Hunter snapped loudly "put it away sir and get out of the car."

"And you re-arrange yourself young lady and do the same" said Grace catching the attention of the fair-haired young girl straddling the man across the front seat. The two detectives turned their heads away but kept a firm grip of the door handles whilst the pair got themselves sorted.

One minute later the driver was standing before Hunter, trying to fasten the belt around his trousers, finding it difficult because of his shaking hands. He was a nervous wreck, avoiding any eye contact and most apologetic. All Hunter could get from him whilst he was checking out his details through the Police National Computer was that he was 'sorry' and enquiring if his wife would find out about this.

Hunter glanced across at Grace. He could see from the look on her face that she was enjoying watching the guy squirm.

The driver checked out; no convictions for anything. Hunter berated him for his actions and told him this was a final warning. He couldn't get away fast enough, slinging the car into reverse and practically throwing the girl's cheap high-heeled red patent leather shoes and matching handbag out from the passenger seat whilst Grace prised her out of the car as it began moving backwards. In less than a minute the blue car was shooting towards the park exit, a cloud of dust spinning up from its rear wheels as it tore along the limestone chip track and out of view.

It was their first good look at her. She couldn't have been more than nineteen. The slim petite girl bent down to slip her shoes back on and then hoisted up her black leggings shuffling the waist band over her slender hips in full view of both of them. "Bastard" she mumbled. There was not a hint of embarrassment.

It was such an ungainly sight Hunter thought to himself.

"Now young lady," began Grace, "you and I are going to have a long chat."

"I not do anything wrong. You cannot prove it."

"Oh believe me we can." Grace grabbed the girl's handbag, unclipped the fastener and turned it upside down. Lipstick, a compact case, half a dozen twenty pound notes and at least ten condoms spilt out onto the grass. "That should be enough evidence for a police caution unless you've been cautioned before and then it's a court appearance."

"Bitch" she snarled and snatched her handbag back. Then she dropped onto her knees and began picking up the scattered contents all the while mumbling beneath her breath.

Grace bent down so that her mouth was aligned with the girl's ear. "I need to ask you some questions miss. If I get the right answers then you and I will part the best of friends. If I don't, it's back to the station, and you make no more money tonight. Have I made myself clear?"

Grace's opening gambit reminded Hunter of his interview technique with David Paynton the previous night. He turned slightly to hide his smile.

The girl stuffed the spilled contents back into her handbag, checked the ground to make sure she hadn't left anything and then hoisted herself up.

Hunter's blue eyes scanned the slim frame of the girl. Then he focussed on her face. Her dark eyes seemed set back - almost sunken. She had applied foundation heavily to hide spots, and blusher to cover prominent cheekbones. He quickly realised she wasn't slim and petite because of her build, but because of her habit. He had seen the tell tale signs so many times during the three years he had served in Drug Squad. This girl was a druggie; heroin he guessed by the looks of her.

"First what's your name?" asked Grace.

"I Tanya. I Russian."

Hunter tried to make out the accent. It had a foreign twang to it but somehow it didn't sound Russian.

"Not what people call you? What's your real name?"

"Tanya. I really called Tanya."

"Didn't I make myself clear?" said Grace pushing her face nearer to the girl. "This is not a good start. It looks like you and I are going back to the station to do a few checks. We'll take your fingerprints and photograph and bring in immigration if you persist with this."

She stood there momentarily, switch-backing her gaze between Grace and Hunter. Then she slammed her hands onto her hips. "Okay it's not Tanya."

And then the foreign accent had gone.

Hunter and Grace stared incredulously at one another.

"It's Kerri – Kerri-Ann Bairstow," she continued in a Yorkshire accent. She looked down at the ground. "I found I could make more money if I gave myself a foreign name and fancy background."

"Right now we've got that sorted, let's stop mucking about because I've got some really important questions to ask, and I don't want any more of your bullshit." Grace placed a hand under Kerri-Ann's chin. "Look at me now. I want to see your face when I ask you these questions"

She lifted her head and Grace drew back her hand. Suddenly she looked sorrowful and lost.

"I believe you use this place quite a lot? Bring your punter's here on a regular basis?"

Kerri-Ann nodded. She began fiddling with her fingers, picking skin at the side of her cuticles.

"How many times a week would you say?"

"A couple of times in mid-week, but quite a lot at the weekend, that's when there's not so many people walking about the place."

"And how long have you been using this park for your sessions?"

"Six – seven months."

"And do you always get the guys to park up where we found you?"

She nodded again. "It's out of the way. Hidden from view if there are people walking round the lake."

"Have you heard about the body which was recovered from here just over a week ago?"

She coloured up, started to twitch nervously then gulped and turned away.

Grace grabbed hold of Kerri-Ann's chin again and fixed her gaze square on. "You have haven't you?"

She shook herself free of Grace's grip. "Course I frigging have. You can't miss it. It's all over the news and in the local papers."

"Look Kerri-Ann this is very important. A young woman's body was dumped in that lake just over a month ago, and where you park up with your punters is in clear view of the jetty over there." Grace pointed out towards the wooden mooring dock approximately thirty metres away. "I need to know if you saw any activity on there during one of your visits here. Especially if you saw anyone carrying anything."

Kerri-Ann tried to look away again.

Hunter knew she was hiding something. "This is very serious Kerri-Ann," he interjected, "a young woman has been murdered and her body dumped over there. If you've seen anything we need to know."

"I don't want to get involved. I'm only talking to you now because I want you off my bleeding back. What if whoever did it comes looking for me?"

"You don't even need to think about that. There is no way we are going to give out a witness's name. Anyway what are you worrying about you've been using a false name for ages - just change it and do your trade somewhere else?" continued Grace.

"I don't know. I feel scared about this."

"Kerri-Ann, listen to me, so far you're our only lead. You really might be able to help us catch this girl's killer."

"I didn't see that much."

Hunter knew from that comment that Grace had managed it. This could be the breakthrough. A tingle of excitement ran through him. He wanted to jump in but he knew this was Grace's call.

Grace touched Kerri-Ann's arm and looked into her sunken eyes. "That's the hard part over. Now just tell us slowly what you saw."

"Look if I tell you will you stop hassling me and let me earn some money? I've got a two year old at home and I didn't see the dad for dust once I told him I was pregnant. I can't manage on the benefits they give me." Her eyes darted between Grace and Hunter.

There was silence for a good thirty seconds.

Grace was about to prompt her again when she suddenly blurted out. "All right if it'll keep you off my back and you promise I won't go to court." She began to pick at her fingers again. "It was either a Friday or Saturday evening. I know that much because those two nights are my busiest time and I was with my fourth punter. Probably be about half past ten."

"Can you remember how long ago?"

"No, sorry. I know it was July time. As you said could have been four to five weeks ago. I don't keep a diary."

"Okay Keri-Ann carry on. You said it was about half past ten at night."

"Yeah that's roughly the time because we got back into town about eleven. Anyway we'd finished and I needed a piss so I got out of the car to go behind the bushes. I was just about to go when I heard muffled voices near that jetty thing and it made me jump. I sneaked a look through a gap and saw these two guys struggling with a bundle half way along the jetty. I thought they were just dumping rubbish and I never gave it a second thought. I had my piss and went back to the car. I haggled with the guy who had brought me here because he didn't want to be seen dropping me off in town. Anyway after arguing with him and threatening to make a scene he agreed to drop me off in a pub car park. Then just after we set off we got cut up by this white van, which came from nowhere. It had no lights on and really freaked us both out. The guy I was with stopped the car for a couple of minutes, let it get a long way from us. He was really freaked out as if he knew who it was. He just kept saying he didn't want to be caught by them. I thought it was a really weird thing to say. In fact he wanted to leave me there and then and piss off back home. I remember it clearly."

Hunter exchanged looks with his partner. This interview had just thrown up something he hadn't expected.

"Kerri-Ann this punter you were with – do you know him?"

"No it was a first time and I haven't seen him since."

"Can you remember what he looked like?"

"Vaguely. He was in his early twenties, quite good looking and he had brown curly hair which was about shoulder length if I remember rightly."

"Where did he pick you up?"

"Down by the industrial estate where I normally hang out."

"Can you remember the car he was driving?"

"Now cars I'm good at – have to be – you know in case something happens. I text it into my phone." She unclasped her red handbag and fished out her mobile. It was a slim pink coloured model. She flicked it open and began playing around on the keys. Just over a minute later she looked back at them before glancing back at the screen. "A silver grey Volkswagon Golf. I've entered the first few letters and numbers but not all the car's number." She turned the screen to enable Grace to see the text written registration.

"YP0Two." Grace read out loud.

"I'm sorry that's all I had time to put in."

"Don't apologise Kerri-Ann that is brilliant. Did you manage to get his name?"

Kerri-Ann started to laugh. "You are kidding aren't you."

Grace blushed slightly. "Sorry, stupid question. Anything else you can remember about him – distinguishing marks, scars etc?"

She shook her head.

"Did your punter drop you back off?"

"Yeah eventually, I got him to drop me off near the bus station. He wouldn't drop me near the pub. He was a nervous wreck."

"Can you remember roughly what that time would be?"

"Elevenish, like I said earlier, or something like that."

"Okay that's good. Now I just want to take you back a bit. We'll not keep you much longer. Did you manage to get a make or number of the white van?"

"No. As I say it just came out of nowhere. It scared us to death. It wasn't a big van like a transit or anything, just a small one. I didn't get a number, it happened so fast."

"Did you notice anything special about the van? Anything written on the sides?"

She seemed to think about it a few seconds then shook her head. "Sorry it was dark by this time and it hadn't got its lights on."

"What about the two guys you saw with the bundle on the jetty."

She shook her head again. "Sorry it was so dark. They were just shapes. I never got close enough to even see what they were wearing. As I say at the time I just thought they were dumping rubbish." She paused and studied Grace and Hunter's faces. "I'm not lying, I really didn't see their faces or anything - they were too far away and it was dark."

"Okay Kerri-Ann I believe you. Well done. Now let's get back to our car and get a statement from you."

As they set off towards the car park Hunter knew that this was just the kick-start the investigation needed.

* * * * *

Stirlingshire, Scotland:

"Still no sign of anyone – could be he's on his hols." Rab Geddes announced flinging open the car door and sliding into the driver's seat. He dropped his gaze and examined his shoes in the footwell.

"Jeez just look at the state of these now - my tramping back and forth through the fields. Your turn next time." He stamped his dusty loafers on the car mat and checked them again.

"Will you shut the fuck up moaning." Billy Wallace leant forward and with the back of his gloved hand rubbed the condensation from his side of the windscreen. Though the lane-lined bushes hid their destination away from view he continued staring out along the uneven track. From an earlier reconnoitre Billy knew that the secluded bungalow they had been searching for lay less than a quarter of a mile away.

This was the third parking spot they had chosen that afternoon, spending time in between going for a drive around so that they didn't attract any unwarranted attention from the locals.

Billy punched a thumb at the electric window switch and the smoked glass rolled down a fraction. Outside a continuous gale whistled through the trees nearby causing an unpleasant sound as resisting branches squeaked and creaked. In the last hour he had noticed that the weather had turned and was coming from the north; the wind had picked up fiercely and was whipping across the fields. He thumbed the window back up. Splodges of rain were beginning to scar the windscreen disturbing his view ahead. He wasn't complaining though. This would mean that people wouldn't be straying far from their homes. The last thing he needed was witnesses.

They had driven the hour or so to Killin early that morning. At first he wasn't sure he had heard the name right when he'd eventually beaten its location out of the mouth of Alistair McPherson four days ago, and he'd had to search it out in the road atlas. But when he had found the small village and confirmed the name it had made him smile.

What an appropriate name for the place. Especially for what he had in mind for his next quarry.

He and Rab had entered the picturesque village just before eleven that morning; approaching the village by crossing the stone bridge which spanned the Falls of Dochart. As they had crossed Billy couldn't help but feel that this was a case of déjà vu and for a few seconds it had puzzled him. Then he realised why as he stared across at the foaming stream which pounded between the huge grey rocks and boulders below him. He had seen this location so many times. It had featured in the 1950s film, 'The 39 Steps;' one of his all-time favourite movies. How ironic that the film was about a fugitive on the run - and he should be here; though in his case he wasn't an innocent man. It had brought about another twisted smile.

They had checked out the place; driving up and down the main street. Rab had made a few enquiries about the man they were looking for; stating he was an ex-colleague, and that they were on a fishing trip and wanted to catch up with him. It had not taken long to find that the guy was a regular drinker in the bar of the Clachaig Hotel, located beside the falls. A quick visit there and the pair had left armed with the man's address. That had been seven hours ago.

Now they lay in wait, watching for the occupant to return to the white-washed bungalow in the middle of nowhere.

Billy climbed out of the car, stretched and then relieved himself by the bushes that were keeping them hidden. He fastened his trousers and then glanced at his watch. "We'll give it another hour," he called back over his shoulder, "and then call it a day if they don't return." He stood there motionless, peering over the top of the brambles, feeling the breeze brush past his face, as his gaze settled on the rear of the premises.

Billy was still there as dusk settled and he seemed unmoved by the sudden biting north easterly and slanting rain.

Then his heart jolted in his chest. A light appeared suddenly in the entranceway followed by another in the right hand corner window. In the warm yellowing light he saw a human shadow inside passing across the room windows. He stood transfixed for several moments watching for more activity inside the bungalow; there appeared to be none. He stretched his gloves tighter over his hands; so tight that he could see the outline of his knuckles pushing against the black soft leather. Then he spun around. "Come on Rab, get your arse in gear he's back."

They crossed the field hugging the bushes, Billy leading, his Crombie flapping in the wind. Rab had to put in a jog every couple of paces just to keep up with him. Then twenty yards from the rear of the bungalow Billy halted and pushed himself into the hedgerow. He stared intently and listened. There was only the sound of the wind and the rain lashing against the tops of the trees.

"Right remember what we rehearsed?" Billy questioned in a hushed gravelly tone.

"Sure"

"Okay let's do the business."

Rab brushed droplets of rain from the front of his jacket and tip-toed towards the door. Billy never let his eyes off him. He watched Rab knock and a few seconds later saw the door open. The man who answered it had put on a good couple of stones over the years and the hair was thinner and greyer but he knew this was the guy they were after.

Billy reached the opening just as the man was asking for Rab's ID and had got a foot in the gap even before he had time to react. "Mr McNab – long time no see." He grinned lopsidedly.

The surprise on Ross McNab's face was a picture.

Billy slammed a clenched fist into his pudgy belly. It dropped him to the floor and then just as he was about to deliver a kick he caught movement through the open door into the lounge to his right. A woman whom he immediately guessed was Mrs McNab stood open-mouthed only a few yards away. He caught the terror in her eyes. He reacted quickly pushing through into the room and even before she had time to scream he had a hand clenched around her jaw.

"Rab get the fat bastard up and get him in here!"

Mrs McNab jerked her head and pushed out with her hands, trying to get free of Billy's grip. He responded by digging his fingers deeper into her mandible and then smacked her across the ear. He felt her jaw pop at the side of her face and she let out a wail as she sank to the floor. She fell away from his grasp; she had collapsed from the pain.

Rab locked onto Ross McNab's arm and was forcing it up his back hoisting him forwards, hustling him into the lounge.

"Put him there Rab," Billy said pointing to a mahogany oval dining table with a seating arrangement of six chairs.

Rab manhandled McNab towards the table, kicked out the nearest chair and slammed him into the seat.

Ross was fighting for breath and beads of sweat appeared on his brow.

Billy checked on Mrs McNab; she was out of it. Then in two strides he was at the side of Ross McNab pulling back his fist before delivering a vicious blow to the man's head. He flopped sideways almost taking the chair he was seated in with him. Rab grabbed him and pulled him back upright.

"Right you fucking bastard do you remember me?" Billy hissed.

The man groaned and brought his hand up to his reddened cheek. "Course I do, how can I forget you? Billy Wallace the bastard who murdered Morag McCredie and her wee bairn," he paused. "For nothing."

Without any warning Billy found himself suffering another flashback. They were becoming far more frequent of late. His mind had transported him back to that night; re-living the horror when that junkie slag had ruined his looks. Almost as if it was happening there and then he suddenly felt a sharp sting across his nose and cheek and it caused him to reach up and stroke the outline of the ugly irregular leathery skin scar, which snaked across half of his face.

"And you're one of the fuckers who helped put me away," he growled.

"And you're going away again for this you bastard. If I was ten years younger…"

Before he had time to finish the sentence Billy smashed his fist into Ross's face instantly breaking his nose.

"Grab his hand," ordered Billy.

Rab Geddes snatched hold of Ross McNab's wrist and forced his hand flat, palm downwards onto the table. He tried to resist but wavered under the dizziness of pain.

Billy removed something from the inside pocket of his Crombie. "Now you bastard, me and Rab here have spent thirty six years in prison because of you and that Campbell who grassed us up. Now it's pay-back time." He sprang the switchback blade into action and hovered it over McNab's hand.

Ross tried to pull away but Rab held him firm.

"I want to know where Iain Campbell is. I know you know where he is." Billy watched Ross's face go pale and saw the stain-patch of sweat spread wider across the front of his shirt.

"I don't know what you're on about. Stop this now Billy. This is your final chance or you'll be back to Barlinnie and you'll nae see the light of day again."

Billy started to laugh and then a look of malevolence crept over his face "You are in no position to threaten me Mr McNab. One more chance. Where does that bastard Campbell live?"

"Don't be so fucking stupid."

Billy slammed down the blade directly over Ross McNab's little finger and used his other hand on top as a lever. The knife sliced through the digit easily and even cut a groove into the dark wood of the table. The finger shot across the surface and a gush of blood sprayed out across the polished veneer.

A guttural scream exploded from McNab's mouth.

Billy started jumping up and down patting his hands together child-like. "Oh, I bet that hurt," he delivered laughingly. "Did – it - hurt?"

Billy saw that McNab was now drenched in sweat. It was running in rivulets down the sides of his waxen face, and his chest was heaving, breathing as fast as if he had been jogging.

Billy then became aware of loud moaning noises behind him. Mrs McNab was coming to. He slipped the knife back into his pocket, took the few steps to where she was laid out and grabbed a handful of her hair, hoisting up her head and shoulders. Her eyes snapped open from the pain. A gurgling sound broke from her and she tried to shout, but her jaw was hanging at an awkward angle, unable to move and make coherent syllables; a clear indication it was broken.

Reaching into one large pocket of his long black coat he took out what appeared to be a small washing up bottle. He popped the plastic top and then squeezed the contents over her head. Then he dropped the empty bottle and let go of her hair and she dropped back onto the carpet into a crumpled heap. She forced open her eyes and then blinked as the liquid trickled over her eyelids and onto her cheeks. Then her face took on a look of unimaginable horror.

From that reaction Billy realised the vapours had invaded her nasal passages.

The smell of petrol soon filled the room.

He took out a disposable lighter from his front trouser pocket and held it above her.

"Now this is your last chance McNab. Tell me where that bastard Iain Campbell is?"

* * * * *

They drove the car back to familiar territory on the periphery of Glasgow and left it parked on one of the labyrinth of roads around one of the notable sink estates of Easterhouse.

The pair wiped much of the interior clean with petrol soaked rags and then Rab dropped the keys onto the driver's seat before closing the door and striding away with Billy.

Billy had thought it all through. He had spent enough time in prison over the years to make his plans and consider all the eventualities. This was all going to plan and he liked the feeling of being in control. He took another look back at the silver BMW. Sooner or later he knew that one of the gangs around here would realise it wasn't a police trap and would nick it. Then hopefully the crew would get involved in a chase with the cops and get arrested.

If by chance anyone had 'clocked' the car near the scene back in Killin then that would throw them off his scent for quite some time: Enough time for him to do what he needed to do.

I've come too far now to be caught.

He checked he still had the package in his coat pocket and then nudged Rab and pointed to a gap between the high-rise buildings. They increased their pace before disappearing below one of the tenement stairwells and melting into the dark.

* * * * *

Barnwell:

For a few seconds the salt in his sweat stung Jock Kerr's eyes forcing him to blink longer than normal. He took a step back from the punch bag, squeezed his eyelids together one more time and wiped away the perspiration from his brow. Shaking away the residue from the back of his training glove he resumed his session, bobbing and weaving around the sand-filled bag hanging from one of the gym's arched roof beams and then he dashed off a series of quick-fire blows to the weighted canvas. The bag barely moved; it was momentum he was aiming for rather than impact. Catching his reflection in one of the mirrors that ran along the length of a wall he had to smile to himself. If he had seen one of his boxing trainees performing like this he would have bawled them out.

Stop tickling it, he would have barked. *Give it a good thumping.*

Thankfully he was alone and wouldn't be embarrassed by his performance. His chest still hurt, especially now that he was breathing was heavy. It was his first time back in his gym since the accident and he'd decided to go in after everyone had finished, just to give things a 'try out'. The session had not gone too badly. Another week he told himself and he should be back to tip-top condition. He gave the bag a final punch, wincing as sharpness dug into his rib cage, and then clasped it firmly to stop it swinging. He caught another glimpse of his image in the mirror; he thought he still looked in pretty good shape for his fifty-six years, though his face looked tired and drawn. He put the hangdog look down to the lack of sleep over the past week, and things had been strained at home. Fiona his wife was pressing him to talk to someone and on a couple of occasions he had reacted towards her like he had done with his son. Unlike Hunter however there was a reason behind her pushing him; she knew what lay behind the attack.

Two nights ago, over a bottle of wine, they had sat down and discussed it all at length; how his past had finally caught up with them, and gone over time and time again the 'what ifs,' were they to finally tell Hunter. He had felt so guilty that Fiona had got dragged into this and had cursed himself for being so naïve in believing that he could have buried everything which had gone before. The crux of all their deliberations was when they should tell Hunter. Fiona felt it was now time, whereas he wasn't so sure. Having made his decision an hour ago he had pulled on his training top and jogged down to his gym.

The last half hour on the bag had reinforced his thinking. It was now time to make that call.

He pulled off his training gloves, slung a towel around his neck, and began to steady his breathing, scoping his eyes around his gym as he did so. For a split second a wave of satisfaction washed over him. He could still remember the sight which had greeted him the first time he had walked into this place thirty five years ago. Then it had been a derelict drill hall once used by army cadets. At the time it had swallowed up all of their savings and had required lots of physical work to lick it into shape to enable him to open it up as a gym. But it had been worth it. Now it was one of the best boxing academies in the Yorkshire region. He had gained a reputation as a boxing coach; he had a good stable of future young champions in-the-making, and as an added bonus it was a profitable business. As he dabbed at the last remnants of sweat from his face he just hoped-against-hope that what he had achieved over the years wasn't going to come crashing down around him because of one night from his past.

He wandered into his office and dropped into the swivel captain's chair behind his old desk, leaned back on its springs and looked around his cluttered room. For a few seconds as he pondered putting off the inevitable his gaze leapt around the walls, checking out the now yellowing boxing promotion posters hung all around; every one of his achievements were recorded on those; all the fights he had won back in his heydays as a professional.

He pulled back his gaze and shivered. He mulled over in his head what he needed to say and then yanked open the desk's top drawer. He ferreted around amongst the loose paperwork until he found the card that had been buried at the back all these years. He scanned the number and guessed he would have to add a nought to the beginning of the dialling code after all this time. He took up the handset and punched in the number and then listened to the ringing tone repeat itself at the other end. It took what seemed an eternity before anyone answered; he had almost given up hope and was ready for hanging up. Then a voice came on he didn't recognise; a woman's voice. It sounded younger than it should have. The voice just said a simple "Hello," to which Jock repeated the same greeting.

"Who is this?" said the woman.

"Jock - Jock Kerr, who is this?"

"Detective Chief Inspector Dawn Leggate," she answered. The voice was slow and distinctive with an air of confidence. "Who is it you are after?"

"Sorry I must have the wrong number. It was Ross McNab I was after."

"Oh you have the right number all right." What the female detective said next took him completely by surprise.

He stopped the call in a daze; trying to grasp what she had just said. Suddenly he felt as though he was in a very dark place.

* * * * *

Stirlingshire, Scotland:

DCI Dawn Leggate pushed her driver's door to and pulled on her windbreaker. Zipping it up she stood motionless for a few seconds taking in the surroundings and preparing herself for what she knew lay ahead. She'd deliberately parked twenty yards away from the scene where the lane opened up to the driveway and where it gave her a clear view of the setting. Ahead, facing her, parked on the gravel hard standing were two marked police vehicles, a fire engine and an ambulance, crowded together blocking the entrance to the McNab's bungalow. Blue strobing lights picked out the shapes of the surrounding trees and hedges, then skirted across the fields, momentarily lighting up the waving fronds of wild grasses before finally washing over the white walls of the secluded dwelling. For a split-second there was darkness as the blue lights spun away and then everything lit up again as they continued their sweeping sequence.

She couldn't help think that the image panning out before her somehow felt staged, almost as if it was an opening sequence to a TV drama: Yet she knew this was for real. Thirty five minutes beforehand the police communications room had rung her mobile just as she was about to fork a mouthful of her microwave lasagne meal-for-one. She had sped up the A84 to make it here in record time. Thank goodness the roads had been relatively clear; she knew she'd driven like a mad women, a mixture of frustration and resolve; but it was her turn as 'on-call' she tried to tell herself after another long day at the office. She just didn't need this pressure at this time in her life.

Another gust of wind rose over the hedges and whipped her ginger red hair across her face. Coaxing the shoulder length strands into a loose pony-tail she bunched it into her jacket's high collar and then continued on towards the McNab's home, slipping on a pair of latex gloves whilst desperately trying to avoid the silvery puddles which had collected in the divots along the track.

Squeezing between the emergency vehicles the only light she could pick out inside the smoke-ridden place appeared to be coming from torches, dancing backwards and forwards, fleetingly appearing through the soot-stained glass windows for a split-second before disappearing again - almost a lighthouse effect. She guessed the fire had taken out the electrics. A couple of the window openings were ajar and wisps of white smoke drifted through the gaps before being caught up and whisked away by the north easterly up into the leaden night sky.

She let herself into the darkened hallway. No one was on the door; the crime scene had not been sealed off yet. She mentally ticked it off as one of her priorities.

She found that the air was heavy with soot and smoke and it immediately clogged the back of her throat making her gag. She clasped a hand over her mouth and loosely pinched her nose.

"Hello – anyone there?" she called out even though she knew there was activity somewhere in the bungalow.

Without warning a bright beam appeared from the doorway to her right. It flashed across her eyes temporarily blinding her.

"Sorry ma'am, didn't hear you arrive," she heard a man's voice say. The light had blanked her vision for a few seconds; she couldn't see a thing.

"The bodies are this way."

She blinked frantically, desperate to see. Gradually through a haze of orange flashes a silhouette appeared before her. She picked out the shape; a uniform cop barred the door. She recognised his face from back at the station but couldn't remember his name.

"They're in a bit of a mess," he said stepping back.

She took out her own 1,000 candle powered Maglite and switched it on. A powerful ray of light leapt from her torch, piercing the drifting fire smoke, and focussed in a circle on the opposite wall of the corridor. She swept it through the open doorway into the room, along the floor, up onto the walls, picking out bits of furniture. From its contents she deduced this was the lounge area of the bungalow. The smell in here was different; soot and smoke the same but in a pungent mix which was somewhat sweeter. It reminded her of a barbeque. Then her beam fell onto the chaos and she immediately realised why. Mrs McNab; she gathered it was her from the remnants of a charred dress which was still smouldering. Most of her upper body was char-grilled black except where the skin had split and cracked from the intense heat and here gashes of raw pink flesh gaped through. Eyes stared back at her and white teeth glistened because the soft tissue of the eyelids and lips had shrivelled away. It was a surreal sight.

"The fire officer says she's been set alight with an ignitable solvent of some type – probably petrol," announced the uniform cop who had followed her into the room. "When I got here they were just dousing her out. He said she had been the seat of the main fire."

Dawn shuddered. She felt her skin go goosey.

"It's even worse back here ma'am."

She followed the light from the officer's torch as it settled on a human form seated at one end of, and hunched across, a large oval table.

Striding over the charred remains of Mrs McNab she stepped warily towards the table arrangement. Moving to the left and right of the humped figure she scrutinised. "And this must be Mr McNab?" she asked rhetorically. He was face-pressed against the table surface, a halo of thick cloying blood surrounding his head. A chunk of flesh was missing from his frontal lobe; it looked as though attempts had been made to scalp him. His skin and clothing were mainly blackened though parts of his bare forearms displayed heat blisters.

"It looks as though he's been tortured," interjected the cop again. The beam from his torch flooded across the grimy mahogany veneer surface and settled on an outstretched hand. "Three of his fingers have been chopped off," the officer continued, "and look at this here." He flicked the torch light over to a package of shop bought fish fingers resting in the centre of the table. "There's a note underneath them. I've already read it but not touched it."

Dawn crossed the officer's ray with her own Maglite beam fixing onto an A4 size silted note. Despite the film of soot she could still make out the black capital letters scrawled across the paper. It read - THESE ARE TO REPLACE THE MISSING ONES.

She tried to catch the gaze of the uniform cop but he was in semi-darkness. Her eyes danced between the disfigured hand of Mr McNab and the fish finger box.

"What sick bastard would do this?" she said out loud. She shook herself back from her thoughts and was quickly turning them into crime scene investigation mode. She went through a check-list in her head; earlier whilst speeding towards the scene she had been told over the radio that SPSA were on their way; getting the Scottish Police Services Authority forensics team here was one job she could tick off.

"And I want you to start the visitor log please." She threw the cop her car keys. "There's a clipboard and paperwork in the boot. And seal the area off with tape before you come back to the house. Oh and before you go - point me in the direction of the senior fire officer." Her instructions were interrupted by the ringing tone of a telephone. It was coming from somewhere back in the entrance hall. She paused in mid-flow waiting for voice-mail or an answer machine to kick-in but that didn't happen. The phone continued to ring unabated. She strode over Mrs McNab's body and tramped into the hallway. She found the buzzing phone on a stand close to the front door. Lifting the handset from its cradle, through the thin layer of latex of her forensics glove she could feel a slimy, greasy film covering it as a result of the fire and she raised it towards her ear; close enough to hear, yet not mark her face.

"Hello," she answered. There was no response but she could make out someone breathing heavily and laboured at the other end. "Hello can I help you?" No response. "Who is this?"

"Jock – Jock Kerr." She thought she heard the man say. She made a mental note of the name for later. She tried to determine the region of the Scottish accent, but somehow it had lost its twang. "Who is it you are after?"

She listened carefully to the answer making another careful record in her head.

When he had finished she answered, "Oh you have the correct number all right. This is Detective Chief Inspector Dawn Leggate. Can you give me your details and telephone number - I'm investigating Mr McNab's murder."

The line suddenly went dead. She was left listening to a long purring noise from the handset. She checked her watch and noted the time; she would make a request for caller ID when she got back to the incident room.

Replacing the phone she stepped towards the front door and took in a couple of deep breaths of fresh air. At the entranceway she took a long look around to see if any neighbours overlooked the bungalow. There were none. This was going to be a difficult case she told herself.

Just as she was fixing her gaze ahead a flitting movement up to her right surprised her. A couple of black shapes flashed in front of a pale moonlit sky. She realised what they were; she was watching bats take to the night.

Dawn stood and watched them, fascinated by their swift movement, zipping and swooping and zooming so close to the trees and then at the last moment diving and swinging away. Living in the city she didn't get to see this type of stage-show. It had made her night.

For several minutes she stood there mesmerized. Then she shook herself out of her reverie and fished her mobile from out of her pocket; it was time to bring in the Procurator Fiscal and then begin calling out the troops.

- ooOoo –

CHAPTER SEVEN

DAY TEN: 2nd September.
Barnwell:

Hunter hooked a bare leg across Beth's hip and pulled her naked body closer. She was warm. He snuggled closer still, moving her fair hair away from the side of her head with his mouth and nose and began kissing the nape of her neck. Her skin was soft and scented. His tongue voyaged downwards into the hollow between her shoulder blades and he caressed her skin gently with short kisses before venturing upwards again, where he settled his lips over the lobe of her ear. She gave off a low pleasurable moan.

"You smell nice," he said softly.

Beth moaned again. "I've not woken up yet Hunter," she murmured – then, "what time is it?"

"The boys are still asleep and I don't have to rush into work this morning" he whispered, moving his lips away, back down to the sensitive area around the nape of her neck.

* * * * *

Hunter stepped out through the French doors of the kitchen and onto the block-paved patio nursing a steaming mug of tea between his hands. He took a long and measured look over the garden. Most of the flowers were beginning to fade and needed deadheading he thought to himself. With the exception of the potted plants most of them were now looking tired. What with the events at work over the past few months he had hardly had time for any gardening. In fact it seemed as though summer had not been part of his life this year. He had never experienced a year like this in his career.

He settled himself down onto one of the four ornate, white metal patio chairs arranged around a round table and set his drink down. He loved the view from here; this was where he and Beth loved to sit on warm summer evenings sharing a bottle of wine, grateful for a little peace and quiet after they had tucked Jonathan and Daniel up in their beds.

He felt totally relaxed for once. He had finally caught up with all those restless nights. It had been his best sleep in ages. It also helped that he hadn't had to go in early to work for briefing. He had arranged to have a coffee and chat with Zita, the reporter with the Barnwell Chronicle, and then he was off to the Forensics Lab to see how Professor McCormack's niece was shaping up with the facial reconstruction.

He recalled his phone call with the Forensic Medical Artist that he'd had yesterday. She had invited him up to see the work in progress. He was looking forward to the trip. From an artistic point he couldn't wait to see the result of the application and flair employed by another artist, as well as talk through the process. And as a cop on the investigation, he was eager to identify their victim and see her likeness. He had also decided to make the trip to Wetherby because he knew it would give him some respite from the investigation.

His partner Grace had been unable to go with him. He had spoken with her just before leaving work the previous evening. Detective Superintendent Robshaw had requested her to join him at Barnwell Country Park that morning where he was making a televised plea for witnesses. He could tell Grace had been nervous about the event and he had reassured her by telling 'she would be fine,' and that it was all good experience for a future promotion board.

Before leaving work he'd asked Mike Sampson and Tony Bullars, the other two members of his team, to make a start on the vehicle owner checks. The information he and Grace had got from Kerri-Ann Bairstow had given the enquiry fresh impetus. Not only had she provided them with a partial index number of a Volkswagon Golf, but through further unrelenting questioning by Grace, they had eventually gleaned that the white van was a Renault Kango make and Kerri-Ann felt confident it was a 53 plate – registered in 2003. They had certainly been glad that the sex worker had developed a system of storing descriptions of people and vehicles to memory as her stock-in-trade method for her own personal safety.

It was a real boost and the investigative machinery had been cranked up as a result. The HOLMES team had submitted the Golf's partial registration number to The Vehicle Licensing Centre at Swansea for a search. At the same time they had extracted the names of all the local owners of Renault vans and tracking down them was now the fresh focus for the MIT teams.

Barry Newstead had been given new CCTV work – to scrutinise town centre footage, especially around the bus station, and also identify and flag up any white vans seen around the country park, including searching through stills obtained from speed site cameras.

The enquiry was slowly, but surely, beginning to pick up pace.

* * * * *

Hunter had arranged to meet the Chronicle reporter, Zita Davies, in a coffee shop which was tucked away inside a ladies high-end fashion shop on the High Street. When Zita had confirmed the location the previous afternoon he'd had to double-check the address back with her, such had been his surprise upon hearing the name of the venue. He had passed the shop so many times over the years, in fact he knew that it was one of Grace's frequent shopping haunts, and yet he had never realised a cafe existed there. He was even more surprised at what greeted him, as he ambled past the racks of ladies clothes to make his way to the back of the shop. The retail part opened up to a bright and airy Bistro style cafe, furnished in a contemporary style, and he noted that original artwork adorned the soft cream walls – though the contempoary painting style was not to his taste.

Zita was waiting for him. She had taken a small round table tucked into a corner of the room. She was wearing a white cotton shirt tucked into a pair of jeans and her shoulder length flaxen coloured hair was tied back accentuating her high cheekbones.

He pulled back a chair, slipped off his jacket, hung it over the back and seated himself opposite.

"I've ordered a pot of tea for us. It is tea you drink isn't it?" She flashed him a welcoming smile. "I've already told them that I'm just waiting for someone and to serve it when you come in. Is that okay? I know you said on the phone you could only spare an hour."

"Yeah thanks Zita, that's fine." He told her about going up to Wetherby and his reason for going.

"Oh wow that's cool. You will let me have an early look at the results won't you?"

"I'll be getting some photo's done of it so I'll get one of those across to you as soon as they land on my desk."

"I appreciate that. Anyway how are things with you?"

He was just about to speak when he became conscious of a shadow falling across the table. He checked to his left and saw a young girl dressed in black sidling towards them. It was the waitress. She was carrying a tray of cups and the pot of tea Zita had ordered. He watched as she set it down in the centre of their table and he acknowledged her with a smile before she spun away.

He picked up one of the cups and locked on to Zita's hazel eyes. A hint of peacock blue mascara lined them; it was the only make-up she wore.

"When you say, how are things with you? I'm guessing you don't really mean in my personal life. You really want to know how the investigation is going don't you?"

She held up her hands in a show of surrender. "There's no flies on you Hunter Kerr. I guess that's why you're a detective." She flashed another bright smile. "Are there any new leads?"

"We have one lead Zita but it's in the very early stages. In fact the team are following it up this morning. If it comes to anything you know I'll give you a call."

Hunter watched as she took her eyes from him and drifted them to the teapot. She lifted the lid, glanced inside and then picked up a spoon and began stirring the contents.

"Will it lead to the killer?"

"I honestly don't know. We only came across the information two days ago and as I say the team are out there following it up."

"Is there nothing you can give me for our next edition?"

Hunter pursed his lips. "Do you know Zita we still don't know who the victim is. We don't even know where or when she was killed. All we know is that whoever killed her wrapped her up in a rug and dumped her in the lake. We're obviously going through the routine stuff to try and identify her, but locally there's no report of anyone roughly matching her description as missing, so we don't even know if she's a local woman or not."

"Nothing to identify her then?"

Hunter shook his head. "Nothing. I'm hoping that the facial reconstruction will help do that. And as I've said, once I get some photo's done you are first on my list to get a copy."

She replaced the lid on the teapot and poured some tea into Hunter's cup. "Well I might be able to help you out in return." She poured herself a cup.

"You mean identify her?"

"Maybe. When I got the info regarding the murder, especially that the victim was maybe Asian, I made a few phone calls to some of my contacts. One of those contacts is a woman who runs an Asian women's refuge across in Sheffield. I've done a few stories in the past about domestic violence and this lady provided me a couple of horror stories which affected Asian women. Anyway she told me that recently a couple of young girls had approached the refuge for support and one in particular had made arrangements to stay there but had then failed to turn up and had not contacted her since. She told me she had tried the girl's mobile several times but it was always switched off."

Zita raised her cup to her mouth and Hunter fixed her gaze.

"It may be nothing Hunter but it's obviously concerned the woman who runs the refuge enough to mention it to me."

"And it's certainly enough for me to raise an enquiry and check it out. Can you give me her details?"

"Can I hold back on them a couple of days Hunter? I haven't told the woman I was going to have this conversation and I don't want to betray her trust. I'll need to get back to her and arrange something for you. I'm sure she'll be alright because she does deal a lot with the police, but just to make sure, if you know what I mean."

"No problem Zita. It's good of you to tell me. And anyway if it comes up trumps you can splash it across the headlines how the Chronicle helped with the murder enquiry."

She fixed him another smile.

As he finished his tea Hunter back-tracked on the information which had already been widely fed to the media and deflected a number of her probing questions regarding the latest lead.

"You can't blame me for trying," she said on more than one occasion as he shook his head at her.

Thirty five minutes later Hunter was following her out of the fashion-shop-cum-cafe and waving her off in her car, she promising that she would get back to him with the details of the name and contact number of the woman who ran the Asian refuge, and he promising he would get photo's of the facial reconstruction to her as soon as they were developed.

* * * * *

It took Hunter just over an hour to drive to the Forensic Lab at Wetherby. As he slowed for the gate he couldn't help but think how long it had been since he had last visited this place; where as in the past it had been he, as the young detective, who had the task of safely delivering evidence, now the job employed civilian drivers to take care of the delivery of forensic exhibits,

He flashed his warrant card to the uniformed gate guard and answered a few security questions before being pointed towards the visitor's car park. Strolling towards the Forensics laboratory he could see that with the exception of the increased protection since his last visit very little of the physical structure had changed. The building was of a 1960s design, flat-fronted construction of concrete and glass, though he could see that new colourful signage did its best to break up the grey drabness.

The reception area was remarkably light and airy and he checked in with the receptionist telling her that he was expected in ten minutes time; at ten-thirty. Arriving early for a meeting was something, which had been drilled into him ever since he was a young cop, and it was advice which he had followed through his service.

Hunter had only just taken a seat when Frankie Oliver, Forensic Medical Artist – he checked her name badge – breezed into reception. She thrust out a hand and greeted him with a beaming smile, showing off a perfect set of white, even teeth. So white in fact that Hunter wondered if they had been cosmetically bleached. Frankie was the same build as her Aunt, Professor Lizzie McCormack, slim and petite. Hunter guessed that she was in her late twenties and he could see that she had been blessed with a faultless skin complexion and pretty features. A hint of mascara framed soft hazel eyes. What made her stand out though was her hair style, short and chopped funky, and dyed jet black with hints of burnt copper.

As she led him towards her lab room Hunter let her know the dual purpose of his visit – fascination with the process together with an artistic eye.

"A detective with a soft side eh?" she commented as she swiped her security card through an electric lock reader. "That's unusual, and refreshing. At least for once I'll know my work will be appreciated." She pushed open the door and held it open for him to pass through. He caught a whiff of her perfume; a hint of flowers; subtle; expensive.

She directed him to her workstation. He could see there were half a dozen other white-coated technicians beavering away in the lab as she pointed him towards a white plinth, approximately five feet in height. Fastened to it was a grey half executed bust. It had all the appearance of a head but without fully formed features. Plastic teeth and prosthetic glassy eyes were set but not covered giving it a surreal effect.

"Do you want me to take you through it?" she asked slapping a hand over the lumpy cranium.

Hunter's gaze was already studying the craftsmanship that had gone into the project. "Give me the full works, I'll let you know if you're boring me."

She laughed displaying those perfect white teeth again. "Don't beat about the bush will you! Okay pin back your lugholes and if there's anything you don't understand stop me. I must warn you that once I'm in full-flow I take some holding back." She moved closer to her sculpture. "Firstly I did a cast of the girl's skull. My aunt helped me with that because the original skull has to be devoid of flesh. In the past I have had to work with a clean skull – you know a skeleton has been dug up - but in this case I have been very fortunate. With your body the majority of its flesh is in place. Anyway I digress." She pinched some of the clay away from the head and worked it into a lump. "We use an oil based clay." She thumbed it back onto the bust. "Sticks easily to the cast and can be manipulated for longer. First, plastic pegs are inserted at specific anatomical sites around the skull to indicate the level of tissue required. Those enable me to begin the muscular build up with the clay – like I have done here." She stroked an index finger around contour lines of the face. "Big muscles which form the sides of the face onto the jaw, round the eyes," she continued stroking the clay form to make her point. "Once the muscle structure is in place I can think about the thin fatty layer which lies on the surface – the connective tissue as it is called. A lot of formation was already there on your body even though it was bloated and disfigured. For instance, creases and folds from the underlying muscle structure especially the mouth and shape of the nose were in place. The nose is generally one of the most difficult facial features to reconstruct, because the underlying bone is limited. However because the girl's face is almost intact this model should be exact." All the time she was talking Hunter through her handiwork she was smoothing her dainty slim fingers around the clay head.

She picked up a cloth from a tabletop next to her and wiped some oily residue from her hands. "Another couple of days and I'll have the face finished. Then it'll undergo a paint job. I can match the skin tone exactly from the body colour. Finally I'll add a similar style and colour hairpiece and you should have a vision of your victim. It won't be an exact portrait but the main features will all be there to enable you to have a near a match as possible for identification purposes."

Hunter thanked her. This is what he had been waiting for. He knew from experience that having a name for the victim always gave an enquiry an extra dimension; family; friends; associates and a background which provided a wealth of additional information to point them in the direction of the suspect, or in this case suspects, thought Hunter. He couldn't wait to see Frankie's completed work.

-ooOoo–

CHAPTER EIGHT

DAY TWELVE: 4th September.

Stirling, Scotland:

"What is wrong with this weather?" muttered DCI Dawn Leggate to herself as she watched the rain roll down the double-glazing of her conservatory blurring the vision she had of her bijou garden. "One minute sunshine, next minute flaming rain."

She caught her spectral reflection staring back at her from the glass.

Jesus I look as rough as I feel. Must stop over-indulging with the wine.

Then she continued with her breakfast. She sawed at her over-done toast and forked in a mouthful with some scrambled egg. This was her first breakfast at home in quite some time; well since Jack moved out just over two weeks ago.

The sound of her mobile rattling on the tiled mosaic surface of the round table-for-two snapped her back from her unhappy thoughts. She followed its vibrating movement for a few seconds before grabbing at it – cursing. She knew from the number on the screen that it was work.

I'm on my day off damn it.

Her mouth and tongue juggled with half chewed food which she finally slotted to one side as she did her best to answer the call.

"This had better be good," she said curtly, nipping her mobile between one ear and her shoulder. She listened to the voice on the other end without interrupting whilst continuing to carve up her breakfast into small portions.

"Okay I'll be in in thirty minutes," she finally responded as the caller hung up. This was one of those times when she needed a cigarette. This had been her longest break from them yet; and she was proud of herself. She had managed to stay off them for eight months, two weeks and five days.

But Christ what wouldn't I give for one right now.

Pushing her plate into the middle of the table, she dropped her knife and fork down with a clatter and then moaned to herself again as she scraped back her chair.

* * * * *

"Okay what have we got?" DCI Leggate demanded as she pushed through the door of the CID office, fighting with her waterproof jacket as she wrestled with one sleeve to free an arm. She saw that the office was buzzing; every member of her team appeared to be in.

"I wouldn't take your coat off yet boss," replied Detective Sergeant John Reed, snatching up his own grey woollen top-coat from the back of his chair and grabbing a file from atop a mountain of paperwork strewn across his desk. "We've got a meeting with Glasgow A Division CID. I said we'd join them"– he paused and glanced at his wristwatch – "ten minutes ago." He slipped past her and held the door back open whilst pointing down the corridor with an outstretched arm urging her to hurry up.

She fought to slot her arm back into her waterproof as she dodged sideways past the DS.

He slapped the folder he was holding into her free hand. "That's the hand-over file of the job. I'll fill you in on the way."

In the rear yard of the station DS John Reed turned the engine over of the unmarked CID car and waited for the screen to demist.

Dawn gave him sideways glance. He was raking his fingers through his dark wavy collar length lanks of hair. He could do with a hair cut-she thought to herself. But as long as she'd known John his hair had always been like that; always looked unruly, and with his constant five-o'clock shadow around his jaw line and upper lip he always appeared untidy no matter how well he was dressed. She tried to think how long she had known him.

On and off it had been just over fifteen years. How time had flown.

John Reed had been her first DS when she had joined CID at Stirling and after three successful promotions she had returned first as his DI and now as his DCI. She trusted and respected him implicitly and had taken him into her confidence on many an occasion. He knew her innermost secrets and had never let her down. He was the best DS she had ever worked with and she had tried to persuade him on many an occasion to take his Inspector's exams but he constantly replied that he was happy doing what he was doing and she had given up bugging him.

"You're going to love this job Dawn," he said driving out of the yard, leaning across and tapping the paperwork now spread open on her lap.

John was the only person she allowed in her department to call her by her first name and only then outside the office doors.

"Traffic spotted a silver BMW in the early hours of this morning cruising around one of the Easterhouse estates. The car's registration number pinged up on their ANPR."

Dawn knew John was referring to the Traffic cars on-board computerised Automatic Number Plate Recognition system linked to the National Vehicle Centre.

"There were three recorded hits for various parts of the registered number. Firstly a hit-and-run accident in North Yorkshire where two people were rammed off the road and seriously injured, secondly it was clocked driving away from the scene of a murder on Sauchiehall Street in Glasgow, and finally as you know from our enquiry in Killin, a silver BMW vehicle's registration number was noted by a local walking her dog after she was suspicious about its activities around the village. Anyway 'traffic' had a hell of a blues-and-two's chase but they finally caught it when it crashed into a lamp post." He tapped the paperwork again. "It was two up and unfortunately the little bastards didn't get hurt – not even a scratch would you believe." He turned and gave her a wry smile before quickly returning his gaze back to the road in front. "And look at the Intel sheet of the two they arrested."

Dawn licked a forefinger and turned several pages until she found the section she was looking for. She started to read the typed sheet following the route of her steadying finger because of the erratic motion of the car; she guessed that John was trying to make up for lost time, but she wished he would just slow down a fraction; she was being bounced uncomfortably around in her seat.

"Driver was Sandie Aitkinson and front seat passenger Bruce McColl. Both are well known and have form for burglary and car crime and a bit of anti-social behaviour, but none for violence. It turns out the car is on cloned plates. We visited the address of the registered keeper according to the number plates on it and they still have their own silver BMW on the drive. Anyway after Traffic checked out the chassis and engine number of the car they discovered that it belongs to someone living at an address at Belshill near Glasgow. We asked uniform to do a visit there for us early this morning and they've found the house broken into and the guy who lived there battered to death."

Dawn gave off a low whistle.

"Told you you'd love it."

"Are the two prisoners saying anything?"

"No one's interviewed them yet, we're letting them stew in their cells."

"Do we know any of the victims of the other two jobs – any links to our case at Killin?"

"The names are somewhere in the file, I can't remember them off-hand. North Yorkshire faxed us a copy of the statements from the man and woman who were rammed off the road. They're from South Yorkshire."

Dawn began to search the folder.

"The murder on Sauchiehall Street happened just over a week ago - and get this it's another retired cop – worked out of Shettlestone nick many years ago."

"Just like our Ross McNab?"

"Exactly."

Dawn pursed her lips and let out a low whistle. "Did they work together?"

"Don't know much about the Sauchiehall Street murder at all, other than he was found dumped near a subway and had been given a real good hiding. His face apparently was barely recognisable – ID'd from his NARPO card. That's why I've fixed up our meet with CID from Stuart Street nick. They are dealing with the job and they're now at the scene of this latest killing in Belshill. It's a DI McBride we're liaising with there."

She knew that name and she was trying to put a face to it. She continued picking through the file and found the faxed copies of the witness statements of the hit and run in North Yorkshire. She spotted one of the witnesses was a DS in South Yorkshire – Hunter Kerr she read.

A Yorkshire man with a Scottish surname.

Then the alarm bells started ringing in her head. Kerr – she had heard that name recently.

Now where was it? Then the light switched on. It was the guy she had spoken with on the phone at the McNab's bungalow. He was a Kerr – Jock Kerr. She recalled him telling her that before he had hung up.

She flicked through the faxed statements. And there it was. The driver injured when his car was rammed off the road by the silver BMW. He was also called Jock Kerr. "This is just too much of a coincidence," she muttered to herself,

"What's that Dawn?" asked DS reed, shooting her a sideways glance. "Didn't grab what you were saying."

"Just thinking out loud." She recounted her thoughts to him.

John shook his head. "I know it's a cliché but I have to say the plot thickens."

Dawn nodded in agreement. Gazing through the windscreen she saw the sign for Belshill. She closed the file.

They entered the old part of the town, driving past row upon row of high-rise old pink sandstone tenements that had been refurbished. Then within five minutes they were turning into a newer estate. The road they finally entered had already been cordoned off halfway along and looked to be busy and organised. They had to leave their unmarked car, some twenty yards from the scene because of the amount of police vehicles, which looked more like they had been abandoned than parked, and they made their way on foot towards the taped off area.

Dawn spotted a number of local press photographers angling up their cameras and she pushed past them to approach one of the uniformed officers guarding the scene. She and John flashed their warrant badges and she asked for DI McBride. She was pointed towards a tall slim man with thinning wavy hair who had his back towards them. He was watching the forensic team erect a blue tarpaulin around scaffolding at the front entrance of a pair of modern semis.

Dawn called his name as she got closer and the detective spun around. She immediately recognised him; she had been on the crime scene investigation and the hostage negotiator's course with him.

He flashed a smile and held out a hand for her to shake.

She took it and introduced her DS.

"You know the reason why we're here don't you Alex?" She recollected his first name.

"Aye, your DS told me over the phone. You've trapped up two who were caught in this victim's car. It was on false plates, wasn't it?"

"Aye," replied Dawn. "And we've linked the car to a murder we're dealing with in Killin on the thirty-first of August - just five days ago. A retired cop and his wife – tortured and then set on fire. A local saw the BMW driving around the village several times on the day of the murders and thought it was suspicious so she noted down its number.

"So I heard. And the same car could be linked to another murder just off Sauchiehall Street. We've got CCTV evidence of a silver BMW driving away close to the scene around the time of the murder. We're currently enhancing the images for a reg number and to see if we can identify the driver. My team are dealing with that. I suppose you've heard that the victim was also a retired cop?"

"Aye."

"Well this latest killing is going to grab you as well. I've just been told he's a retired DS who also used to work out of Shettlestone CID. He retired back in nineteen-ninety-four. Whoever killed him has left him in a right old mess. I've not been inside yet, Forensics are setting up the foot plates for us to walk around the scene, but they've said it's a bad one."

DI Alex McBride's response momentarily rocked her back on her heels.

Three retired detectives murdered, and all from the same station.

-ooOoo–

CHAPTER NINE

DAY THIRTEEN: 5th September.

Barnwell:

Standing in the lounge of the pub holding onto an almost empty beer glass Hunter's thoughts drifted away, his inner vision somewhere else; his mind was revisiting the images he had seen on several occasions that morning.

The bound book of colour photographs had been waiting for him on his desk and he had viewed them the minute he had got in. He had been so impressed with the finished look of Frankie Oliver's work. Especially at the life-like features she had managed to form on the reconstructed head of their victim.

He had marvelled at the artistry of the work so-much-so that he had immediately phoned her up, and as one artist to another he had applauded her skills.

The photo's had been referred to at the morning's briefing. The Chief Superintendent had told the team that these were going out on the local news broadcast later that evening.

That announcement had caught Hunter by surprise and he had shot out straight after briefing to get a set over to Zita at The Chronicle; the last thing he wanted was for her to see them on the TV when she hadn't got her own copies as he had promised.

As he hung around the bar he wondered if his partner Grace would be on the local news broadcast. He recollected the conversation they had had three days previously. He recalled how nervous she had been as she had told him that the boss had requested that she should join him for her first experience of a press conference at the scene of a crime. And he hadn't spoken with her since. He'd been so wrapped up in the incident with his father that he had forgotten to ask her how it had gone.

"Penny for them Hunter."

He hadn't spotted Grace coming towards him until she spoke.

"Crikey you made me jump! I was just thinking about you and your fifteen minutes of fame." He pointed to a large wall mounted plasma TV playing without sound. He could see that the National news was on. "Are we going to see your bright cherubic features then this evening?"

She dug his arm.

"Hey less of the cherubic. That means fat doesn't it?" She took a drink from her glass of white wine. "After spending all morning with Mr Robshaw the other day I didn't even get a look-in with any of the TV crews. It was a waste of bloody time. And I'd got myself all done up for it as well."

Hunter broke into a smile. He knew what his partner was like for her make-up and fashion, even on a normal working day. He guessed she would have spent hours the night before sorting out a suitable wardrobe for her debut TV appearance. Now here she was telling him that she hadn't even managed to get a look-in.

"That's because to the press you're a lowly detective, whilst he's an interesting, high ranking, Detective Superintendent, who's running a murder enquiry."

"Are you saying I'm uninteresting?" She dug Hunter again. "It's us who does the leg work and solves the crime."

"Ha but that's not what the public think." He lifted the pint glass to his mouth and drained the last dregs of his beer. He thrust forward his empty glass. "Fancy another?"

He watched her swill the remnants of the Chardonnay around the bottom of her glass before swallowing the last mouthful. "Just get me a coke. I'll have that then make tracks home, I daren't be late this evening I made a promise to take the girls out for a bite to eat. Besides I need to catch up with Dave, things have not been easy over the past couple of weeks."

"Know that feeling. The job just gets a hold of you doesn't it? I sometimes wonder why Beth puts up with me."

"Must be those rugged good looks!"

"Flattery will get you everywhere," he said taking the empty wine glass from her. "One more won't do you any harm."

"Oh, go on then, you've twisted my arm. Then I definitely must go."

Hunter yawed his way to the bar. The MIT team had virtually taken over one half of the lounge. They had broken away from work early to have a couple of swift drinks, and to watch their SIOs appeal on the local news broadcast, before they all headed for their homes.

Some of them were hanging on to another funny story from Mike Sampson, whilst others were just chatting in general.

He knew it was these moments that bonded a team.

Hunter squeezed himself between a small group of regulars who had congregated at the bar and caught the eye of one of the bar staff. He ordered a pint of Timothy Taylor for himself and a glass of Chardonnay for Grace, and just as he was thrusting his hands into his pocket for loose change a loud cheer and several wolf-whistles went up behind him. He spun round to see a sea of detectives faces all transfixed on the television screen. Someone shouted to the bar-staff 'to 'turn it up' and then Hunter began to decipher the sound. The shot was panning in on their Senior Investigating Officer, Detective Superintendent Michael Robshaw, and the announcer said they were speaking from the lakeside at Barnwell Country Park. The newscaster was dubbing the storyline 'The Lady in the Lake.'

The SIO was commenting on the status of the enquiry and as he began to make his plea for witnesses the scene panned out and was replaced by the stills of the reconstructed face of their victim. Blown up and backlit by the television the result looked even more spectacular.

Someone just has to recognise this lady he thought.

- ooOoo –

CHAPTER TEN

DAY FOURTEEN: 6th September.
Barnwell:

Hunter never heard Grace approaching, his thoughts were elsewhere and he jumped as she slapped a fresh sheet of paper on top of the small pile of vehicle enquiry forms he was checking. The paperwork had been left on his desk from the previous day's tasks carried out by Mike Sampson and Tony Bullars and he was checking if all the outstanding enquiries had been completed before he handed them over to the DI.

"Come on get your lazy butt in gear, we've got a prime witness to interview." She stabbed at the pink coloured form she had deposited across his papers.

Just as Hunter started to read she snatched it up. "Isobel from the HOLMES team has just handed this to me, she said it's the breakthrough we've been after."

He tried to grab back the paper she was waving but she spun quickly away snatching her jacket from the back of her seat with her free hand. She fixed him a look. "What are you waiting for Sarge?"

He picked up his own coat and wrestled the car keys out from a pocket before following on her heels out of the office.

* * * * *

"Are you going to tell me what we've got then?" Hunter asked as he swung the CID car out through the gates of the station's rear yard and drove towards the traffic lights that gave them access to the main road. "All you've said so far is drive to the hospital."

Grace pulled down the passenger seat visor and checked her make-up. She smoothed a hand across her nose and cheek before exchanging looks with Hunter. "We're off to see a junior doctor name of," she paused and took a quick glance at the paperwork that the DI had handed her earlier, "Chris Woolfe. He works on Medical Ward Three at the General. Isobel says that he rang in last night after the late news and said he's certain he knows who the victim from the lake is."

* * * * *

Taking the back roads through the woods Hunter was able to push the car faster than the speed limit because there was no traffic and he made the hospital in just over quarter of an hour. He parked the car in one of the mortuary visiting bays, took the POLICE VISITING card from out of the glove box and slid it on top of the dash and then he and Grace took a rear entrance to one of the lift areas. They knew the hospital layout like the backs of their hands.

"Ward Three you say?" asked Hunter pressing the button for the lift.

Grace double-checked the document and returned a nod.

They rode the lift in silence. It squealed and juddered up the two floors before opening up to a directional sign for the ward they required. They followed coloured coded tramlines painted on the corridor floor, taking a sharp left when the yellow line they were following peeled off from the red and blue ones. Medical Ward Three lay behind a double set of closed doors; Hunter could already hear activity beyond them and they were still a good ten metres away. Dispensing a large dollop of hand wash he pushed through the doors with his shoulder rolling his hands together as he entered the bright fluorescent-lit ward.

It seemed as though he had entered a world of chaos; there was so much activity and it stopped him in his tracks.

For a split-second it reminded him of his experience a fortnight ago to the day when his mother and father had been seriously injured and rushed into Scarborough District Hospital. The thought of it again caused a state of panic to sweep over him. He felt his stomach turn turtle.

Yet even though if gave him bad memories he couldn't help but continue to watch, mesmerised by it all. Everything seemed to be happening behind a screen around one of the beds on the ward.

He shook himself out of his trance, exchanged looks with Grace, shrugged his shoulders and widened his blue eyes. He gave her a 'something's obviously going on' look and then stepped towards the nurse's station; that was busy as well.

After a few seconds he caught the attention of an auburn haired plump woman dressed in dark blue. He snatched a glance at her name badge pinned above her breast pocket; it stated, Helen – Ward Sister. His wife Beth was a sister; he knew she was in charge. He finally caught her gaze and flashed his warrant card. "I bet the last people you want to see right now is us?" he said, rocking his head backwards where he could still hear the commotion.

The Sister let out a sigh. "They brought in a twenty-two year old girl in the middle of the night, suffered a stroke just after she'd had a baby – looks like we've just lost her."

He pushed his warrant badge back into his jacket inside pocket. "We contacted the hospital this morning, we we're told a Dr Woolfe would be on duty here."

"That's right. He's tending to the girl behind the screen."

Hunter and Grace took another look down the ward. The activity behind the shielded bed appeared to be dying down.

"We need to speak with him I'm afraid," said Grace returning her gaze back to the ward sister. "We can disappear for half an hour for a coffee and then come back."

"Is it urgent?"

"Could be. He contacted us last night."

"Okay, just give him a couple of minutes. It looks as though we can't do anything else for her anyway. They've been working on her for over ten minutes now, he'll be calling it time soon and so he should be out in a bit." Her response towards the young girl's death was so matter-of-fact, devoid of any feeling. Hunter guessed her job was very much like his, in times of crisis you remove the emotion in order to cope.

They hadn't even taken a seat in the sister's vacant office before Dr Woolfe tracked them down. Dressed in a white, open necked shirt tucked into a pair of jeans he looked very young. In fact if it hadn't been for his nametag and the stethoscope draped around his neck Hunter would never have guessed he was a doctor. He remembered Grace mentioning he was a junior but this guy didn't even look as if he had started shaving yet.

The doctor shook both their hands and dropped into the ward sister's empty seat behind her desk and then beckoned them to sit in low-set seats positioned next to a filing cabinet opposite.

"We'll try not to take up too much of your time, we can see how busy you are," opened Grace.

"A bit like your job eh? No rest for the wicked." He ruffled his fingers through his light brown, collar length, curly hair, leaned back in his seat and crossed his legs. "Is this about my phone call last night?"

"You left a message with one of our teams stating that you think you know who the victim is?" Grace passed across one of the colour photographs taken of the facial reconstruction.

He accepted it and took a long lingering look, gulped several times, then nodded his head. "The guy on TV said this is the girl who you've found at the bottom of Barnwell lake right?" He sounded nervous.

"Yes a couple of weeks ago. She was murdered and dumped there."

"I can't believe that." He shook his head. "I had a right shock last night when I saw it on the news believe me"

"Do you recognise her?"

"Well it certainly resembles a girl I used to go out with. It looks like Samia, but I can't believe it, she's such a lovely girl – or was - if it's her."

"Samia?"

"Yes, Samia Hassan. She lives – or rather she used to live with her parents in Hoyland before we went out together."

"Are you absolutely certain about that? That photo as you know is just a facial reconstruction, the body was in a bit of a mess I'm afraid," interjected Hunter.

"Even so it's an incredible likeness of Samia. Has anyone else phoned in – her mates from uni, and given Samia's name since you showed it on the news yesterday?"

"You're the first." Hunter paused gathering his thoughts. "You said you used to go out together?" he pointing towards the photograph Dr. Woolfe was still holding.

"We were at Sheffield Uni together. I was in my last year when she came. I took her round on her first student's rag week, that's how we met."

"When was this?"

"Year before I started my training – two thousand and six."

"Do you know how old she was then?"

He thought for a moment. "I'm twenty-three now so I would have been twenty-one back then," he appeared to be talking to himself. "She would have been eighteen – nineteen." He paused and then blurted out. "We went out for a short time - well until we had all that bother." He gulped again.

Hunter directed a quick glance at Grace. She was looking engrossed.

"Bother?" Hunter enquired.

"Yeah from her cousins."

"You've got me hooked doc, tell us more."

"Call me Chris please. Where do you want me to start?"

"From where you think best. I'll stop you if I need to ask a question."

"Well as I say we met on rag week. She was with a couple of girls and she joined our group to go round town. We got chatting – she was doing her first year medicine and she wanted to know what to expect. We just hit it off you know and she'd come round to my place from time to time to borrow some notes and chat. After a couple of months I asked her to go out for a meal and she agreed. Things just worked out for us from there. I was in students accommodation and she was in halls of residence and one night after we'd been to the cinema I asked her if she wanted to stay at mine. After that night she'd stay on a regular basis. Sometimes even at weekends when she should have gone home. That's when the trouble started."

"What trouble?"

"Let me just give you some background. Samia's parents are Pakistani but she was English. She told me they owned a shop in Hoyland and lived in the flat upstairs. She had her heart set on being a doctor but she said that they continually badgered her to go to Pakistan for an arranged marriage to her cousin. Apparently the only way they allowed her to come to University was because she promised she would go to Pakistan to meet the cousin during the summer break. She told me she was dreading this because she had never been to Pakistan in her life and didn't want to marry any cousin. She'd seen a photograph of him and he was a lot older than her – in his thirties I think she said, and she didn't fancy him. She wanted the freedom to chose who she married. I heard her a few times on her mobile having a row with her father over this."

"What about the trouble?"

"That was about a year ago now. I had just finished uni and had started my medical training. She had moved in with me into a newer flat. She hadn't told her parents because she was so scared, though she had told them she was seeing me. They had another blazing row. She told me they were threatening to disown her and that she was bringing shame on the family and that she should marry the cousin in Pakistan. I know it upset her a great deal. She tried to speak with her mother a few times but she would hang up on her. Then one night we had just come out of this bar and this car pulls up. Two Asian guys get out and just set about me, gave me a right hiding. They tried to drag Samia into the car but there were quite a few people about that we knew, thank God and they intervened and phoned the police. The two guys took off before the cops arrived. Samia told me they were relatives; she'd seen them before at her house. She didn't like them. She said one of them had been in trouble with the police. She persuaded me not to make a complaint and that she'd sort it. She guessed it was because her parents had found out about us sharing a flat."

"So you never made a complaint?"

"I wanted to. My face was in a right mess. I couldn't work for a couple of days and I got a rollicking from my consultant for turning up to work all bruised. Said I didn't set the right image for a doctor."

"Was that the end of it?"

"Christ, no. There was a couple more. One night we came home and the flat was trashed, and I mean trashed. Everything was in pieces and they had cut up all of Samia's clothes."

"Did you report that?"

"I did that time. I had to for the insurance. We told the police about Samia's relatives but there were no witnesses and they didn't find any evidence to connect them, so that was that. The final straw came when I was on lates one day. I finished my shift about midnight and I was just walking across the hospital car park when the same two guys waylaid me. They'd wrecked my car. And they told me in no uncertain terms I had to finish with Samia or I would end up at the bottom of a lake. Those were their exact words."

* * * * *

Stirling, Scotland:

DCI Dawn Leggate had finally got home just after midnight. It had been another long day. She took a quick shower, checked her answer machine; there were no messages, and fell into bed.

The alarm woke her at six-thirty am and despite having only had five and a half hours sleep, it had been undisturbed and she felt remarkably refreshed. It was strange, she thought to herself, as she brushed her teeth, but she always felt like this when a big investigation was running. It had to be the adrenaline rush she mused.

She made herself coffee, placed bread from the freezer into the toaster and then dialled Alex McBride's mobile.

She could tell from his voice that she had woke him up. She apologised as he told her it had been two am before he'd finally got to his own bed and offered to ring him later but he responded by telling her he needed to be up himself to brief his own team.

"Likewise, that's why I'm ringing you so early," she replied. As soon as it had come out she could have bit her lip. Her retort had come out all wrong. She hoped he wouldn't take her response as being a dig - that he was still in bed and she wasn't - especially that now they were managing a joint investigation together.

She needn't have worried. He gave her an update of the Belshill murder; she scribbled notes into her police daily journal, her concentration only momentarily distracted when the toast popped out. Then prior to hanging up she thanked him and felt the need to apologise once again for waking him up. Before she rang off DI McBride promised to send over a DS and a DC from his team to join her own morning briefing.

She hit the end call button and then dialled the HOLMES supervisor at Stirling and was brought up to date as to the status of the Killin murder enquiry. She made more notes. It was seven-thirty am when she hit the road.

* * * * *

Entering the office Dawn could see that several new incident whiteboards had been set up. The Glasgow city centre and Belshill murder had a board each and they had been abutted onto their Killin enquiry. These all contained very important components of the investigation and from experience she knew that thorough updates on those charts kept them all in touch with the case. More than anything it helped get a feel for things and could point them in the direction of the perpetrator.

She realised they must have been erected the previous day whilst she and DS John Reed had been at the Belshill murder scene liaising with DI Alex McBride.

Looking at their contents and recollecting the notes she had transcribed in her journal a half an hour ago she knew that the morning's briefing was going to be very intense.

She checked the three timelines – the handwriting was wonderfully neat; she couldn't help but think that was a rarity amongst police officers.

Also attached were photographs of the victims, gruesome Scenes of Crime shots plus crime scene locations and maps of each of the surrounding areas. Her eyes darted from log to log. Except for a few things from the Belshill scene everything was here.

Dawn knew she must find out who'd made the effort and congratulate them.

She opened her journal, picked up a dry-erase felt pen and added further notes to the boards doing her best to replicate the script. At this moment she could see that the chain of events link was the stolen silver BMW presently with forensics.

Ten minutes later, standing in front of the incident boards, Dawn Leggate waited for the incident team to finally settle down. The compilation, which included the three victims names, addresses, witnesses, timelines and photographs took over the entire frontage of the room. She rubbed her hands together and studied the faces of her team. She could tell from their expressions that they were fired up.

Dawn knew that it had been a long time since they had been involved in a major joint investigation and the fact that each of the victims had been one of their own would make them even more determined in their efforts to catch the culprit.

She banged a hand over the nearest board. "Guys we've got a busy day ahead of us, lots of work to do, so give me your eyes and ears for the next half hour," then pointing to the furthermost panel she continued. "Firstly our own Killin enquiry. Ross McNab aged sixty-four and his wife sixty-three were murdered on the afternoon of the thirty-first of August at their isolated bungalow. As you know they were both beaten and Ross was tortured prior to his death. Everything about that scene indicates that more than one person was involved in their deaths. A sharp instrument was used to remove three fingers from his right hand and those have not been found. It looks as though the killers took them from the scene and then left behind a box of fish fingers with a handwritten note which stated," she paused and glanced at a photograph of the message that had been recovered next to Ross McNab's body. 'These are to replace the missing ones.' Before the killers left they set fire to Mrs McNab using an accelerant. The PM indicates that she was still alive when they lit her." Dawn paused for maximum effect. She scanned the detectives' faces again. "A woman walking her dog in nearby fields spotted smoke coming from the bungalow and called the fire brigade. The same woman also spotted a silver BMW driving along a track close to the scene. She had noticed this car earlier driving around the village and thankfully had noted its number because she thought it was acting suspiciously." She added, "She's part of the Neighbourhood Watch in Killin." The DCI glanced at the board again. "The resulting fire has damaged forensics but we might be lucky with the note and box of fish fingers. As you all know Ross was a retired detective. He retired thirteen years ago in nineteen-ninety-five." She took a side-step, "Okay moving on," she stabbed a finger below one of the scenes of crime photo's depicting a battered face, barely recognisable as a man's. "Alistair McPherson, sixty-one years, another retired cop, was found, as you can see, beaten to death, near a subway close to Sauchiehall street at seven-fifty pm on the twenty-seventh of August. We have him captured on CCTV cameras coming out of Lauders bar on that street ten minutes prior to his body being discovered. A very small time frame. CCTV also picked up several sightings of our silver BMW driving in and around Sauchiehall Street before and after the attack. The images have been enhanced but both the driver and passenger had their visors down and so there are no clear images of their faces. What we can distinguish however is that it is not the two young men we have trapped up in the cells." Dawn moved back from the second board. "Finally," she slapped her hand over several photographs, which had all been taken from different angles, of an elderly man slumped upright in a carver type chair. "Donald Wilson a retired DS, sixty-nine years old. His body was discovered two days ago in the lounge of his home at Belshill. His hands had been nail-gunned to the arms of his chair and there was an iron burn mark in the centre of his chest. His throat had also been cut. The pathologist has indicated he was killed approximately two weeks ago; the body had early stages of decomposition. The silver BMW on false plates which we have recovered belonged to him." The DCI latched onto several faces amongst her team. She could see they were focussed. "There are two links to all these three killings, firstly the BMW owned by Donald Wilson, which was stolen from outside his house, and which has been sighted around the locations of the other two murders. The two young men, Sandie Aitkinson and Bruce McColl, whom we still have in custody, who were caught driving it, do have form but it's petty stuff, and one of them has a cast iron alibi for the Killin murder. They are sticking to their story that they found it parked up with the keys on the front passenger seat, and we can't knock that. By the end of play this afternoon the Procurator Fiscal has indicated we should bail them." She was in full flow now. "There is another incident involving the BMW but I don't know if that is linked yet or not. On the twenty-fourth of August, three days before the murder of Alistair McPherson, it was involved in a hit and run road accident in North Yorkshire. The driver and his wife were injured in that accident and we have discovered from statements that they have Scottish surnames." She hadn't told the team about her telephone conversation when she was at the McNab's with the man who had called himself Jock Kerr, though she had previously mentioned it to DS John Reed. That was one enquiry she and her sergeant were going to follow up personally. "Coincidence or not, we will be looking into that as one of the actions. The other link as you all now realise is that they are all retired detectives who at one time worked out of Shettlestone CID. The key tasks, which are being pushed out from this briefing, are related to that. I want to know the relationship, working or otherwise, that these three had and what jobs did they work on together. There are checks to be done with Personnel and the Retired Police Officers Association. I want everyone traced who knew these three. I am convinced our answer lies in their past association. I want the evil bastards who did this trapped up as soon as possible."

- ooOoo -

CHAPTER ELEVEN

DAY FIFTEEN: 7th September.
Barnwell:

Hunter rolled his neck and flexed his trapezius as he made his way along the corridor. His muscle-toned frame felt tight but he was sharp this morning especially after the intense training session and three mile run into work.

He'd risen a good hour earlier than usual, promised Beth that he would get a flyer and take the boys to their football coaching session that evening and then made his way to his father's boxing gym and let himself in. He'd spent twenty minutes working the punch-bag, twenty minutes pushing weights and then ten minutes with crunch sit-ups on incline before the run into work.

As he passed the Detective Superintendent's open door he caught sight of his boss working at his desk; he'd obviously gone in earlier than normal as well.

"Morning boss," Hunter greeted him as he passed.

He had only got a few yards further when DS Robshaw's called out, "Hunter, have you got five minutes?"

"Sure boss." He stepped back into the open doorway and made his way into the tidy office. He stood before him looking down. The Superintendent was just finishing off writing some remarks onto a CPS file. Behind him a sharp light cascaded in from a huge double-glazed window and backlit the SIO with a halo effect. His reflection bounced off the surface of his polished desk. Hunter glanced around the room. It was plush and looked organised. This is what he'd like to aspire to he thought.

Michael Robshaw signed off his paperwork with a flourish, clicked the top back onto his Waterman fountain pen and laid it square across his jotter. Then he slipped off his spectacles and lined them up straight alongside his pen. He raised his head and fixed Hunter with a curious gaze. "I've had a complaint about you."

Hunter screwed up his face. "A complaint about me! What am I supposed to have done now?"

"David Paynton rings any bells?"

Hunter took a long hard look at his boss as he searched for a response. The last thing he wanted to do was give him any bullshit. He had known the Superintendent far too long, and also he trusted and respected him too much to pass off an answer which would be an insult to his intelligence. He had worked with him when he had been a detective constable at Headquarters and Michael Robshaw had been his DI. He knew he had achieved his current status because of his abilities over the years to juggle the management of many successful teams as well as handle the politics which came with the seniority of his rank. He had also on a regular basis spent some personal time with him, training at his father's gym, and he had put in many a run with him during lunch-breaks.

He settled for, "what's he said I've done?"

He interlinked his fingers and rested them just in front of his pen.

"Apparently you and one other, and I'm guessing from the description, that the one other was Barry, waylaid him in the pub a few nights ago and gave him the third degree about your father's hit and run. Says you were trying to fit him up with it."

"Just a minute boss, I never..."

He unlocked his fingers and held up his hand; gave him the stop sign. "I'm not going to quiz you on what you did or didn't say to David Paynton. I'm here to tell you to lay off him. He's flagged as part of an ongoing drug squad operation. He's giving them a couple of major local players knocking out cocaine so they want him around. Besides that, I can tell you he definitely wasn't involved. I got a call from North Yorks police late yesterday afternoon, it would appear that the silver BMW involved in your parents' road accident has been found in Scotland on false plates and two young thieves are locked up for aggravated vehicle taking. I suggest you give them a call." He handed across a post-it that contained a telephone number. "That's the officer in North Yorkshire who's dealing with the incident." He leaned back in his large swivel chair. "Hunter you're a great cop, don't put your career in jeopardy for that little shit, and besides you've still got an unsolved murder here to focus on. Now get ready for briefing you've got a busy day ahead after your interview with the doctor yesterday - haven't you?"

* * * * *

The morning briefing focussed on Hunter and Grace's meeting the previous day with junior doctor Chris Woolfe.

Perched on the corner of his desk nursing his second cup of tea Hunter repeated almost word for word what Dr. Woolfe had said. In addition the doctor had given them the names of a few of Samia's close friends she had made at university who would need to be chased up and he had also made time after his shift had ended to do a composite e-fit of the two Asian men who had beaten and threatened him. Printed copies of the computer-generated images together with a note stapled to them stating that the doctor had confirmed they were good likenesses had been waiting on his desk first thing that morning. Hunter handed them round the office as he briefed; no one recognised them.

The HOLMES team had done background checks overnight on Samia's parent's address; there were only three incidents logged – all 999 calls requesting police attendance for detained shoplifters. A voter's register check confirmed Samia Hassan as listed at that address along with her father Mohammed and mother Jilani and there was no record of her being reported missing.

"We don't know what we are walking into today," Hunter finished off. "The doc is convinced our body from the lake is his ex - Samia Hassan, but no one else has called the name in, including her parents, so we don't know what kind of reception we're going to get this morning when we visit. Grace and I will do a softly-softly approach and check out if she is still living there, or if not, if they have heard from her recently. We'll meet back after lunch for a scrum-down as to where we are once we've done the visit."

* * * * *

Hassans convenience store was nestled between a hairdressers and a small post office on one of the arterial roads that led into the small town centre of Hoyland. It had only taken Hunter and Grace ten minutes to drive there from the station.

As they entered the brightly lit store the first thing that Hunter noticed was the pungent smell of pine air freshener. It was strong but not unpleasant.

To their immediate left a long counter spanned the frontage. An Asian man who appeared to be in his early fifties was working behind it. Hunter checked him out. He was slightly smaller than himself, probably about five-foot-eight and overweight; a huge well-rounded stomach strained the bottom buttons of his blue and white striped shirt and sagged over his trousers. A thick head of greying hair skirted the sides of his head but he was bald on top. His most striking feature was his hooked nose. The image of Samia entered Hunter's head and he couldn't help but think that if this was her father then she obviously didn't get her looks from him; Samia's features were far prettier. Then his eyes skirted around the shop. Most of its brightness came from overhead fluorescent lighting. It was set out like a miniature version of a supermarket, well-packed shelves of fresh produce, tinned and packet foods. The back shelves were stacked floor to ceiling with wines, beers and spirits and close to the door newspapers and magazines took up the remainder of the space. He noticed the large flat-screen monitor suspended from the ceiling directly in front of the counter, its screen split into six sections each portion showing a different part of the store. The CCTV images were of good clarity for a change he thought. He made a mental note; they might need that to back-check footage.

The man greeted them with a cheery yet suspicious smile.

"Don't worry we're not selling anything," Grace said him her warrant card and badge.

Now he looked surprised.

"Mr Hassan – Mohammed Hassan?" she enquired.

He nodded.

"Mr Hassan we're just making some general enquiries regarding an investigation we have running. We're trying to track down people who we think might be of help and a witness has given us your daughter's name Samia. Is she around?"

Good start Grace, thought Hunter focussing on the man's face. Watching and listening was just as important a skill as talking when it came to interviews and having a partner who was on the same wavelength was a big advantage.

He saw the man drop his gaze, only for a second or two but it was enough for Hunter to realise Grace had a hit a nerve.

"Samia, er no she's not here." He stumbled over his words.

"Do you happen to know where she is?"

At that point Hunter became conscious of movement at the back of the store and in that same instant into view appeared a slim, petite Asian woman dressed in a peacock blue sari. A flash of gold came from a necklace that she wore over the bright material. She was tramping towards them and he could immediately see the likeness to the photograph they had of the facial reconstruction; though these features were a lot older. He had no doubt in his mind that this was Samia's mother. She started talking rapidly as she approached them.

Mohammed responded conversing with her in similar tones. The conversation lasted for a good thirty seconds. Hunter could only pick out the words 'police' and 'Samia' as she drew nearer.

"Mr Hassan could you speak in English please?"

He turned back to Grace. "Sorry about that. My wife doesn't speak any English I told her you were making enquiries about Samia. She wants to know what type of enquiries you are making?"

"There is no easy way to say this Mr Hassan but we are concerned about her whereabouts."

His eyes diverted again. Hunter watched them latch onto his wife's. Hers were wide and searching. There was a slight delay in his response. "Why are you concerned?"

"Well we're trying to track her down but we don't know where she is."

Mrs Hassan had started chattering unintelligibly again. Mohammed replied similarly his hands becoming animated.

"Mr Hassan if you wouldn't mind?" checked Grace.

"Sorry," he apologised, "my wife is asking what is going on – why are the police here?"

"Do you know where your daughter is?"

"Of course I do she is in Pakistan," he replied sharply.

"In Pakistan," interjected Hunter. "Are you sure about that Mr Hassan?"

"Of course I am. Why are you asking me these questions about my daughter?"

"As my colleague has already said we have concerns about her whereabouts."

"Who has said these things?   Who is causing us this trouble?"

"No one is causing you any trouble Mr Hassan all we are here for is to check on your daughter's whereabouts," continued Hunter.

"She is in Pakistan."

"Whereabouts in Pakistan?" came back Grace.

"She is staying with my family in a small village in the Punjab."

"What's the name of the village?"

"Look what is this all about. All you keep telling me is that you have concerns about her. What concerns?"

"That she might have come to some harm."

"My daughter has not come to any harm she is with my family." He was starting to get agitated.

Hunter alternated his gaze between the man and his wife. He could sense that something was not right between them but he did not want to damage the enquiry at this early stage. "Mr Hassan - may I call you Mohammed?" He looked for acknowledgement.

The man nodded.

"Mohammed we're not here to cause you and your wife any anguish it's just that a close friend of hers has not seen her for a while and has not been able to get hold of her and therefore reported it to us because they thought it was unusual," he lied. "Now if you can just give us a little bit more information as to where she is so that we can contact her it would be a great help."

There was a delayed response before Mr Hassan answered. "You won't be able to get hold of her it's a small village in the mountains. My family do not have a phone. It is not like it is here in England. They are quite poor. They have to walk miles to the nearest town."

"What about your daughter, did she not take her mobile?"

There was a slight pause then he replied, "it will not work in the mountains."

"When did she go to Pakistan?" interrupted Grace. "And where did she go from?"

"I can't remember the exact date, it was about two months ago. She flew to Lahore from London. I can't remember if it was Gatwick or Heathrow."

Grace scribbled some notes in the folder she was carrying. She held it away from his prying eyes so he couldn't see what she was writing. Then she fixed him with a warm fake smile. "Thank you for that. That's a big help."

"Mohammed just one final thing before we leave you in peace," Hunter continued the deceit, but because of the nagging doubts he had from Mr Hassan's answers he knew they had to get sight of where Samia lived before they left. "It's just a procedural thing but in all cases where someone reports something like this to us we have to check physically for ourselves that they haven't come to any harm in their own home. You do understand don't you? We would be heavily criticised by our bosses if we didn't do a check."

There was an uneasy silence for the best part of twenty seconds. Mr Hassan glanced down, seemed to be checking his hands, then he shot a glance at his wife before returning his gaze back to Hunter. "I don't suppose we have any choice."

"Mohammed it's not a matter of choice, it would just help us with our enquiries. We'd be able to report back to our bosses that we're okay with everything," he added his own fake smile.

Mr Hassan began talking with his wife in Urdu. She huffed and clucked back and made an exaggerated gesture of throwing part of her sari back over her shoulder before turning and making for the back entrance.

"My wife is not happy with this interference. We are very private people. We have not done anything wrong."

"Mohammed we're not accusing you of anything, it's just a formality we have to go through," Hunter replied. "Now if you can just show us her room and then we'll leave you."

Mr Hassan set the lock in the shops front doors, turned a sign around to 'closed' and then pointed them through to the rear of the store.

The entranceway at the back led them into a small semi-darkened stairway. It was cooler back here. Beyond that Hunter could see a large breeze-blocked room that was full of boxed goods. This was obviously the store room.

The bare wooden stairs led up to a door marked private and stepping through they found themselves in a lavishly carpeted hallway. There were five doors off the hall. A couple of those doors were open and Hunter could make out the lounge and what appeared to be a dining kitchen area. He guessed the other three rooms were the bathroom and two bedrooms.

"This is Samia's old room," said Mr Hassan pushing open one of the closed doors.

Hunter and Grace followed him in. Hunter's immediate thoughts were that this room was more like a guest room than someone's bedroom. It was completely devoid of any personal effects whatsoever. He could tell by marks on the wall that there been pictures or photographs hung up at one time but these had now been removed. The bed had a duvet draped over it but the duvet cover and bottom sheet had been removed and were neatly folded and lay across the pillows. Hunter guessed it had not been slept in for some time. Against one wall was a chest of drawers the top of which was bare and next to the window on the back wall was a wardrobe. Hunter slipped past Mr Hassan and moved towards the wardrobe.

"Do you mind?" he asked but didn't wait for his answer as he pulled open one door. He looked inside. It was empty except for a few wire coat hangers dangling from a metal rail inside. Next he checked the chest, tugging open its bottom drawer first, then moving upwards slid out the next three. Whilst he carried out an eye search he asked some background questions of Mohammed - how long he and his wife had owned the business; how long they had been resident in this country; which region of Pakistan they had come from; the name of the village where the family lived and the place and date of birth of Samia. All formal questions but he asked them in an informal way in order to obtain as much information as possible without setting off alarm bells. He made a mental record of the answers to keep him at ease.

Finally he pushed all four empty drawers back into place and then as he straightened himself he did another quick scan of the room setting a mental picture for his next visit, which he knew would not be in the too distant future. This room is soulless he thought to himself. Things are definitely not right but he knew they couldn't move too fast under the circumstances. He had to be patient – make the enquiries first and cover all angles.

"Did your daughter take everything which belonged to her? Did she not leave anything behind?"

"My daughter has gone to join my family back in Pakistan. If you want to know she has gone to marry my cousin out there and make a new life for herself."

Whilst Hunter had been checking out the bedroom with Mr Hassan he had been conscious that Grace had slipped away. He found her in the lounge with Mrs Hassan. She was making attempts to talk with Samia's mother but the woman was having nothing of it, all she kept repeating was, " No speak English."

Hunter knew this would be a good time to withdraw and reconvene back at the station to discuss the next steps.

"Well Mr Hassan thank you for your time. You have been most helpful. You have put our minds at ease I'm sure this can be sorted out now."

"I hope it can officer, I hope it can," he responded.

* * * * *

Hunter and Grace sat in the unmarked CID car, which they had left parked by the side of the store. Hunter had turned over the engine but was sat motionless running his hands repeatedly around the steering wheel and staring through the windscreen, not focussed on anything in particular.

"Are you thinking what I'm thinking?" he asked.

"You bet I am. It is Samia we've found in the lake isn't it?"

Hunter nodded in agreement. "Having just done that search and watching Mohammed and his wife whilst you were talking I'm more than convinced that they're either responsible for or involved in her death. We've got some digging to do to match our hunch."

* * * * *

The entire Major Investigation Team regrouped at two pm having been called together by DS Michael Robshaw who had been sat in with the HOLMES team most of that morning listening to the team's updates. The information had come in so thick and fast that for the first time since the investigation had started just over a fortnight ago he could see a clear picture emerging as to where the murder enquiry was heading.

The time line sequence on the incident whiteboard had been reorganised and updated and new photographs had been added. Only ten minutes previously DC Isobel Stevens, the HOLMES manager, had been feverishly writing, putting the finishing touches to the display panel so that it was ready for the meeting.

Michael Robshaw took a last look at the board then slipped off his glasses to address the team. "Okay guys firstly well done everyone, you've made some significant inroads this morning. As a result of your feedback from the tasks you were given, without being one hundred per cent sure, I think it would be fair to say that I'm pretty confident that we now know who our victim is." He folded his spectacles and popped then into his shirt breast pocket. "Hunter, you and Grace have been to see Samia Hassan's parents. Would you tell the team what you have learned?"

Hunter pushed himself back into his seat and scooted it out from beneath his desk.

"As you know Samia's parents – Mohammed and Jilani Hassan – are the owners of a convenience store in Hoyland. They have lived there for the past fifteen years and have been resident in this country for twenty-four years." He glanced down at the scribbled notes he had made in the car before he and Grace had left. "Samia was born here twenty one years ago on the twenty-fifth of July nineteen-eighty-four." As accurately as he could he recounted the morning's visit to the Hassans, only occasionally reading from his notes.

"I managed to tease out of him that his family, and the place where he says Samia has gone to marry and live is a very small village set into the foot of the mountains twenty miles from a town called Sul Banda. It's apparently in the North East of Punjab, at least a day's journey from Lahore. He says the cousin she has married is also called Mohammed." Hunter's blue eyes moved around the room. "Because of the way he answered those questions, although he was edgy, I'm pretty sure he hasn't seen the news bulletins that were put out yesterday. I think if he had done he would have been far more guarded. However from now on there is no doubt he will be - and especially when he sees this week's local newspaper."

"You did a cursory search as well I understand?" enquired Detective Superintendent Robshaw.

"Yeah - without making it too obvious." He recounted what he had done. "There is nothing left in that flat that would indicate that Samia ever lived there. All her personal effects have gone and there are no photos of her anywhere. Grace managed to check out the lounge whilst I was looking over her room and there were no pictures of her there either. It's as if she had never existed."

The SIO thanked him. Hunter wheeled his chair back under the desk.

Det Supt Robshaw turned and fixed his gaze on Detective Sergeant Mark Gamble, supervisor of the other MIT team. "Mark will you input what your team has found out?"

The Sergeant slipped off the edge of his desk where he had been perched and made his way to the front of the room. He ran a hand through his fair hair before leaning against the side of the incident white board near to where three new photos had been blue-tacked to the panel. The colour shots were of Samia Hassan amongst a group of girls of a similar age. They were smiling, happy images and from the background lighting and red-eye effect it looked as if they had been taken either in a pub or nightclub. There was little doubt that the pictures of Samia were a striking likeness to the facial reconstruction done by Frankie Oliver.

Hunter scrutinised the photographs. This just has to be their lady from the lake he thought to himself.

"My team were given the job of tracking down the girls named by doctor Woolfe who had associated with Samia during her time at Sheffield University. We have so far caught up with four of her closest friends. They all describe her as a very bubbly girl who was intelligent. Two of the girls shared rooms with her for several months, prior to her moving in with the doc. She discussed much of her relationship with all of them at some point and there is no doubt she had formed quite intense feelings for him – well until she informed her parents about him. Samia told every one of her friends that her parents completely disapproved of the relationship and one of the girls told us that one Friday afternoon both her mother and father turned up at the flat they were sharing and had a stand-up row with her and tried to get her to come home, which she refused to do. She saw Mr Hassan smack Samia across the face before they left. Apparently after the visit Samia ended up in floods of tears and said that her parents were threatening to disown her because she had brought shame on the family." The DS looped an arm over the top of the panel and sauntered one leg across the other. He leaned comfortably. "All of them have told us about the attack on Doctor Woolfe by the two Asian guys. They said it had happened one Friday night just as they had all come out of a wine bar near the University. The girls confirm that he was punched and kicked to the ground and that one of the men tried to drag Samia into their car. They describe it as an old battered white Corsa. Anyway they all jumped in to try and help and one of them phoned the police and that was when the guys drove off. Two beat cars turned up with uniform but Samia persuaded the doc not to make an official report and that she would sort it out. She later told the girls the two men were her cousins. They also confirm the damage to the doctor's flat as well and they have confirmed that the e-fits which the doc has done are very good likenesses." He uncrossed his legs, pushed away from the incident board and straightened himself. He tapped three photos stuck to the board. "These pictures have come from Samia's Facebook site. They were posted after she had finished uni. She kept in touch with all four girls and occasionally phoned them. They all say she was down; that her parents were continually pestering her to marry a cousin who lived back in Pakistan and that she didn't want to. The last contact anyone had with her was on the twenty-ninth of July. They have tried to phone her mobile many times but there is no ringing tone. We have a record of her number to see if the 'techies' at headquarters can trace it. We've also posted messages on her Facebook site but that's not been updated since the twenty-ninth either."

Michael Robshaw swelled his chest and removed his spectacles from out of his breast pocket. He took out a handkerchief, wiped them and put them on.

"Thanks everyone, the case has moved on with some real momentum today and I think we all know where it is going. I have no doubt in my mind that we are dealing with an 'honour killing' here. I'm sure you have drawn the same conclusion. Because of the sensitivity and the repercussions it could have I want a sealed lid on this. No one discusses anything outside this room. Everything we do have from here on we follow it up with the utmost discretion, just on the off chance that we might have got this completely wrong. I want no backlash from this." He glanced sideways at the panels. There was a list of 'to dos' which he had written earlier. He returned his gaze back to the room. "Okay everyone these are the tasks and there are quite a few. The majority are phone calls and will involve diplomacy and patience from you guys. For some of these enquiries you will have to work through the British Embassy in Pakistan and Interpol okay?" He checked the first bullet point he had written. "First on the list we will need to check if she was ever on any flight out of this country into Lahore. We will also have to check with Border Control here and in Pakistan and we need to check the

Passport Agency to see if Samia was ever issued with a passport. And now we have Samia's details I want another check done of local dentists here and in Sheffield to see if we can come up with an identical match to our body. I also want triangulation done of her phone number - see if we can pin-point where her last call was made from. Finally," he paused and tapped the two e-fit images fastened to the incident panel. "I want a trawl doing of the intelligence system and I want these faxed to surrounding forces. We need to find out who these two are. My guess is that these are the guys that our witness Kerri-Ann Bairstow saw dumping the body off the jetty." He rested his hands onto his hips and turned to face the detectives. He took in a deep breath. "When we have got all those answers - and only when - we go and pay an official visit to the Hassans."

* * * * *

Hunter slid out the two sports bags from the boot of his car, slammed it shut and then because his hands were full knocked the passenger side back door to with his hip; Jonathan and Daniel had left it open as they had bolted into the house. He heard Beth shouting, "Dirty boots off, now." and "Jonathan where have I told you to put them?" He smiled.

Typical lads.

He had managed to get away from work just after four and he had been glad. It meant he had been able to honour his promise to take the boys to their football coaching session. Besides he enjoyed it, especially the final twenty minutes when the session always ended with a dads' against lads' kick-about. It brought back the memories of when he'd played amateur soccer in his twenties for a Sunday pub team many years ago. In fact the last time he had been able to play regularly was two years ago when he had played weekly five-a-side whilst with Drug Squad.

He pushed through the front door into the hallway to find Beth holding onto the bottom newel post of the spindle staircase bawling up to emptiness, "Put your smelly clothes in the wash basket the pair of you and then get in the shower.

I'll be up in ten minutes to dry you off. And no putting on Sponge-Bob Squarepants until you've done that!"

Hunter used the bottom of his heel to close the front door. Just as he was doing so Beth spun round to catch him. She glared. He held up his son's sports bags.

"What?" he replied, trying to suppress a grin. "I've got my hands full."

"You're as bad as they are," she huffed. "How am I supposed to get them to treat the house with respect if you won't take any notice?" she rebuked him.

He put on his scolded-boy look and leaned in to plant a kiss on her cheek.

She held him off with her hand on his chest but couldn't help but break into a smile herself. "You're sweaty as well. Jump in the shower yourself before you come anywhere near me. Here give me the bags, I'll sort them out and for your sins you sort out the boys."

She relieved him of the sports bags and as she turned he slapped his hand affectionately against her firm bottom before sprinting up the stairs.

"You're not too big to feel the back of my hand yourself Hunter Kerr!" he heard Beth shout from below as he made his way to the boys bedrooms to bundle up their discarded football kits and confine them to the clothes basket.

Fifteen minutes later, clean and refreshed and dressed comfortably in jogging bottoms and T-shirt Hunter stepped into the large dining kitchen; a rear extension of their three bedroom semi.

Beth was at their large cooker removing a dish from the oven. He slid behind her and wrapped his hands around her waist and nuzzled the nape of her neck.

"Smells good."

"Home-made Lasagne."

"Hmm, yummy. Fancy a kir?"

"Oh I'd love one Hunter. I've had a pig of a day. A man had a heart attack in the waiting room this morning. The doctor and I managed to get his heart beating again, thank goodness, but by the time the ambulance came to take him to hospital we were an hour behind with all our patients. And you can imagine that some of them were in a state themselves after witnessing it. I've been in catch-up mode all day."

"And I think my day's been tough!"

Going to the wine cupboard he placed a small amount of Frais des bois in two wine glasses and then added the chilled Muscadet from the fridge. He took a sip and savoured the crisp cold fruitiness of the French aperitif. Then he handed a glass to Beth and letting out a deep sigh slunk into a chair around the farmhouse table centre-stage of their kitchen. He smoothed a palm over the hand-hewn oak surface reminiscing for a few seconds about the time when they had bought this. They'd both spotted it in an antique shop in the village of Settle when they'd spent a week in a cottage in the Yorkshire Dales a few years ago. It was an old battered piece of furniture and only three of the chairs matched but they'd instantly fallen in love with it and on the spur of the moment they'd bought it. It had proved to be an ideal gift to one another; it suited the deliberately designed shabby-chic appearance of the rest of the kitchen.

"I've left the boys in Jonathan's room they're playing on their X-Box," he said casting his eye back to Beth who was slicing through the crusted topping with one hand and sipping her kir with the other. "I called in at mum and dad's with the boys on the way back."

"Oh yes," she replied not turning around. "What did they have to say?"

"Mum was in on her own. I asked her where Dad was and she said he'd had to go back up to Scotland for a funeral."

"Oh that's sad. Anyone we know?"

"She mentioned a name, Archie something, but it didn't ring any bells."

Beth stopped what she was doing and spun around. "This is going somewhere isn't it Hunter?" She raised her glass close to her lips but held it there. "Come on spit it out. I can read you like a book."

He returned the look she was giving him. "It was just the way she said it. She said it was an old friend of his - she couldn't remember his full name. I asked a few questions but I could tell she just wanted me to stop and shut up."

"Well you've given your dad a hard time just recently."

"And rightly so. I saw him arguing with someone, which he denied. Then they were run off the road by some maniac, which I think was linked. And when I push him for some answers he won't talk to me. I know he's hiding something but I don't know what. Now this sudden disappearance back up to Scotland – he's not been back there for years and years. In fact come to think about it I can't ever remember him going back up there."

"You're too suspicious Hunter do you know that. It could be a genuine funeral for all you know. Think about it, all your dad's pals from his past will be getting on in years now."

"I can't help but have that feeling that if I hadn't called in to see them it wouldn't have been mentioned."

"I know what you're saying Hunter but there's nothing you can do about it is there? He'll tell you when he's good and ready. Just give him some space."

"There's something not right," he muttered. "And I'm going to get to the bottom of it."

* * * * *

Glagow, Scotland:

"Cop!" Billy almost upended the tray, containing his fish supper, onto his lap as he fought frantically to get his baseball cap down over his eyes.

"Where?" demanded Rab, instinctively sliding himself lower into the driver's seat.

"There!" Using one hand to point, with the other, Billy pulled harder on the peak, lowering it a little further. Then satisfied that he had hidden enough of his face he lifted his head slightly and peered through the windscreen, setting his sights, twenty yards in front, on the dark haired man in the short grey overcoat who was leaning back against the driver's side of the dark blue Vauxhall Vectra. The man appeared to be scanning the street, and he shot a glance in their direction, but it was only fleeting.

Rab went for the key in the ignition but Billy snapped a gloved hand around his wrist.

"No, just wait! I don't think he's spotted us."

"How do you know he's a cop?"

"I saw him a couple of weeks ago at the bail hostel, talking with the supervisor."

Placing his hands on the dashboard he leant forwards so he could get a clearer view.

"I wonder what he's doing here, in this neck of the woods? And it looks as though he's alone. Just wait a moment and see what he's up to. If he clocks us then we piss off."

Billy pushed himself away from the dash and settled back into his seat. Returning to his supper, whilst watching intently out through the windscreen, he picked out several chips from the polystyrene tray and loaded them into his mouth.

Five minutes later he caught sight of movement; a slim, dishevelled man appeared from a small side street, parallel to where the Vauxhall Vectra was parked, and stopped opposite the plain clothed cop.

"Well just look who it is?" Billy's eyelids screwed into hardened slits as he watched the pair strike up a conversation. "I wonder if we're on their agenda by any chance?"

Watching as the shabbily dressed man accepted a cigarette from the detective, he reached beneath his seat, exploring, until he sought out what he had been looking for. Then hooking his fingers around the steel wheel brace he began to slide it out from beneath its hiding place.

"Once they've finished their cosy chat you and I are going to have a wee word with our pal. I don't like it when people go behind my back"

- ooOoo -

CHAPTER TWELVE

DAY SEVENTEEN: 9th September.
Sheffield:

"What's that address again?" Hunter asked pulling the car into the kerb.

Grace slid the handwritten note over the handbrake to where Hunter could see it and ran a French manicured finger nail beneath the scribbled destination he had been searching for over the last five minutes.

Zita had telephoned Hunter yesterday afternoon. She had got back to him with the address of the Asian Women's Refuge and had fixed up a meeting with its owner – her contact.

They had found the street easily enough - just off the Wicker in Sheffield, but all the buildings looked the same; three storey Victorian red-brick houses with their soot encrusted frontages from past industry and with dusty windows. At first glance it appeared as if the majority of them were empty, or more likely were used as storage for the small shops or last remnants of businesses, which still operated in this run-down area. However Hunter and Grace knew that behind one of the doors was the refuge. However, given the absence of a number and knowing that the secret address would have no signage advertising itself, finding it was proving extremely difficult.

"Give the woman a ring Grace, tell her where we're parked and ask her to come out and make herself known, otherwise we'll be here all day."

Grace reached into her handbag, mumbled to herself the telephone number she had scribbled on the inside leaf of the folder, and tapped it into her mobile. Within seconds there was an answer and Hunter listened to the one sided conversation from Grace. Less than thirty seconds later Grace ended the call and slipped the phone back into her bag.

"She'll be down in a minute. She's been watching us drive up and down from her office somewhere up above us but because we're in an unmarked car she didn't come down."

Hunter turned off the engine and as he had parked on double-yellow lines he placed the 'police visiting' card on the front of the dashboard.

A sharp rap on the front nearside door startled them. Hunter looked sideways to see a middle-aged Asian woman crouched down by the door looking in at them. He took in the details of a smile but most of her face was partially covered by a white cotton veil.

Nahida Perveen greeted them with an energetic shake of her hand.

Dressed in a long white cotton dress, embroidered with a gold neckline, Hunter could see she was tall and slender though he still couldn't make out her features because of the veil.

"Sorry I didn't come down and make myself known. We have to be very careful here as you can guess. I forgot to ask Zita what you looked like and some of the husbands and fathers of the women who are staying here will do anything to find this place." Her voice was almost perfect BBC English.

She led them through a solid wooden door into a dark entryway. Hunter could just pick out detailed Victorian tiles, which covered the lower half of the entrance hallway. They followed her up a stone stairway to the first floor where the lighting was better. "We have ten ladies with us at present but I don't think any will make an appearance. They've gone through such a lot and have come here for safety until we can help them turn their lives around. They knew you were coming but you still won't see any of them. Some of them don't even trust the police unfortunately," Nahida said as she took them to the top of the stairs, only occasionally looking back as she spoke.

Hunter still couldn't make out her face.

She showed them through another locked door, guided them along a corridor and then showed them into a room, which Hunter guessed put them somewhere at the back of the building. It was a huge sitting room, brightly lit, with a high ornate plaster ceiling. It was furnished with four sofas and three armchairs, all draped with patterned throws; none of the fabrics matched. They were arranged around two low wooden coffee tables. The carpet was thin, stained and threadbare. Hunter could see that the place had been furnished on a tight budget.

Nahida chose one of the chairs and pointed out one of the sofas, as the place for them to sit. She crossed one leg over the other and leaned back.

That was when Hunter caught sight of her badly scarred face. A clump of pink leathery flesh marred the left hand side of her head.

"You're probably wondering how I got this scar?" she said.

Hunter diverted his gaze and latched onto her almond eyes. He suddenly felt embarrassed. He had held on too long looking at her face. He could feel his cheeks flush.

"Don't be embarrassed." She smiled. "I've lived with this for almost twenty years. That's what made me set up this place." She pulled back her cotton head covering a fraction; it was enough for Hunter to see the full extent of her injuries. The scar wound its way from the side of her left eye over her ear down towards her jaw. A portion of her hair was missing. In its place was a lumpy piece of scarred flesh.

"My boyfriend did this with drain cleaning fluid – a powerful acid." She re-covered her face. "This ended my career. You see I was a TV news journalist working in London – an in-front of camera reporter." She gave them an awkward smile.

"I'll not bog you down with the details because I know you're here on other matters but it will give you an awareness of where I am coming from. The man who did this; my boyfriend, was chosen for me by my parents. He came from my parents village in Pakistan; he was from a family who had been very good friends with them. My father and his father had been business partners before my parents came to live here. I quickly discovered that his values and culture were entrenched in something I didn't really understand and I knew it wasn't going to work within weeks of meeting him. Firstly he wanted me to pack in my job. He started to accuse me of flirting with my colleagues. After nine months I told him I had taken enough and told him I wouldn't be going through with the marriage. I left him one night whilst he was at work and went to stay with a friend – another reporter. He started pestering me with phone calls threatening me so I changed my number. Then he'd turn up at work and security had to intervene. Anyway one night we were celebrating a colleague's birthday in a bar one evening and he turned up. He started accusing me of having an affair and then just threw the cleaning fluid in my face. Fortunately some quick thinking by my friends prevented me from serious injury – they poured drink all over me and then used water from behind the bar, but it still left me with this." She smoothed a finger over the scar. "The police arrested him but he was given bail and fled back to Pakistan – to his family. He's still on the run out there." She shrugged her shoulders. "I continued my career as a journalist but it was all desk work. My editors didn't say as much but I realised my career in front of the camera was over and so I persuaded the company to make me redundant and I used the money to come up here where no one knew me and set this place up, so that I could help protect other Asian women from what happened to me."

"And have you been able to help many?" asked Grace.

"Hundreds over the years. Word of mouth and contacts through solicitors have made this a very popular place for women to turn their lives around."

"And I gather from what you've told Zita that you believe our victim contacted you for help and had made arrangements to come here but never turned up and also that you haven't been able to get hold of her since?" Hunter said.

"That's right. I've tried her mobile several times since our meeting and there's no answer. In fact I rang it as late as yesterday and now it appears to be dead. Not only that, but I saw the news the other evening, and the reconstructed face you showed looked exactly like the girl who came to me for help. When we met she called herself Samia."

Hunter and Grace looked at one another. Grace opened up her folder and slid out an A4 size colour copy of the facial reconstruction. She also took out copies of Samia's photographs from her Facebook site, which her friends had made them aware of. She slipped them across the coffee table to where Nahida had a better view.

"Is this the girl you met?" asked Grace.

She lined up each of the photographs and picked up one, which showed Samia holding up a drink to camera. She scrutinised it for just a few seconds before setting it back on the table. She tapped the photograph and raised her eyes to fix Grace. "This is definitely the Samia I met and spoke with."

"When did she come here?"

"Oh she never came here at all. She originally left a message on our answer machine and left her mobile number. It would have been a good six months or so ago now. I arranged to meet up with her at a coffee place at Meadowhall. It's a place I always use. It's public and it's busy. I also need to suss out the people I'm meeting with before they find out where we are. You wouldn't believe the things the husbands and parents do to try and track down the girls who flee here. I have had people posing as police officers, social workers, solicitors. You name it I've had to deal with it." Nahida leaned forward clasping her hands intently. "I suppose my job is a little bit like yours when I meet up with the people who request my help. I have to sort out who is genuine and who is not."

Hunter knew exactly where she was coming from. He pursed his lips and nodded.

"Can you remember what she said to you?" continued Grace.

"Not word for word but I can give you the gist of our conversation." She settled herself back. "She told me she wanted to get away from her parents but needed somewhere she could hide for a while – where she couldn't be found, whilst she sorted somewhere permanent to go. She said her parents were putting pressure on her to go out to Pakistan to marry a cousin out there and that she didn't want to go. I told her that I could help her out with that. Samia told me that she was being constantly watched since she had finished University; that her parents wanted to know virtually her every move. She also told me that she felt she was being followed and mentioned two cousins. At our first meeting she also gave me details of other problems she had encountered because of a relationship with a young doctor. At the end of that meeting I gave her a number of options which included talking to the police as well as meeting me again. She felt she couldn't go to the police because she didn't really want to get any of her family into trouble. She felt it would just make things worse for her. She really just wanted to get away."

"Did you meet again?"

"We did but that didn't go to plan. She contacted me a couple of times from her mobile and told me she couldn't get away without anyone knowing. Then right out of the blue about six weeks ago Samia rang me. She said she was on a train coming to Meadowhall and asked if I could meet her again at the coffee place just by Marks and Spencers. She was in a bit of a state when I finally got there. She was agitated, looking all around her. I have to say she made me nervous even though I've been involved in so many of these. I was really glad that there were a lot of people around us. She told me she'd managed to sneak out of the flat whilst her father was at the warehouse and she'd brought some things for me to store for her until she could get everything together so she could leave. I could see she was in one hell of a state and I did suggest she should come with me there and then. I could arrange with the police to pick up her other bits she needed later, but she didn't want anyone else to be involved, especially not the police. I didn't want to leave her to do that but she said everything would be okay; she was confident she could finish getting together the last of her things. And in a couple of days, she said, she'd contact me and arrange to be picked up."

"Can you remember when that was exactly?"

"It will be in my diary."

She pushed herself up out of the seat and left the room, but she was only gone a few minutes before she returned carrying a red knapsack in one hand and a large journal in the other. She set the knapsack down on the coffee table, covering the photographs of Samia, then she sat back in the chair, crossing her legs again and flicking open her diary across one thigh. Following a roving finger she drifted her eyes over several pages checking each one before moving onto the next. After a couple of minutes she paused and stabbed at a page. "It was Monday the twenty-eighth of July." She announced looking across at Hunter and Grace. "She was already at the coffee shop waiting for me."

Hunter gazed across to Grace and caught her eye. He knew from the briefing two days previously that her friends had last reported speaking with her the day after - the twenty-ninth of July. Since that day on no one had heard from Samia.

Nahida closed her diary. "From what I remember it was about half ten, quarter to eleven time in the morning. As I said she was really agitated. She was convinced someone was following her. I said I could call security or the police if she wanted and I would bring her to this place, but she said it was only a feeling she had, that she hadn't seen anyone. Also she wanted to pick up some final things before she left home permanently." Uncrossing her legs she leant forward and tapped the red knapsack. "This is what she handed me and asked me to keep it safe for when she got here."

Hunter leaned across and pulled the bag towards him. "Have you had a look inside?" he asked sliding open the top zip.

Nahida shook her head.

He could see that the top section of the bag contained items of clothing and he began to lift out each piece separately laying them down across the coffee table. He counted out two pairs of jeans, four T-shirts, a hooded sweat top, several items of underwear and a pair of trainers. He ran his a hand around the inside lining; he'd emptied that section. He switched his attention to the side pockets. He found make-up and a few items of jewellery – a mix of expensive gold items, a bracelet, two necklaces and a pair of gold loop earrings, together with inexpensive costume jewellery, which consisted of various bead bracelets. Finally he zipped open the front. He had to give the insides a second glance and he couldn't hide his surprised look. With forefinger and thumb gripping the top edge, as though it was a priceless object, he removed the item and carefully placed it over the laid out garments. It was a British passport. He opened up the back section for Grace and Nahida to see.

The personal details and photograph left them in no doubt that this belonged to Samia Hassan.

- ooOoo -

CHAPTER THIRTEEN

DAY EIGHTEEN: 10th September.

Barnwell:

Jock Kerr poured himself a generous shot of Laguvulin single malt.

Just a wee dram after a hard day in the gym.

He pushed back his reclining captain's chair and propped his feet up onto the desk. Swilling the golden liquid around the crystal tumbler he cradled it against his upper chest allowing the peaty aroma to tease his sense of smell. Reminiscing once again, his eyes roamed around the room leaping back-and-forth between the many framed photos and the promotion posters which adorned the walls of his office; all significant memories of his past boxing career. Then he recalled just how it had all come to a crashing halt. Just when he'd been on the cusp of greatness, with a Commonwealth medal to his name, it had all ended prematurely when one single punch, thrown after the bell during a bout, sliced open an irreparable deep wound above his right eye. At the tender age of twenty his career was over; that one punch had ended everything and had landed him where he was now – in one hell of a mess.

He knew that deep down some of it had been his own fault – if only he had known at the time what he was getting into.

Foresight is always a wonderful thing.

Back then he had been a young naïve man with a living to make and his fists were the only tools of his trade. He'd actually used that phrase to the two detectives when they'd interviewed him three days ago back in his native Scotland.

Detective Chief Inspector Dawn Leggate and Detective Sergeant John Reed had picked him up from Motherwell railway station and driven him to a quiet hotel where they'd questioned him in the empty bar area. They'd chosen that place, they'd told him, because they did not want anyone to know he was back in Scotland helping them with their investigation. Initially they had asked him all kinds of questions when they had collected him - not about the murders of the three retired detectives - but about whether he knew if he had been followed or not during his journey. And they had driven a long circuitous route to the hotel. Jock had watched the DS constantly check his mirrors, satisfying himself that they did not have a tail.

That was when he had told them about bumping into the bald headed man in Staithes whom he had recognised from his past and then the subsequent hit and run where he and his wife had been badly injured.

The DCI had said to him that it confirmed their worst fears.

They had talked for well over two hours at the hotel, between them piecing everything together. Jock had been able to give them much of the background to it all and although initially he sensed that the two detectives had been suspicious of what he told them; he knew the signs from his experience with his son, once they had back-tracked over everything and double-checked his story with snippets of information from their briefing notes they had ended the interview by telling him that they were extremely grateful for his help. They said it had significantly moved on the enquiry.

Before they had dropped him back at the railway station they had advised him on his personal safety and the DCI had given him her direct mobile number.

Time and time again during the past two days he had run through in his head everything they had talked about; checking that he hadn't left anything out, though he knew deep down he hadn't; it had been locked away in his memory for so long now. He shivered, staring back at the framed photographs. He'd done his best to bury the past but it had caught up with him.

What a bloody mess.

He swilled the single malt around the glass then drained it in one gulp. For a second he considered pouring himself another but checked himself. He had to keep a clear head. It was time for home.

He placed the tumbler onto his desk coaster and locked the bottom drawer containing his bottle of whisky before pushing himself up from his seat.

Then he made his way through his gym, returning the odd misplaced dumbbell weight to its respective place on the rack before taking a last look back; like he always did, and turning off the lights prior to locking up.

Outside the temperature appeared to have dropped. He shivered again and zipped up his hooded training top. The car park was empty save for his rented Toyota; the insurance company was still assessing the damage to his own car.

That was when he noticed the padded envelope on the step. He glanced down and gave it a puzzled look. Then he surveyed the car park again – this time with a critical eye; it was quiet.

Bending down he picked up the small brown package. There was nothing written on it. He turned it over. On this side he saw that someone had scribbled in thick black lettering 'JOCKS GYM.' The quality of the handwriting was poor.

He felt the envelope; there appeared to be something lumpy inside. He pulled at the sticky fastening and peered into the void.

Suddenly startled by what he thought he saw he recoiled in horror dropping the package. It caused the contents to roll out onto the concrete and it confirmed what he had seen. He let out a gasp as his stomach leapt up to his throat. Three severed human fingers lay at his feet.

-ooOoo–

CHAPTER FOURTEEN

DAY TWENTY: 12th September.
Barnwell:

Hunter leaned back in his seat, stretched up his arms and then folded them across the back of his head, interlacing his fingers. Physically he felt drained yet mentally he was energised. Since his and Grace's meeting with the owner of the Asian Women's Refuge; Nahida Perveen, the investigation had clicked up a gear.

Discovering Samia's passport had been the catalyst. Fingerprints found on it matched those from the body.

He mulled over in his head what they had uncovered over the past few days. The team had tracked down a dental practice in Sheffield; she had signed up to a practice near to the University. Records held there matched the x-rays from her post mortem. They now had official confirmation that their body recovered from Barnwell Lake was that of Samia Hassan.

Phone calls to the UK Border and Immigration Control, and the British Embassy in Lahore had confirmed that no air ticket had been purchased in Samia Hassan's name; there was no record of her passing through Immigration Control in the UK, or of her arriving at Allama Iqbal International Airport in Lahore.

On a local level they had tracked down and interviewed several more friends and acquaintances of Samia through her Facebook site. They had reinforced many facts they already knew; the attack on Dr Woolfe, the burglary and damage to the flat, and Samia's fear of a forced marriage, and they had also determined that no one had spoken with her since the twenty-ninth of July. Now they were attempting to track down the police officers who had turned out to those incidents in the hope that one of them might just have recorded the name of Samia's cousins who had been implicated.

Hunter knew it was a long shot.

Civilian Investigator Barry Newstead had been assigned to Meadowhall to liaise with the police and security team based there in order to gain access and view CCTV footage. Nahida had been able to provide the times, dates and the exact place where she had met with Samia and he had been given the job of locating all that footage and of checking if anything could be of help to the enquiry.

There had been a meeting with Duncan Wroe from Scenes of Crime and his counterpart from The Forensics Science team, and Task Force had been booked for that Sunday to execute a warrant at the Hassans shop and residence.

Things were coming to a head Hunter mused as he looked up from his desk and viewed the work in progress from the incident white board. Long lists of actions and names had now been added to the timeline. In big red capitals 'MOHAMMED HASSAN; JILANI HASSAN and SAMIA's COUSINS?' had been ringed as the main suspects.

As he re-checked the incident board he knew that everything was taking shape, especially now as the raid at the Hassan's was in two day's time.

"Who's the redhead with the gaffer?" asked Tony Bullars pushing through the doors into the office.

His entrance brought Hunter back from his thoughts. He unlocked his fingers and came out of his stretch. "Redhead?" he asked.

"Yeah, good looking, late thirties. I've just come past the office and they seem to be thick-as-thieves together. The door was open and she sounded Scottish - like your mum and dad." He dropped some paperwork in front of Hunter. "That's the operational order and the warrant for this weekend's raid at the Hassan's. The magistrate asked me a few questions but nothing I couldn't handle. I just flashed my bestest smile at her and she signed it up."

Hunter smirked. Tony had always been a ladies' man for as long as he'd known him. Tall and slim, blue grey eyes, chiselled facial features, gelled and styled light brown hair and always immaculately dressed. He was twenty eight years old, still single and he was a charmer. In fact Hunter couldn't recall there being a time when he'd ever met him in the pub twice with the same girl. He glanced quickly at the warrant lying on his desk then back up at Tony. "Bully, don't give me half a story. What do you mean good looking redhead, Scottish accent, in with the gaffer?"

He shrugged his shoulders. "I smell cop – and senior cop at that." He tapped his nose and turned away. "Get you a cuppa?" he shouted back making for the office kettle.

Hunter's head was suddenly elsewhere, especially with everything that had gone on with his father. The recent discovery that the offenders who had been arrested in the car which had run his parents off the road were from one of the sink estates near Glasgow came to mind. He had managed to track down the officer in the case from North Yorkshire only to have been told that he had handed over the paperwork to a female DCI up in Stirling. After several phone calls he had finally managed to determine who the Detective Chief Inspector was and had now left four messages for her, none of which had been returned. Over the last few days whenever he had thought about it he couldn't help but sense that he was being deliberately kept out of the loop.

He rubbed his chin and pondered whether this was the DCI who was running his father's investigation. Well there was only one way to find out.

He picked up the signed magistrate's warrant for the Hassans. It was a good excuse to get a foot in the door.

He made his way down the corridor and could see that the Detective Superintendent's door was slightly ajar. He slowed his pace and strained his ears hoping to pick up some of the conversation. A woman's voice drifted out. Definitely Scottish, though he couldn't make out what she was saying. He paused at the door for just a second then rapped.

"Come in"

Hunter entered Michael Robshaw's office. The redheaded female was in one of the comfy armchairs in the office looking relaxed. She glanced up at him and flashed a smile. He remembered what Tony Bullars had said. She certainly was attractive and looked to be in her late thirties. She was wearing a well-tailored dark blue trouser suit over a white cotton blouse. A visitor's badge had been clipped to her jacket breast pocket; he couldn't make out the name. A folder lay open across her lap. He drifted his gaze and tried to get a glimpse of it. She snapped it shut almost as if she had guessed what he was doing.

He returned a false smile to her, nodded and then turned to his SIO. "Got the Op order and warrant for the Hassans this Sunday boss." He held out the documents.

"Okay Hunter." He reached across and took the paperwork, gave it a quick once-over and then dropped it onto his jotter. "I gather no problems with it."

Hunter shook his head.

"Smashing. Everything is in place as well?"

He nodded again.

"Right thanks for that, tell everyone briefing's at seven thirty am Sunday."

It felt like he was being dismissed. He turned to the redhead. "I couldn't help but notice your Scottish accent. My dad's from Glasgow." That was a good opener.

"Oh yes – yes. I'm from Stirling."

"This is DCI Leggate," interjected Det Supt. Robshaw.

"Not DCI Dawn Leggate?"

"Yes," she responded, sounding surprised.

"I've been trying to track you down for the past few days. I was told by North Yorkshire Police that you had taken over the job investigating my parents' hit and run. Apparently you have arrested two for it."

"Oh yes –yes of course. You're Hunter Kerr?" Her voice seemed hesitant to Hunter.

"Have they been charged?"

"Has your father not said anything to you?"

"No I didn't know if he knew or not. It's been like getting blood from a stone just lately."

"Well things have been discussed with him. He knows where we are in our enquiry."

"Can you tell me then?"

"Well – er."

For a second Hunter thought she appeared flustered.

"You should know better than that. Confidentiality DS Kerr."

"But this is different. I'm a cop."

"So you should be even more aware then. I'm afraid I can't tell you anything. It's an ongoing investigation. I suggest you speak with your father." Her return was abrupt.

"Sorry to interrupt Hunter but I have a few things to discuss with DCI Leggate," Detective Superintendent Robshaw interposed. "If you could excuse us."

Hunter knew from their reaction that there was something more to this but he was being dismissed.

"And if you could close the door behind you Hunter? Thank You," added Michael Robshaw.

* * * * *

Hunter sank back in his chair and rested his eyes. He felt drained and had a thumping head and the TV was interfering with his thoughts; everything was spinning around in his head. He heard the patter of Beth's slippered feet come down the stairs and enter the lounge; she had just tucked up Jonathan and Daniel in their beds. He snapped open his eyes.

"You look tired," she said dropping down on the sofa with a big sigh. "Boys were lively tonight?"

"Sorry Beth I should have taken them up tonight and given you a break." He tried to focus on the TV programme but it was washing over him.

Beth pushed herself up and turned towards him. "All right Hunter what's the matter? You've been at odds with yourself since you got home. Something gone off at work?"

He shook his head. "It's my dad again." He told her about the brief meeting with DCI Leggate earlier in the day. "I called in at mum's on the way home but they weren't in and I've rung their mobiles and dad's gym but there was no answer."

"Look Hunter do you think you might be reading into this more than you should be?"

He pursed his lips. "I thought that myself, but it was the way both the superintendent and the DCI reacted when I tried to probe about mum and dad's incident. She gave me all the confidentiality crap. You know cops don't do that with other cops."

"She might just be a stickler for procedure Hunter. She's from another force, she doesn't know you from Adam."

"No there was something in the way she answered me. She was bullshitting."

"Well you can't do anything about it can you? You're going to have to wait until your dad tells you himself."

He closed his eyes again.

I'm going to get to the bottom of this if it is the last thing I do.

- ooOoo –

CHAPTER FIFTEEN

DAY TWENTY TWO: 14th September.
Barnwell:

By seven-thirty am the incident room at Barnwell police station had become badly overcrowded with Murder Squad detectives, Task Force Search Team members, Scenes of Crime Officers and Forensic specialists all squeezing into any space they could find. There was standing room only.

A large scale street map and a blown-up, colour, aerial photo of the Hassans store, taken by the Force helicopter, together with a hand drawn layout of the property; both store and ground floor flat, dominated one of the white boards at the front of the room.

Hunter led the briefing; he was orchestrating the raid. He handed around photocopies of the operational plan setting out the purpose of that morning's sortie and then quickly got into his preamble. He summarised the investigation to date and then outlined everyone's tasks. Although the team now had the Hassans as TIE's; Trace, Interview, Eliminate, the team still had not been able to identify the attack site where Samia had been killed. That was the crux of the day's task ahead and the purpose of the warrant and he deliberated over his final words; he wanted no stone left unturned.

Shortly after eight am as the Police and Forensic teams were heading out of the station's yard, daylight had just broken through a heavy grey sky. The day ahead looked promising.

Hunter and Grace were leading the convoy and in less than quarter of an hour they were hitting the outskirts of Hoyland. Hunter eased off the accelerator, but only a fraction and he took the turning into the side road at the side of the convenience store quicker than normal, braking sharply to avoid a parked car close to the junction. He mumbled an apology to Grace as the car rocked to a halt. He felt wired. A highly charged tingling sensation surged through him. He was always like this on raids: a flash from his Drug Squad days momentarily took over his thoughts and then just as quickly disappeared as he took in the sight of Hassans convenience store.

In less than twenty seconds they had the premises surrounded. Hunter glanced at his watch: twenty past eight on a Sunday morning and he was surprised to find that the shop was already open.

He and Grace pushed through the entrance doors, Hunter holding out the warrant, whilst Task Force, Scenes of Crime and Forensics disembarked, sealing off the area and sorting out their equipment.

Mohammed Hassan was behind the counter serving a customer with an edition of one of the morning's papers. His jaw dropped when he saw them enter. But that was only briefly. Within seconds he had composed himself and then his face took on a hardened look.

"What is the meaning of this?" he demanded.

"We have a warrant to search these premises Mr Hassan," returned Hunter thrusting the rolled up magistrate's document towards his face. He threw the customer a 'I want you to disappear now' look and followed up by using his head to indicate the door. The customer took the hint – leaving quickly.

"What for? I have done nothing wrong."

"When we came the other day making enquiries about your daughter Samia remember me asking you a series of questions as to her whereabouts and you told me she had flown over to Pakistan?"

Hunter paused and studied Mohammed's face. Tiny beads of sweat suddenly appeared on his forehead.

"Well we now know she was never there because as you will have realised by now from the local news broadcasts we have recently found her body. She has been murdered and I suspect your involvement in her killing."

"No, no you have got this all wrong. I haven't done anything to Samia."

"Mr Hassan I am arresting you on suspicion of your daughter's murder," finished Hunter.

Ten minutes later, in handcuffs and protesting loudly, both Mr and Mrs Hassan were helped into separate marked police cars just as officers were finishing off sealing the frontage of the store with crime scene tape. The premises were now secure and ready to be searched.

Hunter took out a protective forensic oversuit from the boot of his car and quickly slipped it on then watched everyone else kit themselves out as he picked up his clipboard from the back seat. He made a bee-line for Duncan Wroe the Scenes of Crime manager, and the Task Force Sergeant; he wanted to double-check their tasks. He saw that Grace had already taken responsibility for the search of the rear store-room with her team.

For the next three hours Hunter repeatedly moved from one doorway to another through the building watching the Forensics Team photographing, swabbing walls and furniture, lifting carpets and selectively drop various items into evidence bags, whilst Task Force overturned chairs, sofas and beds and rummaged through and behind units and cupboards. The work was slow and methodical but the exhibits were soon stacking up on the landing ready to be removed for tests.

Just as Hunter was about to call time for lunch-break the first positive call went up.

"Got something Sarge." It came from one of the Task Force officers working in the kitchen area. He strode excitedly to the door and waited in the opening; he didn't want to contaminate the search grid. A slightly built, dark haired female greeted him with a broad grin across her face. He saw that the white forensic suit she had on hung loosely in baggy folds around her such was the slimness of her frame.

"Is this what you're looking for from your list?" She proffered him an A4 folded document. He slotted his clipboard beneath his arm and took it from her quickly casting his eyes over the DVLA V12 form. As he peeled over the front sheet with his latex gloves he couldn't help but break into a smile himself; it was a registration document for a white Renault Kango van – on a 53 plate.

* * * * *

Hunter loosened his tie away from his collar and undid his top button. He glanced across at Tony Bullars. "Right let's see if we can wrap this up," he said pushing open the interview room door.

The two detectives strolled into an already warm and stuffy room and eased themselves down on seats opposite Mohammed Hassan and his solicitor. Mr Hassan was looking very uncomfortable; a damp patch stained the front of his shirt.

Another hour of questioning and I'll have Mr Hassan soaking wet with sweat.

Hunter pushed his legs under the table and dropped his paperwork and exhibits onto the veneer surface with a resounding slap for effect. He slowly and deliberately unfastened his cuffs and rolled his shirt-sleeves back to reveal sinewy muscled forearms.

Tony Bullars flicked on the tape recording machine.

"Mr Hassan you understand why you have been arrested, don't you?" opened Hunter. "We have explained to you that your daughter's body has been recovered from Barnwell Lake and that she has been murdered."

Mohammed nodded.

His bearded overweight solicitor began making notes.

"Mr Hassan. I would appreciate a verbal answer. The tape cannot pick up nods."

"Yes, yes," he stammered. Then he licked his lips. "But you have got it wrong I haven't done anything bad to Samia. I haven't killed her."

"We'll get around to that in a minute." Hunter steepled his fingers and looked over them. He tried to lock onto Mohammed's eyes but his were darting around; he was avoiding making eye contact.

A classic sign of guilt.

"When I was at your place a week ago you told me that Samia had flown to Pakistan to get married to a cousin of yours. Do you remember telling me that?"

"I can recall saying something like that but I think you misunderstood what I meant."

"Why would I misunderstand you?"

"Because I might not have explained myself."

"Would you like to explain yourself now then?"

"What I should have said is that I guessed Samia had flown to Pakistan to marry my cousin. You see she packed up all her things a couple of months ago and she told me she was going to Pakistan to marry my cousin."

Hunter gave a wry smile. He pulled his fingers apart and pushed himself back in his chair. "Well that is very interesting she should say that to you Mr Hassan because we have statements from several people which clearly state that she did not want to go to Pakistan to marry any cousin of yours. In fact those witnesses have said that you were forcing her to go there."

"They are lying."

"Why should six different people all say the same thing? That you were trying to force her to go to Pakistan, to force her into a marriage with someone she didn't know."

"She probably told them one thing but really meant another. Samia was happy to marry my cousin."

"If she was happy to marry your cousin why should she pack some of her things together with a view to taking refuge away from you?"

"That is a lie."

"No it is not Mr Hassan. We have a statement to that effect and we also have the things she packed ready to leave you. We also have a statement from someone who states you went to Sheffield whilst she was staying with friends and you argued with her about going to Pakistan to be married and when she told you she didn't want to go you slapped her across the face."

"They are lying. We rowed because I found out she was living with someone. She was bringing dishonour upon herself."

"Because she had a white boyfriend?" Hunter saw Mohammed's face colour up.

"No, no, you are trying to put words in my mouth. She was bringing dishonour upon herself because she was sleeping with him before she was married."

He wanted to probe him further about the involvement of the two men who had assaulted Doctor Chris Woolfe and who had then tried to drag Samia into their car, but at this stage the team had not been able to identify them and he didn't want to alert Mr Hassan to the fact that they were even aware of this incident for fear his two relatives would go to ground, or even disappear out of the country – if they hadn't already done so. Anyway he still had something else he wanted to hit him with. "I put it to you Mr Hassan, because Samia had made her mind up not to enter into a forced marriage and to get away from you that you decided to do something about it?"

"No, no that is not right."

"That you were angry with your daughter. That by her refusal to agree to marrying your cousin, you thought she was bringing dishonour to yourself and so you murdered her."

"No. You are making me out to be a bad man."

The solicitor stopped scribbling and gave a loud throaty cough. "I think my client has fully answered all your questions relating to this terrible act perpetrated against his daughter. If you press him any further you will be in danger of intimidating him."

"Oh I wouldn't want to do that," Hunter returned sarcastically. He leant forward pushing his arms flat across the interview table and interlaced his fingers. He fixed Mohammed with a glare.

Mr. Hassan stiffened.

"Okay then Mr Hassan, seeing as everyone is lying against you and your solicitor is unhappy with my line of questioning about you being involved in the brutal murder of your daughter."

"Detective Sergeant Kerr, that is out of order" interjected the solicitor.

Hunter shrugged his shoulders and returned a look of innocence towards the solicitor. "I apologise if you find my questioning offensive, but my job is to discover the truth in this matter and all your client has given me are answers which are evasive. I don't want to get into a cat fight here on such an important issue so I'll move on – okay?" He paused. "Mr Hassan this morning when we searched your flat - ."

"You had no right to do that," Mohammed interrupted.

Hunter raised his clenched hands a fraction then dropped them back down with a thump.

Both Mohammed and the solicitor jumped.

"Sorry about that," Hunter exclaimed, unlocking his fingers. "Now where was I before I was so rudely interrupted? Oh yes, this morning when we searched your flat – with a warrant," he added in an exaggerated tone, "we found this at the back of one your kitchen drawers." He slid out a clear plastic exhibit bag, which contained the registration document for the white Renault Kango van. "I am showing Mr Hassan exhibit RA One." He slid the document into the centre of the table. "This VR Twelve relates to a white Ranault Kango van registered in two-thousand-and-three. Is this yours Mr Hassan?"

He watched Mohammed blush. A droplet of sweat ran down the side of his face.

"It was mine. I used the van for collecting stock from the warehouse."

"Where is it now? It's not at your premises or parked nearby."

Mohammed Hassan's gaze galloped up to the ceiling.

"Mr Hassan, can you give me an answer?"

"It, it," he stammered, "it has been stolen."

"And when was it stolen?"

"I – I can't remember exactly," he paused. "I think it was taken a couple of months ago."

"Did you report the theft to the police?"

"No."

"And why didn't you report the theft of your vehicle Mr Hassan?"

"Because I didn't think it was worth it."

"You didn't think it was worth it?" Hunter returned dryly.

"Well it wasn't worth that much."

"Detective Sergeant Kerr," interjected the solicitor again. He rested his pen on his notepad and stroked the line of his beard to its point. "Is there some significance to this line of questioning or are you on some fishing expedition?"

"No I am not on some fishing expedition. There is something I am working towards."

"And what would that be?"

"Mr Hassan – your client – has so far indicated that everyone is lying against him and also there is a big coincidence here that I am struggling with"

"A coincidence?"

"Yes a coincidence that your client owns a white two-thousand-and-three plate Renault Kango van and a similar one was seen in suspicious circumstances at Barnwell Country Park shortly after we think Samia's body was dumped in the lake."

"You say shortly after you think Samia's body was dumped."

Hunter wished he had chosen his words more carefully.

"I gather by that comment you do not know for certain that was what exactly happened."

Hunter knew the solicitor had the advantage.

"These might be coincidences Sergeant Kerr, I'll grant you that, but as you well know coincidences do not make for a case. Now unless you have any pertinent questions for my client, I suggest we finish things here...that is unless you have something more concrete?"

At that moment Hunter knew the solicitor had the upper hand. He realised it would be futile to carry on unless he wanted to reveal the information about the two men seen dumping Samia's body and whom the team strongly felt were related to the Hassans. Hunter pushed himself back in his chair and pasted on a false smile. "Mr Hassan I am going to bring this interview to a close. We have a number of further enquiries to make especially to track down your Renault van which has been so conveniently stolen, but I'm sure that when we will find it there will be some further questions for you."

Hunter picked up his papers and the exhibit bag and scraped back his chair. Maintaining his false smile he nodded to Tony Bullars to turn off the recording machine and then he cast Mohammed Hassan a threatening look. "In the words of The Canadian Mounted Police – we always get our man." Then before the solicitor even had the chance to challenge he spun around and strode purposefully out of the interview room.

Closing the door behind him Hunter kept his hand firmly gripped around the handle. Almost as if he was squeezing the very life out of it. In the corridor he turned to Tony. "Fuck, fuck, bastarding fuck." He muttered through gritted teeth.

Tony smirked. "I gather by that outburst Hunter, that one is a tad fractious and frustrated. You could always resort to torturing him for a confession."

His colleague's words lightened his mood and his mouthed creased into a smile. "Now, now Bully, you know that's not my style." He winked and let go of the door handle. "That smug solicitor may have won that battle but he hasn't won the war."

* * * * *

Hunter knew the minute he walked into the incident room that there would be an air of expectancy waiting. Half a dozen faces of the murder squad including Grace and Mike Sampson's all stared in his direction. He raised his hands in a surrender pose. "Sorry guys I failed. No cough, no job. It's back to the grindstone I'm afraid."

Watching the detective's part to continue their tasks he beckoned to Grace and dropped himself down in his chair opposite her. "You have any joy with Mrs Hassan?"

Grace shook her head.

Hunter dropped his shoulders and sighed. "What a bummer." He began picking at his nails as he recounted the interview to his partner. "And I'm afraid SOCO can't help us either," he added, "I rang Duncan Wroe ten minutes ago and he says the Hassans place is definitely not the attack site."

"Me and Mike haven't made any progress either," exclaimed Grace picking up where Hunter had finished. "We couldn't get any momentum going with her. Every time we asked a probing question she'd say she couldn't understand what we were saying. Going through an interpreter as well as a solicitor was bloody awful." She tried to put on a brave face. "Do you know I even tried the motherly daughter approach to empathise with her. You know, tell her what I'd do if it was my daughter and I thought my husband was responsible, but she just sat there stony-faced. The woman is a real heartless bitch. I'll tell you what though I'll be ready for her next time."

Hunter nodded and examined the cuticles of his nails he had been picking. Then he glanced up at Grace again. "The one solid thing from this though is that it reinforces my belief that these two are guilty of some involvement in their daughter's death. Not one of them has shown any sorrow or remorse." He dropped his shoulders. "Unfortunately a jury won't convict them for that. I hate to say this but we're going to have to release them on bail." He spread his hands flat over his blotter and pushed himself up off his desk. "Come on, no time for dwelling on our misfortunes. We owe this to Samia if nothing else. We've still got to find the white van. If that was used to dump Samia's body – and my guess from Mohammed's reaction, and comments, that it was – then it should have some forensics." Hunter headed back towards the doors. "And we'll also seize Mohammed's and Jilani's mobiles before they leave. With a bit of luck once the techies sprinkle their magic dust over them it might give us the two names of the faces from the e-fits."

- ooOoo –

CHAPTER SIXTEEN

DAY TWENTY FOUR: 16th September.
Barnwell:

"I'm glad you accepted my invite," Michael Robshaw said on a soft note and watched for a reaction as he gazed into Dawn Leggate's hazel eyes. He noted that tonight their colour was accentuated by the application of a thin line of brown eyeliner to her bottom lashes.

He had managed to get a table at The Stables restaurant; telephoning that morning immediately after Dawn had accepted his invitation to dine. He had booked one of the tables where there was the view into the old cobbled courtyard.

As he held her gaze Michael also registered the colour of her upper eyelids as well; a dusting of two tones of brown powder to the eyelids; not too dark, not too light, and her face had a thin layering of tan foundation. He couldn't help but think how that little bit of make-up had enhanced the prettiness of her features; she hadn't worn any make up on her first visit to his office four days ago.

"I'm glad you invited me." She pulled away from his gaze and lifted her wine glass. She took a sip of her chilled Pino Grigio. "You know what it's like staying in a motel. No matter how nice they are you can't beat your own home. It's nice to have a friendly face to talk to."

"I thought you were down here with your DS?" he responded suddenly feeling embarrassed that he might have stared just a little too long into her eyes. He dragged back his gaze and took a swig of his beer.

"He's gone back to Stirling to brief the team. Now that it looks as though Billy Wallace and Rab Geddes are down here, they've assigned me six officers to see if we can track the pair down. He'll be back down tomorrow with the team."

"Sorry I can only supply one officer to you, but as you know we're up to our necks with our own murder. The person you've got though is local and a good detective to boot."

"Will they report back to DS Kerr?"

"No the officer is from our Intelligence Unit. I've briefed him and told him the importance that he only discusses things with your team for the moment."

"Good. I'll keep you up to date with everything. By the way do you think I got away with it the other day when Kerr asked me all those questions?"

"Not one bit. Hunter doesn't miss a trick. He knows you're hiding something just like he knows his old man is holding back." He set down his pint. "Anyway why hasn't Jock said something to him yet, especially after this latest incident – the severed fingers left as a warning?"

"When he came up and gave us the background to all this he said he'd like to tell his son himself and in his own time. He said he had a special relationship with him and wasn't quite sure how to break it to him just yet. He wasn't sure how he was going to react. I think he's hoping we can get these guys and that will be the end of it all - but I'm afraid it will only be the beginning – they'll want their day in court and the media circus are going to love this story. And that's if we get to them before they get to Jock. Billy and Rab are real nasty pieces of work – pure evil. I've already told you how they tortured those retired detectives before they killed them. I offered to move him to somewhere safe but he said no. So I'm juggling four of the team with obs on his house and his gym. It's not a perfect situation with those resources but we'll try and cover as best we can and hopefully catch them. One thing is for sure, Jock is going to need as much support as possible and the sooner he tells his son the better." She set down her glass and ruffled her fingers through her mane of auburn rinsed ginger hair.

Michael found himself staring again and he had to mentally check himself. *You daft pillock, she's only agreed to go out for a meal. Behave yourself you're acting like a love sick teenager.*

"What's Hunter like? Is he a good cop?"

"Very - one of the best I've worked with. Completely dependable and a good DS as well - can get the best out of anybody. Sails a little bit close to the wind sometimes but he's good at covering his back. I've had to pull him up a couple of times when the District Commander has got a whiff of his antics, but I always back him and give him a little rein because he always gets results. He's never let me down yet." He took another drink of his beer and picked up the menu. He was feeling hungry.

He scanned the selection; he could just make out the choices without his reading glasses. "Have you decided on what you want to order?" Michael waved the menu. "I can recommend the mussels as a starter. Cooked in brandy and cream – I had them a couple of months ago."

"Yummy sounds good. I'll give them a try."

"I'll tell you this for nothing," continued Michael setting down the menu, "Hunter will be devastated when he finds out this business with his old man. I do know how close he is to Jock. I've drunk in their company and trained with the pair of them. I'm shocked myself about what's gone on. Until you turned up at my office and we had that conversation the other day I had no idea about Jock's past."

"Oh well *c'est la vie.* Anyway less of the job talk for now and let's order I'm ravenous."

Michael watched her long fingers clasp the wine glass and set it against her ruby glossed bottom lip whilst she scoured the menu. He realised it had been years since he had felt like this.

The conversation flowed easily as they ate, Dawn occasionally falling into fits of giggles as he regaled her with some of his *faux pas* early on in his career. Inevitably as the evening went on some of the chat focussed on aspects of their job before finally coming around to their personal lives.

Michael began to explain that he had been divorced for eight years. "I was furious at the time because I never saw it coming, but when I look back on it now I can't blame her. I suppose you could say I'm married to my job, and I do love it. I've always been a detective and I've just never taken my foot off the pedal. Even when we went on holiday with my son and daughter I couldn't wait to get back to work. The worst thing I had to reconcile myself with after the split - and I've managed to do it slowly over the years – is that deep down I know I've brought this all on myself."

"Do you still see your ex and the kids?"

"Yes. She's remarried now. But to be honest, we probably see more of each other than when we were married. I get the odd invite to go round for a meal. And I also get to see the kids as much as I want. They're teenagers now and I keep telling myself to ease off the job otherwise I'm going to miss the best times of their lives."

"So why don't you do it. What's stopping you?"

"I'll let you into a little secret. I've put myself forward for a Detective Chief Superintendent's post which I know is coming up at Headquarters. It's less hands on, I know, and more nine-to-five but I can officially retire in three year time with a thirty year pension and I've promised myself I'll go and spend more time with my son and daughter and pick up my life again." He picked up the bottle of Merlot he had ordered with their meals, saw that it was still half full; they had talked more than they had drunk, and replenished their glasses. "Now I've told you my deepest darkest secrets what about yourself?"

Rolling her wine glass between the palms of her hands Dawn opened up by likening herself to him; a career detective devoted to work – but also ambitious. "I don't mean to the point where I'll trample over anyone to get what I want to achieve." He saw that she appeared to be searching his face for a look of understanding to the comment she had just made.

Michael nodded approvingly – inviting her to continue.

"Don't get me wrong, I'm not a hard-nosed bitch. It's just that over the years some of the older end - especially male supervisors have dismissed me when I've wanted to take a particular route towards something, or they've taken credit for something I've done. So I just want to show them I'm as good as them or even better." She smiled "Am I scaring you?"

He almost laughed. "Not one bit. I know exactly what you mean." He took a sip of the red wine and then nodded towards her hand. "I've noticed the wedding ring. How's your hubby cope with the job?"

He suddenly noticed Dawn's eyes glass over. She set down her wine and began twisting the gold band around her finger. "He's left me," she replied. Her voice was suddenly brittle.

"Oh I'm sorry."

"Don't be, you weren't to know. You know what you said earlier about not seeing it coming – so wrapped up in your job. Well snap – that's me as well. I found out a month ago. The bastard. He had been seeing a colleague from his office for the last two and half years. When I thought he was away on conferences he was in fact screwing her in a hotel somewhere. It all came out after I took a phone call from one of the hotels where they'd stayed – he'd left behind his mobile." She stopped twiddling with her wedding ring and picked up her wine glass. "He didn't even try to deny it. Said it was my fault – I was never at home – always at work – and what did I expect. He's moved in with her and consulted a solicitor – he wants a divorce."

"Dawn I'm so sorry." He fixed her teary eyes. "I know what you're going through." He raised his glass. "I know a good cure for the blues though – I'll order another bottle of red. Let's get drunk."

For the next hour they continued drinking. Michael did his best to brighten her mood with more of his 'office' stories. It worked; she was soon in fits of giggles again.

Draining the last of his wine he peered over his glass and searched Dawn's face. He studied her eyes and she returned his look with her own probing intent.

He reached across and lightly touched her hand. "I'll order a taxi. Do you fancy coming back to my place – for a nightcap – instead of going back to your lonely hotel room?"

"Will we regret this in the morning?"

"I'll regret it if you say no."

A smile lit up her face. "You've talked me into it."

His heart lifted.

-ooOoo–

CHAPTER SEVENTEEN

DAY TWENTY FIVE: 17th September.
Barnwell:

Marcus Hill had been a police officer for fifteen years and he had developed 'a nose' for sniffing out when something wasn't right. And just now, as he watched the grey Ford Mondeo in the distance, circling, ever so slowly, around the recently cropped wheat field, he had that feeling that something was wrong.

Firstly, because the farmer who owned this field had a red Nissan Navarro, and besides he'd only ever seen the farmer's tractor going around in that field. And secondly, there had been quite a few complaints over the years about fly-tipping in this locality. Thirdly, the lane just above the field was where a couple of burned out stolen cars had been found in recent months.

Marcus had first spotted the Ford Mondeo two minutes earlier. He had been making his way back to the station for his meal, having spent the last twenty minutes driving around the countryside section of his beat - where the roads were less congested, and where the scenery was better. It had been an unusually quiet afternoon, and he was taking every opportunity to savour the tranquil moment - these instances were few and far between - especially on the afternoon shift.

The car had attracted his attention because it had emerged from a copse of trees, which he knew was the site of a ruined eighth century chapel. He had an interest in local history, and he knew it had protected status.

Marcus pulled his police car off the road and drifted up onto the grass verge, settling next to a gap in the hedge, where he hoped for a better view. He saw that the Mondeo had also come to a stop, but such was the angle of its parking that he was unable to get a view of its number plate. He watched as the passenger door opened. A man dressed in a long dark coat disembarked.

Leaning across the passenger seat of the police car Marcus strained his eyes to get a clearer description but he was just too far away. He watched on as the dark clothed man made his way to the rear of the Mondeo where he popped open the tailgate.

Marcus decided he had seen enough. His suspicions were aroused. He radioed in, using his personal airwaves set, informing the communications room operator what he could see, and asked for back up. Then he pulled back onto the road and set off towards the track, half a mile away, where he knew he would be able to get access to where the Mondeo was.

The public bridle-path he turned onto was rutted and undulated and lined by heavy hawthorn bushes, and it took him much longer than he had anticipated finding an opening into the field.

Marcus spotted the gap at the last moment, and pulling the steering hard left, bounced up and over a tufted incline, and dropped down hard onto the recently harvested field. The heavy landing knocked the wind out him and he slammed on the brakes. The police car skidded to a halt. As he grabbed his breath he scoured the fields to gather his bearings. He espied the Mondeo twenty yards away, though he realised, when he saw that both front doors were open, and the car devoid of passengers, that he had lost the element of surprise.

He flung open his driver's door and sprinted towards the car, giving an update over his personal radio, whilst at the same time searching the field with his eyes to see if anyone was making a run for it.

There was no sign of life. He guessed they had dashed into the copse where the old chapel was. Once his colleagues arrived Marcus knew that there would be nowhere for them to hide. They'd surround them and soon flush them out.

He stopped at the Mondeo, craning his neck inside, through the open doors, just in case one of them was laying low in the seats. The car was empty. Then he made his way to the rear where the tailgate was still up.

Now let's see what you were up to, shall we!

What he found in the boot momentarily startled him - curled up in the foetal position lay a man, and he'd seen enough corpses in his time to realise this man was dead.

The sudden rustle of leaves coming from the coppice behind him made Marcus jerk up his head. Emerging through the bushes and into relief he saw a stocky built man. A black woollen ski mask covered his head. He reached for his baton and simultaneously depressed the emergency button of his radio – his Status-Zero alert – a signal which overrode all other communications on that channel and let colleagues know that he was in imminent danger.

Marcus never heard the footsteps behind him and never felt the blow to his head, though his ears registered the sharp crack as his skull fractured.

The very last thing he saw, before his vision pitched into darkness, was the galaxy of stars which exploded inside his head.

- ooOoo -

CHAPTER EIGHTEEN

It took Hunter ages to find a parking spot. He had never seen the police station car park so full of cars. And inside the station was no different. The rear foyer and corridor was crammed with uniformed officers all milling around. He didn't identify any as regular faces.

Pushing through the double doors into the first floor stairwell he recognised one of the duty group sergeants. He was carrying a clip-board and seemed deep in thought.

"What's going on?"

The uniformed Sergeant looked up. "Oh, morning Hunter. You mean the Task Force officers? Haven't you heard?"

"Heard what?"

"Marcus Hill was attacked last night. He's in a bad way."

"Marcus!" Hunter knew Marcus Hill. A few years ago Marcus had joined Hunter's team as a CID aide, but had then passed his sergeants exams and decided to go back into uniform where he would have the regularity of 'acting-up.' He had only spoken with him a couple of weeks ago, when he'd bumped into him in the canteen. He'd seen the smile on Marcus's face as he'd told him that he'd just passed the last round of sergeant's boards and was waiting for a suitable vacancy.

"What happened?"

The Sergeant outlined the circumstances. "Fractured skull. And he suffered a bleed to the brain. They operated on him late last night and he's heavily sedated. We won't know anything else about his condition until later this morning."

"Have you got the person who did it?"

The Sergeant shook his head. "He called in a grey Mondeo, that he thought was acting suspiciously, in one of the fields opposite the Crown Inn at Barnburgh, and called for back-up.

Then he went status-zero, but it took the first car a good ten minutes to get to him. By that time the Mondeo, and whoever had attacked him, had left. We've got everyone available out looking. Task Force are going out to do a thorough search of the area."

Hunter laid a hand on the sergeant's shoulder. "Okay let me know how you go on, and keep me updated about Marcus." He turned and made his way up the stairwell to the MIT room, his thoughts drifting.

Shouldering his way through the doors Hunter immediately felt the atmosphere in this office at a complete contrast to the one he had been greeted with downstairs. This place was buzzing. It brought him back from his gloom.

He slipped off his jacket and wrapped it around the back of his chair. He caught his partners gaze. She was just putting a mug of coffee down on her desk opposite.

"Morning Grace. Have you heard about Marcus?"

"Yeah, terrible isn't it."

Hunter nodded. He pointed towards his murder squad colleagues who were at their desks, cradling their own hot drinks and chatting excitedly in small groups.

"Something going on that I should know about?"

"That's appeared this morning."

Grace thumbed a sign towards the white incident boards at the front of the room. Beside them, stacked on a trolley, was a large flat screen TV on 'stand-by' and a DVD player.

"I called in to speak to Isobel first thing this morning and she told me we were in for a treat this morning. She said there'd been a breakthrough – but she wouldn't tell me what."

Before Hunter and Grace could discuss things further they were interrupted by Michael Robshaw and Barry Newstead making a noisy entrance. The team watched Barry swagger to the television, his face beaming, as he switched on the monitor with a hand held remote, whilst the SIO took up centre stage in front of the boards.

"Okay everyone settle down." I'm guessing you've all heard a whisper that progress has been made in this case, especially after the disappointment we had from the interview with the Hassans." Michael Robshaw swung his eyes from Hunter to Grace. "And that's no reflection on you two by the way. We had nothing to go on." He paused and broke into a grin. "That was until yesterday afternoon." He began rubbing his hands together. "When Barry discovered what you are about to all see. All yours Barry," introduced the SIO.

Barry Newstead smoothed a hand down over his loosened tie. He took in a deep breath and made a vain attempt at pulling in his beer belly. "As you know, I was given the task of visiting the security team at Meadowhall to see what, if any, CCTV footage they had of Samia Hassan and see if there was anything of significance which could take the investigation further. Well thanks to the dates, times and precise location which refuge owner Nahida Perveen provided I was able to isolate the cameras which might have captured images of Samia. This is what I have found. The footage is disjointed because I have just taken clips from hours of original CCTV film and cobbled it together onto one disc."

He took a step back away from the large TV screen and pressed the remote. The interior of the shopping mall flickered onto the forty-eight inch screen.

"Okay this is where we first pick up Samia." He pointed to the television using the remote and homed in on a young, pretty, dark haired Asian woman strolling through the ground floor of Marks and Spencer's store and out through the entranceway, which gives access to the mall. The murder squad detectives were quickly glued to the pictures playing out over the TV. They witnessed Samia weave her way through a throng of seated people centred round an open plan coffee lounge and then take up a place at an empty table. "You'll see at the bottom right is the time and date of the footage; the fourteenth of March – a good six months ago. I'll fast forward it a bit." He flicked a button on the hand-held and then used the remote to point out another woman joining Samia at the table. "That's Nahida Perveen. I'll not go any further but I can tell you they have coffee and are obviously in conversation for about twenty five minutes and then Samia leaves and makes her way back into Marks and Sparks before heading off onto the train." Barry clicked the remote again.

"Okay this is the second piece of footage. We jump forward to the twenty-eighth of July."

Again images played out of Samia walking through the ground floor of Marks and Spencer's and out towards the coffee lounge by its entranceway. On this occasion Nahida was already at a table and Samia joined her. Barry speeded up the footage showing Samia handing over a red knapsack and then froze the picture. He turned to Hunter. "I think this is the same knapsack in which you found Samia's clothing and passport, is it not?"

Hunter nodded.

"Okay there's not much conversation on this occasion," Barry increased the speed of the footage for just a few seconds then hit the play button. "They're only together for approximately ten minutes and as you can see they split up and leave." Barry froze the DVD once again, pulled his eyes away from the screen and scanned the room. He had the attention of every detective. "Now this next bit is very interesting," he continued, clicking the remote back into play mode.

All eyes in the room watched Samia travel the escalator to the first floor of Marks and Spencer's, stride through the aisles and then go out through the exit. At one stage it looked as though she was heading for the ramp to the train station, but then changed direction towards the car park and she also appeared to be continuously glancing behind her.

"At this stage, like you, I was wondering why she was looking around as much as she was so I pulled up footage from other cameras and I found this." He clicked the remote again, changing the image. The shots were back inside Marks and Spencer.

The picture zoomed in and a grainy image of an Asian male, mid to late twenties, dressed in white t-shirt and jeans, came into focus. He was dodging from one rack of clothing to another clearly acting suspiciously.

"As I pan the shot out you can now see that this guy is following Samia and I'm guessing because of her reaction she has sussed this. Okay I'll play it out a bit more."

The picture juddered for a split-second and then the drama was back on. Samia was picking up her pace slipping between parked cars. In the background, visible but out of focus, the Asian man took something out of his pocket and put it to his ear.

"He's on his mobile."

The team watched Samia taking a final look in the direction of the Asian man before dashing into one of the glass-encased stairwells, which gave access to the ground floor car park.

"And finally this," exclaimed Barry. The image changed again to a low-lit underground car park. The view was wider and longer, taking in a considerable amount of the car park, but the action being played out was clearly unmistakeable. Samia sprinted out of the stairwell like a chased rabbit, looking back over her shoulder. Then from out of nowhere, in fact a blur at first to the right of the screen, another Asian man, taller and much stockier than the first man, steamed into her as if she was on a rugby field, bowling her over onto the concrete floor. He was on top of her in a split-second, straddling her prostrate body, one hand covering her mouth to prevent her crying out and the other in a clenched fist pummelling her upper torso. Seconds later the man who had been initially following her emerged from the stairwell also at considerable pace, slipped on a wet patch at the bottom of the stairs, caught himself, re-balanced, and then joined in the attack. It was all over in thirty seconds. Samia's body quickly slumped under the onslaught. The stocky man pushed himself off her and then sprinted away out of camera view, whilst the first Asian man stood over her looking around, but there was no one else in sight. Less than a minute later a white van entered the picture and pulled directly across Samia blocking the cameras view. Barry gazed over the room. He could see that all eyes were fixed; the detectives seemed unable to pull themselves away from the scenes unfolding before them. He turned back to the screen just in time to see the two Asian men bundling Samia's limp figure towards the rear of the van. Then as if she was a rag doll they slung her into the back. The doors were slammed shut, both men jumped into the front of the van and then it was tearing away.

"All that took less than three minutes," Barry told them. "The last footage I have is this." He ran the picture. It was a short snippet of the white van heading towards the exit of the ground floor car park, at the point before it entered the major road system around the Meadowhall Centre. Barry freeze-framed the close-up image, which was obviously just below the security camera. Clearly visible were the faces of the two Asian men who had attacked and abducted Samia.

The eyes of the murder squad darted between the e-fit images on the incident board and the TV screen – there was no doubting that the facial features were an exact likeness. Just as important was the index number on the front number plate of the van – it was the same registration as that on the VR 12 vehicle document which had been recovered from the Hassans.

- ooOoo -

CHAPTER NINETEEN

DAY TWENTY EIGHT: 20th September.
Barnwell:

Clicking the remote 'stop' button Hunter stood transfixed beside the large TV monitor at the front of the incident room; it had not yet been removed from the department. It had been the third time he had watched the attack and abduction of Samia.

He shook his head as the later, violent images played out again inside his head. He couldn't help but cringe as he thought about the sheer brutality, which had been meted out to her. Samia was such a slight young woman. She'd not resisted or put up a fight and yet those two men had beaten her mercilessly and tossed her into the back of the van like she had been a sack of rubbish. He also reflected upon what Grace had told him from her attendance at Samia's post mortem; of the catalogue of injuries inflicted upon her and the violation she had suffered prior to her death.

What he'd like to do to those two bastards.

As he shook himself out of his reverie he found himself trying to squeeze the very life out of the plastic TV remote. He found himself flushing as he glanced around, hoping no one had noticed as he set it back down on the trolley.

Hunter made his way back to his desk, dropped down onto his chair and began to immerse himself in the paperwork which had so readily accumulated over the past couple of days; the majority of it was written off 'actions' or reports as a result of his team's footwork and foraging. As he pored over their content he recounted what they had learned to date.

The MIT teams had not eased up since Barry had discovered the CCTV footage; the investigation was now at the manhunt stage. The blown up footage of the two Asian men had been given to the Intelligence Unit and they had circulated it throughout the South Yorkshire Districts as well as neighbouring police forces. On the back burner was a visit to the Crimewatch studios, but they wanted to exhaust their own enquiries first. The pictures were so good that everyone was confident it wouldn't be long before they were caught.

Simultaneous checks were also being carried out at scrap dealers and car dismantlers for the white Renault van. It hadn't been found dumped and burnt out after all this time, and therefore experience from other murder enquiries told them that if it wasn't still secreted away somewhere, then these were the usual disposal places for such evidence.

Also, now that they had the fixed time and date parameters of the attack and kidnapping of Samia the technicians at force headquarters had been able to make a quick examination of the SIM card memory and mapping hardware inside Mohammed Hassan's seized mobile. There the 'wizards' had got a crucial breakthrough. From the downloaded data they had discovered activity on his phone within minutes of his daughter's abduction and traced a name and phone number. On Mohammed's database they had the name Ari registered in his contact details. They had also confirmed that the same number had been dialled persistently during a number of days following Samia's kidnapping, with the last call recorded at ten-thirty-three pm on Friday the first of August. Since then there had been no activity to this number and the technicians were reporting that the line was now dead; the phone switched off - but more than likely dumped, especially since the raid at the Hassans.

Hunter recalled what Kerri Ann Bairstow had told them about seeing a white van driving away from the country park either a Friday or Saturday. He had no doubt in his mind now that this was the date when they had dumped Samia's body into the lake, and that meant she had been held captive for almost five days.

He felt the hairs at the back of his neck prickle; though the post mortem report had shown that she had clearly been raped and butchered he couldn't imagine psychologically what she must have gone through during all that time. Her suffering must have been off the Richter scale he thought to himself.

Hunter continued picking over the reports. He now knew that enquiries had revealed that the mobile number which Mohammed had contacted was a 'pay and go' phone bought in Sheffield with cash, and the details of the purchaser entered on the system were false. Nevertheless from discussions during briefings the murder squad were confident Ari was the real name Mohammed had entered into his contacts register.

Together with the photographs from the CCTV footage Hunter knew this was as good as they were going to get.

"Hunter didn't you hear what I said?"

Grace calling out his name broke his concentration. He looked up from his paperwork and caught her glaring at him. She was holding the handset of the phone away from the front of her face pointing at the receiver.

"Sorry Grace I was elsewhere."

"Yeah I could see," she replied. "I just said they've found the white van." There was a high pitched note of elation in her voice. "It's Communications on the phone. Uniform have found it at a car dismantler's in Rotherham. A low loader is on its way to pick it up and SOCO are heading out there."

Hunter snapped the top back onto his pen. "Then why on earth are you dilly-dallying about Grace. Get your butt in gear girl - we haven't got all day." he cried jubilantly.

* * * * *

Later that afternoon Hunter drove the unmarked CID car into the force's forensic examination facility and swung it into an empty parking slot. Excitedly he jumped out, slamming the car door behind but forgetting to lock it and at a quick pace made for the drying room. Grace jumped out of the passenger seat and half-skipping followed in his wake.

Duncan Wroe, dressed in a blue all-in-one, was just edging backwards out of the rear of the white Renault.

Giving it a quick once over Hunter thought it looked in remarkably good condition to say it had been languishing in a car dismantler's for several weeks, though it was missing its rear number plate.

Hunter stopped at the door and shouted to Duncan.

He turned and acknowledged them with a wave, a small fluorescent light in one hand and a bottle of Luminol blood reagent spray in the other. He sauntered towards them.

"Hi Hunter, Grace. Wondered how long it would be before you got here." He set the spray down on a table.

"We wanted to give you enough time to work your magic on it Duncan," Hunter replied.

Duncan smiled and mussed his fingers through his tousled lanks of fair hair. "Too early for miracles just yet I'm afraid, though I have made a start on it." He picked the Luminol spray back up. "Come on, slip on some overshoes and I'll show you what I've got so far."

He peeled away leaving Hunter and Grace to fit on the blue latex shoe coverings, kept in a dispenser by the entrance door. Duncan still continued talking as he parted from them and Hunter found himself hobbling after him, trying to fit on one shoe protector whilst at the same time hanging onto what the SOCO manager was saying.

"I've only done a preliminary examination you understand. The van's been out in the open for months and will need at least a couple of days in the drying room before we can bottom it. However I have made a start." Duncan stopped by the open rear doors, resting against one as Hunter and Grace caught up.

"Is it the right van?" questioned Hunter, finally snapping both the forensic overshoes in place and then pointing at the absence of the rear number plate.

"Absolutely. The engine and chassis number are a match. This is definitely the van belonging to Mr Hassan."

"And what have you got so far Duncan?" asked Grace.

"Well I have found traces of blood – just small amounts. I've given it the once over with the Luminol and it shows up under the fluorescent. Whose it is at the moment I won't be able to say but my guess is Samia's. Her throat was cut I recall and I would think despite the fact she was bundled up in the carpet some will have seeped out. I'll swab it and send it to the lab."

"Anything else?"

"The impossible I can do, miracles take a little longer Hunter. Once it's thoroughly dried out I'll be checking it out for fibres and DNA. I've got the samples from the carpet she was wrapped up in and so I'll be able to examine them under the lighting equipment and get the frequency and wavelength of the fibres to see if there is a match – to confirm if this was the vehicle she was carried away in before she was dumped in the lake."

Hunter returned a thank you smile. "All very technical for me Duncan but I have faith in you."

"In layman's terms it's a bit like the fluorescent lights in a nightclub picking out white clothing."

Hunter and Grace nodded understandingly.

"I'll also be checking for soil samples in the wheel arches and on the wheels and see if I can marry them to the samples I've taken from the car park at the country park. Lastly we'll swab the cabin's interior and see if there is a DNA composite for the driver and passenger. With a bit of luck in a day or two I should have all the answers."

* * * * *

Hunter found Barry Newstead bending over his desk as he pushed through the office doors. Grace was only a few strides behind.

"Caught you!" Hunter said. "Snooping through the bosses things whilst he's away?"

"It would take a real detective to ever catch me doing that," Barry returned craning his neck back over his shoulder. "I thought you'd disappeared for the day I'm just leaving you a note before I knock off." He finished scribing on an A5 pad, then tore off the top sheet and spun around to hand it to Hunter. "A couple of things I wanted to leave for you before tomorrow morning's briefing."

"What's that Barry?"

"Firstly we might have identified Samia's cousins – the two men from the Meadowhall CCTV footage. I've been chasing up the Intelligence Units throughout the Force and Sheffield think they have a positive ID on the pair. It looks as though they're known to Drug Squad, so I'm just waiting on final confirmation of that. It looks promising."

"Great stuff. And the second thing?"

"Remember we set up a trace search of the part index number of the Volkswagon Golf which that prostitute Kerri-Ann Bairstow gave us belonging to one of her punters?"

Hunter pursed his lips. "Yes?" he retorted.

"Yep. Well you're going to love this. Guess who it comes back to? You've already interviewed him."

Hunter shook his head. "Surprise me."

"Mr Chistopher Woolfe. An address in Sheffield,"

Hunter's eyes widened. He locked on to Grace who had the same surprised look.

"Told you. You'd love it."

Hunter brushed past Barry and snatched up the phone, punched in a number and waited for a response. His feet were tapping ten-to-the-dozen. After a brief conversation he slammed the handset back onto its cradle and then turned to Grace. "Have you got anything pressing this evening?" he enquired, searching her face.

"Nothing that can't wait. I'll just make a quick call to Dave to sort out the girls and then I'm with you."

Hunter patted Barry on the shoulder. "Cheers for this. Now I've got some arse to kick."

* * * * *

Hunter listened as the footfalls padded towards him. He took his eyes off the car park for a few seconds whilst he checked his watch; he and Grace had been waiting in the entranceway to the hospital generator plant room for just over half an hour.

Whilst they had been there the last light of dusk had faded into early evening. The car park security lighting had activated giving everything a blue white tinge.

Hunter narrowed his eyes as he focussed on the shadowy outline of the man passing across his vision only a few yards away. He recognised him from their previous visit to Barnwell General Infirmary.

"Good evening Dr Woolfe," Hunter greeted him, stepping out of the shadow of the doorway. Grace slipped in beside him.

Hunter saw the doctor physically jump, slapping a hand across his chest, covering his heart.

"Christ you made me jump!" Chris Woolfe returned with a startled look on his face.

"Good."

The doctor suddenly looked perplexed.

Hunter took a few determined steps towards him and then stopped just inches from his face. "Give me one good reason why I shouldn't haul you down to the station right now for perverting the course of justice!"

Even in the low-light cast from the glow of the overhead security lighting Hunter could make out that Chris Woolfe had coloured up.

"I – I," he spluttered.

"Why after contacting us and giving us all that information about Samia's cousins assaulting you and threatening you, didn't you tell us that on the evening of Friday the first of August you recognised them leaving the country park in their white van?"

The Doctor dropped his head onto his chest.

"You could have saved us a lot of time - do you not realise that? Instead you gave us a storyline half pointing us in their direction. Is it because you were with a prostitute that night?"

He raised his head and nodded. "I'm close to finishing my time as a junior Doctor. If the hospital finds out about this I'll not get a post. Believe me I didn't want to obstruct your investigation I thought if I gave you enough to lead you to Samia's cousins and help catch them this wouldn't come out."

"Well it's backfired hasn't it? Do you know we've wasted time tracking down the owner of a VW Golf for weeks as a potential witness and all this time it was you. Now I'd be very careful how I'd answer this next question. Did you see the two men dump Samia's body in the lake?"

The doctor shook his head vigorously. "Christ no! I didn't spot them until they'd cut us up in the car park. When I saw who was in the van I thought they were after me again. You know because of my past fling with Samia. I thought they'd followed me there and I was going to get another hiding. When they just drove away I couldn't fathom it out. Then of course when I saw it all on the news I put two-and-two together and realised what I had seen." He paused and dropped his gaze again. "I'm sorry. If it hadn't been for the prostitute I would have told you all this."

"You might be able to save some face here Doc. Can you definitely say you recognise the two people in the white van as Samia's cousins who previously beat you up?"

Chris Woolfe nodded. "Yes it was definitely them."

- ooOoo -

CHAPTER TWENTY

DAY THIRTY: 22nd September.
Barnwell:

"These are our targets," announced Detective Superintendent Michael Robshaw, holding aloft a pair of A4 size colour photographs to his audience of detectives; they were blown up head and shoulders mug shots of two Asian men, holding in front of them custody reference boards, which indicated to the team that at some stage they had both been arrested and charged.

"Ari and Pervez Arshad, twenty-nine and twenty-seven years old respectively, from the Attercliffe area," he continued. "These photographs were taken just over five months ago when they were arrested and charged with witness intimidation after an assault on a young man at a taxi rank. Three witnesses stated that Ari and Pervez pushed in on a queue and when a twenty-two year old man challenged them they both set about him. They punched him to the ground and statements from the witnesses state that Ari jumped several times on his head - with both feet. That young man is now permanently brain damaged and the three witnesses who initially came forward have now refused to give evidence in court after being visited by the pair." The SIO turned and pressed the images onto the incident white boards directly beneath the two earlier e-fits joining the blown up CCTV image of the two Asian men caught on camera driving away from Meadowhall in the white Renault van.

All could now see that there was no disputing the likeness.

The Detective Superintendent returned his gaze back into the room. "These two are well known to the Sheffield police and also to Drug Squad. They have been strongly suspected of knocking out cocaine and heroin to the clubbers for some time but subsequent raids have only found enough gear for possession charges. Ari has also been arrested twice for assault and aggravated burglary when it's believed he went round to collect drug debts owed to him - though once again victims and witnesses refused to give evidence in court." Michael Robshaw paused and scanned the room. "However their luck has finally run out. We now have clear identification which places these two at the scene on the night Samia's body was dumped, by our witness Christopher Woolfe, who had previously been assaulted by the pair – and he is willing to testify in court. So not only do we have CCTV footage of these two abducting Samia, we can also now place them on the night her body was dumped in the lake. What we don't have at present is their precise address. I have already learned that they no longer live at the flat they were at when they were arrested five months ago. That has been let to another couple and was occupied by them on the date of Samia's abduction. Detectives from Sheffield have paid this couple a visit and given the place the once over. There is no suggestion that these two people have any links to our targets or to the Hassans and therefore our priority now is to identify where they are currently living and bring them in. Tasks today relate to their known associates with a view to tracking them down."

DC Mike Sampson half raised his arm. "What about bringing Mohammed Hassan back in now that we know about Ari's number being on his mobile?"

"Not yet. I don't want him to know just how much we've got from the technicians until we have Ari and his brother Pervez in custody." The Detective Superintendent reached behind him tapping the incident board. "All our efforts now are focussed on these two. Good hunting everyone."

* * * * *

Prompted by an early finish from work; they still hadn't discovered the Arshad's address, Hunter had made a last minute decision to make a detour on his way home and call into his father's gym for a quick training session to unwind.

Might even get some time with dad!

Removing his training bag from the boot he took a casual look around the grit surfaced car park. He noticed they were a good dozen cars at least - more than usual at this time of day.

Must be a few in. It occurred to him that he might be able to get in a bit of sparring for a change.

As he set his bag down to close his boot he suddenly spotted movement in one of the parked cars. A grey Mondeo, with its engine revving, was parked at the end of the row. It looked out of place here; not the type of car he normally saw in the car park – most of the trainees who used his dad's gym were young men using age old 'bangers' - the best of them done up with body kits, which shouted 'boy racer.'

After everything which had gone off recently he had a sense about this; something didn't appear to be quite right. And weren't they looking for a grey Mondeo, in relation to the attack on PC Marcus Hill.

He slammed the boot shut and slipped down the side of his car to get a better look at the parked Mondeo and especially to view the driver and passenger. From where he was, his initial impression was that the two men in it seemed to be concentrating their stare upon the entrance doors to his father's gym.

He slightly dropped his stance and shifted for a better angle. The passenger was the nearest. He appeared to be a middle-aged man with long straggly greying hair and a salt and pepper neatly trimmed beard. Unfortunately he was too far away to pick out any other features. The driver, also middle-aged, had thinning crew-cut sandy hair. He had his head pushed back against the headrest, and there was something about him he recognised, though he couldn't put his finger on it.

As Hunter took another step towards the front of his car he saw the passenger suddenly sit bolt upright and stare in his direction - he had been eyeballed.

He was given no time to react as the Mondeo roared into life, its front wheels whipping up gravel as it jolted forward, fish-tailing for a split second before straightening up and shooting out of the exit onto the side-street.

He had just enough time to log its number in his head.

As he listened to the squeal of tyres disappear into the distant estate he felt his hackles raise. It had been the look the passenger had thrown him – a cold-bloodied granite stare - an animal-like expression he had seen only a few times in his career – usually when someone had expressed their wish to kill him.

He knew those two meant business and he had disturbed them.

- ooOoo -

CHAPTER TWENTY ONE

DAY THIRTY ONE: 23rd September.
Barnwell:

Billy Wallace looked up to the heavens to see if there was a break in the clouds as more drizzle floated from a murky blue, cloudy sky, adding to the shiny black wetness of the tarmac surface around him. He gave off an involuntary shudder as he felt the droplets run down his neck and trickle onto his back.

It had been raining on and off most of the day, but that had not been a bad thing he had told himself as he had sloshed amongst the puddles earlier that afternoon. It had enabled him and Rab to do what they had needed to do and not draw suspicion to themselves as they had scoured the streets with their collars up and chins tucked firmly into their topcoats whilst they had searched out their target address.

He wiped drips of rain from his hair as he stepped inside the entranceway of the smoking shelter at the rear of The Station public house, his slate grey eyes scanning the car park before resting his gaze upon the modern railway building that housed the ticket office and waiting room that was only fifty yards away. He strained his ears, waiting for the sounds of the engine clonking over the tracks and checked his watch; the connection train from Edinburgh was due in any time.

He stroked his recently grown beard that now covered his craggy features and hid most of the hideous scar, which normally made him stand out, whilst once again mulling over the decision he'd been forced to make. He knew that they needed some extra muscle to finish the job and he'd had to call in some favours with old contacts during his flying visit back to his hometown two days previously. He had been uncomfortable with that; he always liked to know who he was working with – needed that level of control and trust -

but on this occasion it was out of his hands. It had cost him a few grand as well, but he knew it would be worth it.

"Get that down your neck."

The appearance of Rab Geddes made him jump. He was edgy.

He took the pint of lager from his partner in crime and stepped to one side to allow him into the shelter.

Neither of them smoked but they were using it so as not to draw attention to themselves; two strangers with Scottish accents would make them stand out - he had told Rab.

"Not arrived yet?" said Rab sweeping one hand over his newly grown hair before slurping the top off his bitter.

It had been a long time since Billy had seen Rab with hair. It was still sandy in colour but it was now thin and wispy and he realised why he had taken to shaving his head on a regular basis over the past ten years.

Nevertheless despite their appearance he knew this was necessary to disguise their features for just a few more days.

"Nope. It's a couple of minutes late," Billy replied, sliding the cuff back of his coat, looking at his watch again. He glanced back towards the station. The hazy sun was dipping below the rain clouds towards the horizon, another half an hour and then darkness would cover them.

His thoughts drifted back to their recce earlier in the day. After they had finally found the house, Billy had done another circuit of the streets surrounding the semi as he guessed somewhere close would be cops keeping watch; and he'd been proven right.

Although he hadn't spotted anyone who stood out as a cop he had found the unmarked police car on the second sweep. He had to smile conceitedly to himself as he checked the Peugeot over. Despite all these years in prison, though the make and models had changed, the police radio in the centre console was still a dead giveaway. He mentally noted its number and position; it would have to be taken care of so they could make their getaway after the job.

He guessed the detectives would be in a house somewhere nearby keeping observation, though he dare not stand around to check as that would make him vulnerable to capture, and so he and Rab had driven back to the railway station finalising their plans. Billy had made sure the car had been parked well away from view. They still had the Mondeo and he knew that yesterday afternoon it had been clocked by that nosy bastard at Jock's gym, so they had to keep it low profile for a few more hours. After that it could be dumped.

In the distance he heard the rumble of the train and it brought him back from his thoughts. "Come on Rab they're here," he said nudging his partner and then swallowed the remnants of his glass in one gulp. He swiped the residue from his mouth with the back of a gloved hand, then removing his handkerchief from his trousers pocket he wiped it around the edge of the glass several times; no room for error he told himself as he held it up to the light before setting it down on a bench.

As he stepped out into the car park he pulled up the collar of his coat.

"Got the masks?" He enquired, turning back to Rab who was catching him up with a shortened jog.

Rab took out two black woollen ski masks from his jacket pocket and waved them towards Billy.

The corners of Billy's mouth creased into a malevolent smile.

* * * * *

The late evening news was just starting. Jock Kerr slid a coaster across the surface of the coffee table and set his steaming mug of tea down before flopping down onto the sofa. He was just going to shout through to Fiona, who was in the kitchen opening a fresh packet of shortbread biscuits for supper, to let her know the news was on, when the telephone rang. One of the house handsets lay on the table in front of him and its display was glowing with the ringing tone. He snorted as he glanced at the clock on the mantelpiece even though he knew the time. He snatched up the receiver.

"Hello," he said gruffly.

"Do you know who this is?" Jock heard the gravelly voice say down the line.

"I always said I'd catch up with you and I have done. Your day of reckoning is almost here."

Then the line went dead.

Jock sat transfixed, the receiver pressed firmly to one ear, listening to the continuous purring down the line. In a flash an image from his past flooded into his mind as he recognised the voice and suddenly his head was in turmoil. As he started to push himself up from the sofa, without warning, there was an abrupt explosion of glass, shards flying everywhere, and the fabric vertical blinds drawn across the lounge window erupted from their fastening, as a weighted lump slumped through the shattered opening.

Jock froze. His eyes registered what lay before him but his brain was grappling with the vision; confusion, disbelief and fear were all manifesting at the same time. The head and bare shoulders of a man's lifeless body lay flopped over the windowsill entangled amongst the wreckage of the blinds. A chill ran through his body as he momentarily sat riveted staring at the unkempt lank of hair hanging from the bloodied head. At the same time he became conscious of an awful gut-wrenching smell emanating into the room.

Then he was jolted back into action by the piercing screams of his wife who had appeared in the doorway and was holding her face in her hands. He launched himself from the sofa and made a dash for the hallway. Flinging open the front door he leapt out onto the path. Having jumped out from a brightly lit house, for a split-second his eyes only registered blackness, but quickly his sight re-adjusted and in the darkness he saw that slumped half-inside, half outside of the front window was a naked man. The paleness of the flesh told Jock that he was dead.

Then out of the corner of his eye movement at the top of his drive grabbed his attention. He could make out a tall silhouetted figure who appeared to be looking in his direction. Behind the shadow he could see, pulled against the kerb, was a hatchback car. Its engine was revving loudly. In the half-light he could make out at least a couple more people both in the front and rear all staring in his direction.

He turned his gaze to the body and then quickly snatched it back up the drive. His eyesight had now fully adjusted to the surroundings of the night.

He saw that the figure in the long dark overcoat was peeling up a ski mask. The action appeared to be slow and deliberate. He first caught sight of the beard and then as the woollen mask was lifted over his head the straggly wavy hair dropped to the man's collar and the remainder of his facial features were revealed.

A shiver ran down Jock's spine. Despite the greying beard and hair he recognised his nemesis after all these years.

Billy Wallace's eyes were wide and staring and glistening with hate.

In the distance Jock could just make out the faint wail of a siren; he knew the police were on their way and a wave of relief washed over him.

There was a stand-off as Jock scrutinised Billy who was motionless staring back at him. Then he saw him lift his hand and drag a finger across his exposed throat – a slow slashing movement. He saw Billy give him a menacing smile before turning and easing himself into the front passenger seat of the car behind. The door was still open as the wheels squealed on the wet tarmac as it shot away from the kerb and screamed towards one of the side streets.

* * * * *

Hunter sank into his armchair with his tumbler of single malt whisky. He savoured the moment of his first sip, feeling the pleasant after burn, first tickling the back of his throat, then his gullet, and finally his stomach. It was a wonderful feeling. Removing the glass from his lips he eyed the contents and then swilled the amber liquid around listening to the chink of ice against the cut glass.

It had been another long day.

He took another small sip, this time holding it in his mouth. Momentarily he closed his eyes as the oak-aged flavours caressed his taste buds. Then he swallowed.

Moments like this were rare these days.

An hour ago, as promised, he had managed to get home - just in time for Beth to make her 'girls' night' appointment. He hadn't even had time to take off his jacket before she was kissing him on his cheek and telling him his salmon was in the microwave and just wanted heating up, and there was some salad in the fridge.

"I'm only round the corner at Julie's," she shouted back over her shoulder. "You know where I am. See you about eleven," she finished as she disappeared out of the door.

He'd only just managed to get Jonathan and Daniel settled down. They had finally let him go after three short stories. As he'd ruffled their hair affectionately and kissed their foreheads before tucking the boys up it had jolted his conscience; he sometimes wished he had more time for this.

He picked up the remote from the coffee table and powered on the TV; he would try and lose himself for a couple of hours before Beth got home.

He took another glug of whisky and listened to the sounds of the house. The central heating pipes creaked somewhere upstairs beneath the floorboards. He pushed himself back into his armchair feeling himself relax. He swilled the contents around again; the tumbler was almost empty.

One more, and then that's it.

He enjoyed a drink at home but it was never more than a couple to unwind. He'd seen too many of his counterparts use it as a crutch to ease away the tensions of the day and now found themselves relying on it too much. For some, drinking had become second nature and he'd seen the disastrous consequences which had resulted. It had made him determined not to go down that route.

Twenty minutes later as he set down his second empty glass he could feel his eyes becoming heavy. He knew it was a clear sign he was almost at the edge of exhaustion.

Time to call it a day.

He couldn't even stay awake for when Beth got home. Never mind, he knew she would understand.

Just as he pushed himself up the phone rang.

He eyed the handset and saw his parents name's light up on the screen. He slipped it out of its stand.

His mother's voice screamed down the line. The panic in her cries rattled him to the core. He tried to interrupt whilst he made sense of her high-pitched ramblings. Finally, unable to get a word in, he just shouted, "I'm on my way!" and then ended the call.

He speed-dialled Beth's mobile; she was only two minutes away, and then bolted upstairs to sling on his jeans and a sweat top. By the time he had got downstairs Beth was almost falling through the front door. Her face flushed.

"Sorry about this," he said, snatching up the car keys from the hallway table "Something's happened at mum's! I'll ring you as soon as I find out what!" He shouted as he popped open the locks of his Audi and yanked open the driver's door.

* * * * *

Hunter raced at break-neck speed towards his parents' home. The tiredness he had experienced ten minutes earlier had gone, and it was if he had never touched a drink that night. He was as alert as ever and his mind was trying to make sense of the hysterical screams he'd heard over the phone.

Within twelve minutes of leaving home he was screeching into his parents' road.

What greeted him shook him. It was mayhem.

The street seemed to be awash with police officers, and emergency vehicles of all descriptions lined the road, their whirling blue strobes dancing around, lighting the area as if it was a disco. Blue and white crime scene tape was everywhere – sealing off the approach to his mother and father's semi and keeping neighbours back.

His stomach turned over; he knew this was the scene of a major incident.

He slewed his car into the kerb and leapt from it, leaving the driver's door open as he launched into a sprint. He could see his parents' house less than fifty yards away but he couldn't get anywhere near for abandoned vehicles. A young uniformed officer was about to head him off as he dipped quickly beneath a strand of waving incident tape, then he moved aside as Hunter flashed his warrant card and raced past.

Slackening his pace, as he neared the drive, he swore he had never seen as much activity; uniformed cops, plain clothed detectives and Scenes of Crime officers were swarming all around the front of the house. Despite attending so many crime scenes this seemed so surreal; this was his old home; he had moved here when he had been twelve years old and had spent his teenage years growing up in its warm and loving environment. And this was the street where he had met Polly, who had lived four doors away and whom he had fallen madly in love with as his first girlfriend. It was here where he had first heard the news that she had been found murdered. Finally it was this place where he had made his most life-changing decision – telling his parents that he didn't want to take up his place at university to study fine art – instead, he wanted to be a cop and catch his girlfriend's killer.

A lot of water had flowed under the bridge since then.

He focussed his gaze as he entered the top of the drive. Much of the activity was centred at the front lounge window, which had a huge gaping hole in the double-glazing with just a few fragments of glass jutting from the frame. Two forensic officers appeared to be draping a plastic sheet over something half-inside, half-outside the window and as he rushed into the drive Hunter realised what it was. From the light coming through the gap from inside his parent's house he could clearly make out the naked shape of a gaunt lanky man through the semi-opaque sheet. This is what his mother had been in such a state over.

On the front lawn the skeletal frame of a forensic tent was just in the process of being erected by SOCO; he recognised Duncan Wroe.

Then he spotted his boss emerging from the front door. In the hallway, behind him, stood the red-headed Scottish DCI he had spoken with ten days ago; he tried to recollect her name but suddenly his brain was mush.

"Hunter!" shouted Michael Robshaw.

Hunter's pace had dropped to a fast-walk as he made towards them.

"What the hell is going on?" he demanded. "Who on earth's this?" he shouted pointing towards the cadaver.

"Where are my mum and dad? Are they hurt?" He machine-gunned the questions one after another in quick succession.

Detective Superintendent Robshaw held up a hand just as DCI Dawn Leggate stepped over the threshold to join him.

Hunter pointed his finger towards her. "Why's DCI Leggate here?" He'd recalled her name. "What's she got to do with this?"

"Whoa just a minute Hunter, calm down, both your parents are okay. Shook up - but neither of them are hurt. As we speak they're on their way to the Victim Interview Suite at Maltby police station. The FME is on route as well to check them over."

"Who's that?" Hunter asked again, pointing towards the naked corpse.

"Steady down Hunter and we'll tell you."

He watched his Superintendent glance sideways at the Scottish DCI.

She shrugged her shoulders and took a deep breath, pushing her hands into her rainproof jacket. "That's the body of a junkie."

"A junkie?"

The DCI nodded. "He was abducted two weeks ago near to where he lived in Glasgow."

For a second Hunter was dumbfounded. Everything was spinning round in his head.

"What's having the body of a druggie from Glasgow thrown through the front window of my mum and dad's home got to do with them?" He wanted answers and he wanted them quick.

"It's all linked to an investigation I'm involved in," the DCI responded.

He switched his gaze between the Detective Chief Inspector and his boss. He pointed his finger at her again as if it was a weapon. "I knew you were down here for something. What's this shit you're hiding from me?" He asked angrily.

"That's enough Hunter," interjected Michael Robshaw. "Don't say something you'll regret later." He took a step towards Hunter. "DCI Leggate is here under my sanction, and she and her team have actually been trying to protect your father. Now as I have already told you, your mum and dad are safe and should be at Maltby police station by now. I want you to go there with DCI Leggate and when you get there she and your dad will fill you in with everything you need to know."

* * * * *

Given the time of night, the main roads were quiet, enabling Hunter to step on the accelerator of his Audi as he headed towards Maltby Police Station.

Beside him sat Dawn Leggate.

"The junkie's name is Fraser Cullen. He was a snout of one of my DSs."

Hunter was watching her out of the corner of his eyes. The DCI never took her eyes away from the windscreen.

"It's a long story, but basically, me and my team have been investigating the murders of three retired detectives for the past month, and just over two weeks ago Fraser contacted my DS and told him he had information regarding one of the murders. Fraser gave us the names of two men who had beaten to death a retired detective in Glasgow. Ten minutes after the meeting between Fraser and my DS we got an anonymous phone call to the effect that someone had seen Fraser being bundled into a grey Ford Mondeo. We've been searching for him, the car, and the two men he named since that call."

There was the mention of the grey Mondeo again, thought Hunter. The same colour and make of car that was involved in the attack on one of his uniformed colleagues, and which he had disturbed in the car park of his father's gym yesterday.

What the fuck is going on! "I don't get it. What's the relevance of Fraser's – whatever his name is – dead body being thrown through my parents' front window? Are you saying my dad's involved in drugs?"

"Cullen. Fraser Cullen. And no, it's nothing to do with drugs. As I've said, it's a long story, and soon you'll be told everything. Let's just see if you're mum and dad are all right first. That's the main priority. Then if your dad's in a fit state to talk he can tell you everything. I promised him faithfully he could be the one to tell you when the time came."

Hunter's head was in a whirl and he was doing his best to focus on his driving. He gripped the steering wheel so tightly that a tingling sensation shot through his fingers and up into his forearms. It brought him back from the muddle his brain was desperately trying to make sense of. Glancing down at his hands he realised they had turned partially white; he realised instantly that he needed to rid himself quickly of his frustration and vexation.

He spotted the road sign for Maltby police station – the journey had flown. He flicked down the column indicator and turned left off the main road.

Pulling into a visitor's bay he killed the engine and took a deep breath.

DCI Leggate reached across spanning her palm across Hunter's forearm.

He stared at her.

"I'm not trying to wind you up DS Kerr, believe me. I made a promise to your father and I'm simply keeping it. In another ten minutes you'll know everything." She closed her grip. "Some of what you are going to hear is not going to sit comfortably so I'm warning you to be prepared."

Hunter led the way into the station; he had been here before. They both flashed their warrant cards to the receptionist and she buzzed them through into an internal corridor and then pointed them through to where they needed to be.

The Victim Reception Suite was where rape victims and abused children normally came to be supported, examined and questioned by video evidence. He had used a similar room at other stations elsewhere when he had been in CID.

Hunter pushed through the door into an overbearingly warm room that had been furnished as though it was someone's front lounge. The instant he stepped into the room his mother launched herself off from the sofa and flung her arms around his neck.

Hunter felt her body convulse as she mumbled his name. It momentarily took him aback; he had never ever witnessed an outburst like this from his mother. He had always seen her as such a strong character.

It also had the effect of deflating his anger and frustration, bringing him to his senses. He looked over her huddled shoulders at his father who was slowly rising from one of the seats in the room, face expressionless, almost as if in shock.

Hunter gently eased his mum away catching the look in her face. Her eyes were bloodshot; she had obviously been crying for some time.

DCI Leggate took over the support of his mother, guiding her back to the sofa and taking up a seat next to her.

Hunter lowered himself onto the arm of one of the chairs facing them all.

Dawn Leggate flashed an awkward smile at Jock. "I've not told your son anything yet Jock, but now it's time for him to know everything. We agreed that if things ever came to this then it would be the right thing to do, didn't we?"

Jock nodded. He had a forlorn look on his face.

DCI Leggate turned her gaze back to Hunter. "Before your father tells you his bit I'll tell you where I fit into all this."

Hunter slipped off the arm and dropped onto the seat cushion.

"Just over three months ago two prisoners serving life for the murder of a twenty-four year old woman and her five year old daughter were released from Barlinnie prison after spending thirty-six years behind bars. Those two prisoners are Billy Wallace and Rab Geddes. I don't know either of these two - way before my time - but I have since learned their history. Billy had the nickname Braveheart in his younger days. He had a fearsome reputation and used to boast that William Wallace was his ancestor. I'm not sure that's true, and to be honest knowing what I now know about Billy Wallace I for one feel that it's an insult to a great Scottish hero. Billy comes from bad stock. His father Gordon did time for a couple of warehouse robberies and was involved in the black market during the nineteen-fifties in Glasgow. Throughout the sixties Gordon built up a bit of a criminal empire and formed one of the leading gangster families in the suburbs, offering protection to pubs and clubs and at one stage he was peddling guns around to arm criminals." She leaned forward clasping her hands intently. "Gordon introduced his son into the fold when he was about eighteen. Billy was a real tough nut who could handle himself and he quickly made a reputation for himself because of the extreme violence he would use, even when he didn't need to. Rab Geddes was a lifelong school friend and between them they began to run the Wallace family business. Billy started to push drugs – something which was unheard of amongst the gangs and began to make himself quite a wealthy young man. Then things took a turn for the worse for Billy and his family. The police began to crack down. A few rogue cops who had been taking backhanders to turn the other cheek, or in some cases lose evidence, were investigated and dismissed and many of the different gang members had their collars felt. Rival gangs started to turn in against one another. The Procurator Fiscal together with CID from Shettlestone nick – east end of Glasgow – began looking at the Wallace gang round about nineteen-seventy and Gordon decided to call it a day, happy to live off the wealth he had amassed from his earlier criminal activities. His son Billy didn't, and one night back in nineteen-seventy-one when he went to collect a drug debt, things boiled over. He couldn't find his dealer who had ripped him off and so in a fit of temper he shot the guy's girlfriend and her five-year-old daughter before setting fire to the flat. Within days snouts from opposing gangs had dropped Billy and Rab for it and detectives managed to get a breakthrough when they found a witness who had been there on the night of the murders and provided crucial evidence. The upshot was that they were both arrested and as a result of the evidence were convicted of the murders and sent to prison for thirty-six years. You will have gathered by now that Billy is a bit of a psycho, and even in prison he continued his violence. He was responsible for at least one prisoner's murder and he was also involved in the stabbing of two others." DCI Leggate pushed herself back into the sofa crossing one leg over the other. "He also vowed revenge against the team of detectives who'd arrested him and also the main witness who had helped convict him. And that's where I have come in. Several weeks ago Billy and Rab disappeared off the radar after they did a bunk from a bail hostel. Shortly after, four people – three men and a woman – were brutally murdered. The man and woman were from my neck of the woods – Stirling, the other two men lived near Glasgow. The men are all retired detectives – the same detectives who were responsible for getting the convictions and putting Wallace and Geddes behind bars. My team from Stirling are involved in a joint investigation with Glasgow CID and we have enough evidence to link Billy and Rab to the murders." She uncrossed her legs and sat forwards. "Your dad recognised Billy Wallace this evening and we have circulated the number of the grey Mondeo he was seen making his getaway in. There are a lot of officers on the ground looking for them as I speak – but then you'll have guessed that."

The mention of the grey Mondeo again flashed an alert inside his head. Now he remembered where he had seen the driver before. The newly grown, thinning, sandy hair had tricked him. He was the bald headed man at Staithes whom he had seen his arguing with his father that morning. Suddenly it was all fitting into place.

The DCI continued. "Me and my team are down here for two reasons – one to track down Wallace and Geddes, and two, and just as important, to protect the main witness from that trial back in nineteen-seventy-two – your father." She looked across to Jock. "I'll let you take over."

Hunter turned towards his dad, saw him take a deep breath and then glance towards his wife. He tried to search out his dad's look but just as he had done so many times over recent weeks he avoided eye contact, instead staring down at his hands, which he rolled around one another.

"This is very difficult for me son," he began. "I've not tried to hide this from you I just didn't know how to tell you what you're about to hear, especially with the important job you have. I suppose naively I hoped it would never come to this. What do they say about the best laid plans?" He gave a resounding cough.

Hunter saw tears well up in his father's eyes.

"You know I've told you all about my younger days as a boxer and how my career ended and how me and your ma came down to Yorkshire where you were born and I set up the gym?"

Hunter nodded. He suddenly felt his stomach knot as he watched his dad wipe the corner of an eye with the back of a hand.

"All that is true but I have never told you why, have I son?" He made eye contact with Hunter for the first time. He lifted himself slightly and took his wallet from his back trouser pocket, fished into one of the sleeves and extracted a crumpled yellowing piece of paper and proffered it.

Hunter reached across and took it. It was a yellow-aged Sellotaped news cutting, which he unfurled to get a fuller view. He glanced at the headline. It read: GLASGOW GANGSTERS SENTENCED FOR BRUTAL SLAYING OF MOTHER AND DAUGHTER. Below that was a smaller sub heading: SUPERGRASS TURNS QUEENS EVIDENCE. Hunter read most of the article before stopping.

"That's what I've been trying to avoid all these years, you finding out the full facts. My names' not Jock Kerr – or rather my birth name wasn't that."

Hunter suddenly felt as though he had been punched in the guts. His stomach turned and ached. He checked the looks on his mum's face and then on the Detective Chief Inspector's'. He knew from the exchange they gave him he had heard right. His head started to throb.

"I'm sorry son, I know this has come as a bit of a shock but now you know. I've been living under an assumed name for years. I was forced to change it after the trial. I took on your grandfather's name from your Mother's side and the Procurator Fiscal and the detectives on the case helped me to relocate to Yorkshire."

"So you're the supergrass in the article?"

"No – no, nothing like that. That was editorial licence. Let me tell you the full story before you judge me."

"I think you'd better."

"After I had to give up my boxing I didn't know what to do, and Billy's dad – Gordon Wallace – came to me one night when I was in the club having a beer, said he'd heard good things about me and maybe he could put some work my way. He knew I was good with my fists so he offered me some door work looking after a couple of clubs. I didn't know who he was at the time. Then one day he turns up at the flat I had with your ma and says he wants me to keep an eye on his son Billy. He told me that some people were after giving him a good hiding and asked me if I'd drive him around and watch his back. Said he'd pay me a hundred pounds a week. Well I jumped at the chance didn't I – where else could I earn that type of money? They gave me a Mercedes as well to drive. All he said to me was I wasn't to ask too many questions but just watch his son's back. Well the first time I picked Billy up he introduced me to his pal Rab and he asked me to drive them to this tenement because he had some business to sort out. I had no idea what he was up to until he and Rab came running back to the car and they asked me to get them out of there. There was blood everywhere. Billy said that the woman in the flat had slashed him with a knife. Then he told me that he'd shot her. They set fire to the flat as well. He was flashing this shooter about and I was really freaked. I drove them to some wasteland and watched them bury the gun and then they told me to drop them off. I was physically sick when I got home. Then the next day I saw on the news that they'd not only killed a woman but a five-year-old wee bairn as well. I told your ma what had happened and she told me to go to the police. I didn't at first but I did give them a call and gave them Billy and Rab's name. I don't know how but a couple of days later two detectives came to the flat and asked me about the murders. I told them everything and they told me to find somewhere else to live until the trial. I knew I wouldn't be safe especially once I found out about the gangster connections and so I agreed a deal with the police. I said I would give evidence if they gave me a fresh start and they did. I stopped being Iain Cambell." For a second Jock closed his eyes. "Little did I realise what repercussions there would be. Do you realise now why I wanted to hold this back?"

"And that guy I saw you arguing with in Staithes?"

"Rab Geddes. It was sheer bad luck he recognised me, especially after all these years. Apparently he'd just dropped off an old friend of his after a stag night up in Glasgow."

For a few seconds Hunter felt as if a great weight was pushing down on him. He was trying to make some sense of what he had just been told. Suddenly it made him question himself; to wonder who he was.

"This may seem a strange question dad. Is my name really Hunter Kerr?"

His father looked shocked. "Of course it is. Only I changed my name. It was done by deed poll. Your mum was already a Kerr so she reverted back to her maiden name. You were christened Hunter and your birth certificate says that."

Hunter dropped his head into his hands and rubbed them around his face. He could feel a migraine coming on. He hadn't suffered one for ages. He knew in another hour or so the pressure would be so great that he would see flashing stars and then be physically sick.

- ooOoo -

CHAPTER TWENTY TWO

DAY THIRTY THREE: 25th September.
Sheffield:

Hunter adjusted the rear view mirror – turned it towards his face. He stared at his reflection and noted the dark rings, which circled his eyes. He stroked his jaw-line – he was also in need of a shave.

Overall, you look like shit Hunter Kerr.

"You look crap," said Grace.

It was almost as if she had heard the voice inside his head. He glimpsed across at her relaxing in the passenger seat.

"I feel it. I've had very little sleep the past couple of days."

"Your dad?"

Hunter nodded. "He and my mum are staying with us after what's gone on."

"They'll catch this Billy Wallace and his mate soon and then you can all put it behind you. It sounds to me as though they've got them bang to rights and they'll be going back inside and die in prison." Grace examined her fingernails, which she had done the previous evening. The pearlescent polish glinted in the sunlight.

"We won't be able to put it behind us though will we? It's always going to be there isn't it?"

She turned sharply and fixed him a glare. "Oh for goodness sake Hunter, stop feeling sorry for yourself. How will it affect you in the future? It's your dad this has happened to."

"Grace he's not the man I thought I knew. All these years he's lied to me."

"Listen to me Hunter. This is me talking to you not only as a friend and colleague but one wearing an impartial hat. Your father has not lied to you and never has done. Yes he's held back the truth but that is not lying. And the way I see it he did it with all best intentions, especially with the job you've got. How could he have told his son – a cop – that he was involved with gangsters in his past? Think about it for a second – would you tell your sons?"

He held her stare. He had no response. He hadn't looked at it like that.

"And from what you told me it seemed to me as though he had little choice. He was only twenty two at the time with all kinds of problems to deal with – mainly how to make a living for him and your mother after a promising boxing career was in tatters. I'm sorry but I don't agree with you on this one. I feel for your dad. It must have been a living nightmare for him the last couple of months. Can you not imagine what must have been going on inside his head? He was trying to protect your mum and you from this. You need to take a long hard look at yourself Hunter. You've only got one set of parents. You know how much they've been there for you and how much you've got in common with your dad. He's your friend as well as your father. If you carry on like this you'll be in great danger of destroying your relationship. Anyway what's Beth say about all this?"

He faltered with his reply. He'd already had a similar hushed conversation with his wife. Finally he said, "practically the same as you." He felt a lump emerge in his throat.

"Well there you are then. Listen to her. I don't know what you men would do without us women. For god's sake take him out for a beer and clear the air."

At that moment static over their radio airwaves broke into their conversation.

He, Grace, and the majority of the MIT team had been on plot since seven am that morning, their unmarked cars at various locations dotted around Parkhill Flats in Sheffield lying in wait for Ari and Pervez Arshad.

Excitedly, they pushed themselves up from their lounging positions.

Grace yanked across her seatbelt.

Hunter started the car and strained his ears to listen to the report coming over the police radio net.

The information he was listening to spirited his thoughts away from the problems of his father and conjured up fresh images, specifically the ones he had seen in the office the previous afternoon, after Superintendent Robshaw had bounded into the office, excitedly announcing to the squad that they had found the hiding place of Samia's killers. Drug Squad had just contacted him, he had lauded. One of their informants had given an approximate location of Ari and Pervez. They had a flat somewhere in the huge complex, which the team were now staking out. He added that the pair had acquired false passports and were making plans to leave the country in the next few days. Hunter had watched the whole squads faces light up with looks of jubilation.

"They should be coming into view in the next minute or so," Grace exclaimed out loud, ear close to her personal radio.

Hunter was listening to the same transmission. DS Mark Gamble and DC Paula Clarke were on foot and had Ari and Pervez in their sights. They were passing out the targets' descriptions and current location.

He had parked on one of the estate roads slightly above the concrete monoliths, which he had read somewhere were now an icon of sixties architecture. He could see for himself that many of the blocks were in the throes of refurbishment and their frontages had a vibrant colour scheme mix of red, blue and yellow in an attempt to hide the drab greyness of the structures.

Within thirty seconds Hunter had them in his vision.

He followed the two Asians' movements. They appeared to be in no hurry and were sauntering across a grassy slope a hundred and fifty metres below. The pair seemed to be dressed identically in dark hoodies and baggy jeans and he could just make out, thanks to the glint on gold from the bright mid-morning sunshine, that both of them had a number of lengthy chains hanging around their necks dangling to mid chest. They were huddled together and appeared to be in deep conversation.

Just as Hunter hunched himself forward, to keep them in his sights, the pair made a surprise sharp movement. They stopped in mid-step and spun around to get a look behind.

Something had spooked them guessed Hunter.

He was right.

A split second later the brothers were off and running, and just coming into view he spotted DS Mark Gamble scrambling after them. His voice was screaming over the airwaves letting everyone know that the foot surveillance had been compromised.

Hunter hung on to the two fleeing figures watching where they were heading before he made a move. He gripped the handbrake with his left hand and lightly touched the accelerator with his right foot. He felt the engine surge. He was ready for a quick getaway.

The pair suddenly dropped out of view disappearing into a line of trees at the edge of the estate but Hunter knew they were making for the road.

Hunter could hear that Mark Gamble was doing his best to keep the commentary going, his voice trailing off now and again breathlessly, as he tried to make ground. Then within seconds his excited tone was alerting the team.

"They're getting into a new shaped silver Astra!"

Hunter craned his neck scouring the road system beyond the line of trees. He heard the Vauxhall before he saw it as the rubber of the tyres screeched on the tarmac. Then it sped into his sightline, heading away from the estate in the general direction of the suburbs of Halfway. Hunter locked the steering wheel sharply and pulled away from the kerb. Whipping through the gears quickly he soon made the end of the road and he guessed he would be a fraction in front of the speeding Astra. He could hear over the radio that two other unmarked cars were in hot pursuit but trailing.

Hunter reached the junction in a matter of seconds and slung his car at an angle to stop the Vauxhall turning in and forcing him to make a costly u-turn. He gripped the steering wheel tightly and braced himself.

Ten seconds later the Astra gunned into view rocking out of a right hand bend and veering towards them.

Hunter gritted his teeth and in one swift movement spun the steering wheel sharply, hitting the accelerator and then the brake almost simultaneously, with the result that his car jumped forward into the carriageway making the impression he was going to deliberately collide.

The action had the desired effect. There was a long screech as the Astra tyres grabbed the road surface and then it slewed sideways, its nearside wheels smashing into the opposite kerb edge.

Hunter could see Ari, the driver, fight with the wheel, trying to straighten out the car as it bounced back into the centre of the road. His actions were in vain. It bucked violently and scythed sideways, whipping into a screaming 180-degree turn before finally smashing its back end against a concrete lamp stanchion.

Hunter threw open his door, smacked the release button of his seat belt and flung himself out of the car. He instinctively knew Grace would be following.

Ari was just as quick in his movement, kicking open his door, which smacked Hunter's legs and rocketed him sideways. It gave him just the few seconds break that he needed and he was out of the blocks like a sprinter on a running track.

Catching his balance Hunter momentarily winced at the pain to his right thigh, but then the adrenalin kicked in and he set off in pursuit.

Ari had gained just ten yards on him. Hunter could make out the word SEMTEX in large white letters across the back of his black designer hooded top and couldn't help think how much he'd like to demolish him once he got hold of him.

Within moments his chest was pumping in and out in rhythm with his arms and legs. His lungs clawed for air as he put in that extra burst. In less than fifty yards Hunter was in grabbing distance and he lashed out with a swift kick. It connected, banging one leg into the other, sending him sprawling into a heap. Hunter was on top of him and wrestling an arm up his back before he had any time to react.

He let out a loud scream as Hunter yanked his shoulder joint against its socket.

"You're breaking my fucking arm!"

"Think yourself lucky it's not your neck." Hunter snarled. "You're nicked!"

As he turned round to drag his prisoner back he saw for the first time the chaos behind him. Uniform and CID cars were strewn everywhere and Grace was just snapping handcuffs on a dishevelled Pervez's wrists; he was being restrained by Tony Bullars who had been the lead car in the chase prior to the crash.

As Hunter neared, still jamming Ari's arm up his back, forcing him to walk on his tip-toes, he could see Pervez doubled up, frantically rubbing at his face and moaning loudly.

"What's the matter with him?" he asked, releasing his prisoner to Mike Sampson who was waiting with snap-on cuffs.

Pervez snapped up his head.

Hunter could see that tears were streaming down his face and that he was having difficulty opening his eyes.

"That fucking bitch has CS'd me," Pervez moaned.

"Stop rubbing your eyes you'll only make it worse," Grace retorted with a smirk, slipping her CS gas canister back into her jacket pocket. She turned to Hunter. "I thought he was going to attack me so I gassed him."

"Fucking liar I said I was coming quietly."

Hunter kept a straight face.

"I don't know Grace, what have I said to you about police brutality and that temper of yours?" He opened the back door of his car and guided Ari onto the rear seat. "I wouldn't dream of doing anything like that. I don't know I can't take you anywhere."

He turned to see her rolling up her eyes and shaking her head in mock despair and he shot her a wink.

"Well done everyone," he exclaimed slamming the car door shut. "Let's wrap this up and get these two back for questioning."

* * * * *

Barnwell:

Hunter picked up one of the Pakistani passports from his desk, flicked through the inside pages and added a few more notes to his pre-interview record. He set it back down amongst the pile of evidence laid out across his and Grace's desks.

Upon their return to Barnwell with their prisoners the team had emptied the contents of the Vauxhall Astra's boot, which Ari and Pervez Arshad had been arrested in after it had crashed. They had discovered personal clothing belonging to the pair in three holdalls together with two single journey airline tickets to Allama Iqbal Internationa Airport in Lahore and two Pakistan National passports, which displayed Ari and Pervez's photographs but under other names.

The Drug Squad informant had been spot on about the brothers making ready to flee the country thought Hunter, as he put the finishing touches to his notes. He looked across at Grace who was still logging the evidence.

The Incident room was empty. DS Mark Gamble and DC Paula Clarke had shot out to Hoyland – to the Hassan's convenience store; they were going to re-arrest Mohammed and Jilani, now that the Arshads' were in custody, whilst the other two members of the team DCs Andy France and Alex Mills were still across in Sheffield, trying to determine an address for the brothers. They had refused to divulge their place of abode to the Custody Sergeant and nothing in their possessions helped to highlight one. However they had recovered both the brothers' mobile phones which were with the technical experts in the hope that they could locate the last spot where a signal was emitted. It was a long shot.

"Ready?" he asked. He and Grace had been given the task of interviewing Ari Arshad whilst Tony Bullars and Mike Sampson had the job of questioning his brother Pervez. They were already in one of the other interview rooms.

Grace nodded.

Hunter pushed back his chair and gathered up his notes. He took a final lingering look at the incident board time-line sequence, confirming and double-checking in his head that he had it all lodged and ready for when he needed to dig in to his memory banks during the interview. He pursed his lips and nodded to himself. He was prepared.

"Okay Grace let's put this job to bed."

* * * * *

Ari Arshad presented a cocky look despite the painful pink flesh graze to his right cheek. That had been caused when

Hunter had tripped him prior to his arrest and he had already bleated to the Custody Officer that he had been assaulted when he had been booked in.

He was leaning back on the rear legs of his chair, arms folded defensively.

The duty solicitor who had been called in was seated next to him scribbling notes into his legal pad. The minute the two detectives had walked into the room Hunter saw him check his watch and make a note of the time.

Hunter dropped his paperwork and the evidence on the table in dramatic fashion.

It made the solicitor jump and he scowled back over his spectacles.

Hunter cracked a false apologetic smile. "Sorry about that," he said raising his eyebrows and taking his seat opposite. He nodded to Grace and she started the tape recording machine.

Hunter went through the customary preamble to an interview, flicking open his folder even though he knew in his mind he wouldn't need to refer to it.

"For the tape can I confirm you are Ari Arshad?"

The prisoner exchanged a look with his solicitor who shrugged his shoulders and returned a nod.

Ari rocked slightly on the back legs of his chair. "That's right, I am the one and only Ari Arshad," he sniped.

"And not Habib-ur-Begum as it says in the Pakistan National Passport which we found amongst your possessions?"

"No comment."

"Why were you in possession of a false passport and a one way airline ticket to Pakistan?"

"No comment."

"Okay if that's the tack you wish to take Ari I'll ask you a less incriminating question. Just for the record what relation are you to Mohammed Hassan."

He glanced at his solicitor again who gestured with raised eyebrows that it was okay to answer.

"Mohammed is my uncle."

"And so Samia Hassan, his daughter, is your cousin?" Hunter removed a photo of Samia from beneath his papers. It was a blown up shot from the Meadowhall CCTV footage.

"For the tape I am showing the defendant a colour photograph of Samia Hassan. Is this the Samia we are talking about?"

Ari nodded, "yes."

"When was the last time you saw Samia?"

He bunched his shoulders. "Can't remember."

"Rough guess. Couple of weeks, couple of months?"

"Couple of months I guess."

"Where was that?"

"At my uncle's place."

"What address is that?" Hunter was hoping for a slip up. They still did not know the attack site.

"His shop in Hoyland."

"You have already been told the reason for your arrest this morning haven't you?"

"Yes, but that's shit. I haven't murdered Samia. You've got the wrong man Mr smart detective."

Hunter rolled with the sarcastic retort – let it wash over him. "I'm guessing you've seen the TV news and the newspapers headlines about Samia's murder?"

"Yeah."

"When did you first become aware of her disappearance?"

"Can't remember."

"Who told you about it?"

"My uncle – I think?"

"Can you remember when that was?"

"Nope."

Hunter knew he needed to move things forward. He replaced the photograph in his folder and took out another. It depicted the white Renault van, which had been recovered from the Rotherham car dismantlers. "Ari, slight change of questioning now. Do you recognise this van."

Hunter clocked a reaction in Ari's face.

He dropped his chair back on to its four legs but he did not respond.

"I'll ask the question again. Do you recognise this white Renault van?"

Ari coughed. "I think so."

"You think so?"

"My uncle owned a similar van."

"This is the van owned by your uncle – Mohammed Hassan – I can confirm that from its index number. Have you ever driven this van?" Hunter knew from Duncan Wroe's SOCO report that Ari's fingerprints and DNA were all over the van and that he had been seen in the Country Park by Doctor Christopher Woolfe.

There were a couple of seconds silence then he replied softly, "Yeah I used to do deliveries for him."

"When was the last time you drove or were in this van?"

There was a delayed response again. "Can't remember," he returned.

"Let me help you remember. Have you ever been to Meadowhall in the van?"

Now there was a clear reaction. Ari locked his arms tighter and his face hardened.

Hunter waited for twenty seconds but there was no reply. "I'll ask the question again. Have you ever driven or been in this vehicle to Meadowhall shopping centre?"

Ari turned to his solicitor as if seeking to be helped out with an answer. His solicitor picked up on the look. "DS Kerr is this line of questioning going anywhere?"

Hunter opened up a CD case and took out a DVD and slid it across to Grace. She rose from the table and slotted it into a small TV/DVD player set on a shelf in one corner of the room. The screen flashed immediately from dark grey to blue.

Hunter turned to the solicitor. "There is some significance to this line of questioning which your client obviously finds uncomfortable answering. Could it be that he has something to hide?"

"DS Kerr that is out of order."

Hunter diverted his gaze and fixed Ari with a determined stare. "Mr Arshad, my question relating to your use of your uncle's white van at Meadowhall has in my view hit a raw nerve. I am therefore going to show you some CCTV footage which may help jog your memory."

He turned and nodded to Grace who hit the play button on the TV. Over the next five minutes the horrific sequence of events depicting the attack upon Samia by Ari and Pervez in the underground car park at the Meadowhall shopping complex played out across the screen. The whole time Hunter explored his prisoner's face. He watched him attempt to put on a front as he surveyed the damming evidence but Hunter could see from the continued jump in the young man's Adam's apple that he had him rattled.

He heard Grace pause the TV and knew it had finished. "Do you want me to play that again or are you happy for me to ask you questions in relation to what has just been played on the TV?"

Complete silence.

"You have just watched an attack upon Samia Hassan in the underground car park at Meadowhall shopping centre which was carried out by two men on the twenty-eighth of July this year. Do you recognise the two men you have seen carry out that attack?"

Complete silence again. Ari's eyes widened. He glared back in defiance.

"Mr Arshad I would appreciate an answer. From what you have just been shown do you agree that the one of the people who beat Samia Hassan until she was unconscious was yourself?"

Ari unlocked his arms and slammed them onto the table. "No comment. No fucking comment."

The solicitor reached across and nervously tapped Ari Arshad's arm. "DS Kerr I would like ten minutes with my client," he announced.

The ten minutes went beyond twenty minutes. Hunter leaned against the wall of the interview corridor, his eyes fixed on the gap at the bottom of the door. He knew that right now there was some serious client solicitor storyline being hammered out behind it. A smile played on his lips; they had Ari on the rack.

Then just as he was checking his watch again the door opened and the solicitor stuck his head around it. "My client is ready to answer your questions."

Hunter and Grace started afresh. Grace switched on the tape recording machine and Hunter reminded Ari of his rights. "Okay before we had a break you were shown CCTV footage of an attack upon Samia Hassan by two men. Was one of those men you?"

"Yeah, but I didn't kill Samia?"

"And who was the other person who carried out the attack with you?"

"You know who it is. It's Pervez, my brother."

"Why did you attack Samia."

"We were forced to do it."

"Forced?"

"Yeah, you don't know what my uncle Mohammed is like. He's a violent man we're scared of him. He told us to do it."

Hunter knew that this didn't sound right, especially given the criminal records of the pair, but he encouraged him to continue.

"Mohammed used to ring me lots, telling me that Samia was dishonouring the family. He told me she was sleeping with a man outside of marriage and wanted us to warn her off and get her to come home. Then a few months ago he came to see me and Pervez and said we had to do something about Samia. She was refusing to marry a cousin of ours after agreeing to the marriage and he wanted us to make her go to Pakistan. I told him we couldn't do that but he threatened me and Pervez. He is a very violent man. That day at Meadowhall, me and Pervez were making deliveries for our uncle and he phoned me up shouting and swearing. He said Samia was at Meadowhall threatening to run away and he told us to go and get her and bring her back. I know on that footage it looks worse than it was."

"Looks worse than it was," interrupted Hunter. "You beat her unconscious and threw her in the back of the van as if she was a rag doll."

Ari shrugged. "We didn't mean to beat her like we did, we just got carried away."

"So what happened after you left the car park."

"Uncle Mohammed met us on an industrial site near Rotherham town centre and took her out of the van and drove her away. We didn't kill her. The last time I saw her was when we helped put her in the back of Uncle Mohammed's car."

Hunter hadn't expected this response. He now needed to hit him with Christopher Woolfe's evidence and they also had the SOCO evidence of the fibres from the rug, which she had been wrapped up in prior to being transported to Barnwell Lake where her body had been finally dumped. Ari's account did not cover these elements. His spirit lifted.

"You say you took Samia out of the van and put her in her father's car?"

"Yeah."

"Was she conscious or unconscious?"

"Conscious. She was struggling."

"Then why did you get need to get rid of the van. To dispose of it at the car dismantlers like you did."

Ari dropped his head for a few seconds then returned his gaze towards Hunter. "Because Mohammed just told us to. If he tells you something you obey."

"Did you do this straightaway?"

"No we hid the van in a garage for a few days then took it there."

"Did anyone else use it?"

"No we hid it."

"Ari I've let you go on a bit but that's because I wanted to give you enough rope to hang yourself. What you have just told us is complete bullshit. And how do I know that? Well firstly, how do you account for fibres being found in the rear of the van? The same fibres, which match those of the rug, in which Samia's body was found, when it was dragged up from the lake. Before you try and dig your way out of that one I also want to introduce some other evidence as well. Do you remember a few years ago when Samia was at University and she had a relationship with a young man who was training to be a doctor?"

Ari's eyes rose up towards the ceiling.

"A young man, who you, and your brother assaulted, because of that relationship?"

His eyes lowered. "No complaint was ever made about that."

"No it wasn't but we know that on a later occasion you and your brother paid him a visit when he was working at Barnwell Infirmary and warned him off, and also damaged his car. And the bad news for you is that he just happened to be driving his car at Barnwell lake on Friday the first of August, the night you and your brother dumped Samia's body in the lake, and he recognised you driving your uncle's white van away from the scene."

He saw from Ari's changed expression that he had him. The man closed his eyes a few seconds then snapped them open. "I've told you what happened, now I'm saying fuck all else."

Hunter tried a few more probing questions which Ari batted off with 'no comment' and he realised he had lost the impetus of the interview. He made a decision to sum things up, draw it to a close, and then returned him to his cell.

* * * * *

Hunter and Grace waited in the custody suite. Tony Bullars and Mike Sampson had not fared any better with Pervez Arshad who had also made no comment to the majority of the questions, and once he had been shown the CCTV footage of the attack upon Samia had refused to even talk to the detectives except to demand to be locked up back in his cell.

They still had to interview Mohammed and his wife Jilani. At least Ari's evidence had implicated Samia's father and would provide a wedge, though Hunter doubted the truth of that, especially as they knew that Samia had been violently raped prior to being murdered. From his experience that just didn't feel like something a father would do. He knew they had made in-roads that afternoon but they were still no nearer to getting a clear-cut confession to the murder of Samia.

As they all made their way back to the incident room for de-briefing Hunter knew the priority was to find the attack site. That would provide them with so many answers and much needed evidence to swing the enquiry.

- ooOoo -

CHAPTER TWENTY THREE

DAY THIRTY FOUR: 26th September.

Barnwell:

Hunter pulled another bacon sandwich from the pile, which Angie the cleaner and his partner Grace had made. He'd heard the pair chatting and laughing, in the small kitchen next to the incident room, during the past twenty minutes.

Most of the team were in, hugging mugs of warm tea or coffee, munching on the surprise breakfast, and gossiping, waiting for the early morning briefing.

Looking around the room and listening, Hunter knew that this enquiry had just turned the corner, even despite lacking the confessions, in relation to Samia's murder. The implication from Ari that his uncle Mohammed was also responsible for his daughter's final days and hours was the starter for the day, and with a bit of luck might just be the lever for obtaining the proper story.

Grace walked into the room with another plateful of sandwiches. "That's it, all the bacon's gone now," she said plonking the plate down between hers and Hunter's desk.

"What muck have you two raked up on someone then? You were going at it hammer and tongs back there." Hunter bit into the warm bread.

Grace flopped into her seat and leaned across her desk. "You will never guess what I've just found out from Angie," she responded in a hushed voice.

"Go on enlighten me."

"The boss is only having a thing with that DCI from Scotland."

"You are joking?"

"Nah, nah. One of her friends is waitressing at the Stables restaurant. The pair have been in there most evenings."

Hunter shook his head in amazement and grinned. "Well the crafty bugger. I'll have to give him some rib over that."

Grace smiled herself and settled back in her chair.

Hunter took another bite of his sandwich. The mention of DCI Dawn Leggate caused him to drift away for a few moments. His parents were still staying with them as Billy Wallace and Rab Geddes still had not been caught. He'd wanted so much to sit down and sort things out with his dad but since the revelation he had not had the opportunity because of the investigation. He had spoken to Beth about it when he had finally fallen into bed the last few nights and she had told him that what she had seen of his father had been a pitiful sight. She said he had been moping round the house like a caged animal and certainly wasn't eating properly. Hunter's mum had also taken Beth to one side and told her that his dad was desperate for some time with him to explain everything.

The sooner we put this enquiry to bed, the better.

"You lot owe me a gallon of beer," announced Barry Newstead, pushing through the incident room doors.

It broke Hunter's daydream.

"You are going to really thank me for this," he continued, waving aloft a clear plastic wallet containing a CD disc. He strode towards the large TV, switched it on with a podgy index finger, inserted the disc into the DVD player and snatched up the remote. "I spent most of yesterday afternoon with the neighbourhood team for the Parkhill Flats. Did you know most of it is covered by CCTV?"

The plasma screen fluttered into life.

"There are twenty odd cameras fitted around the outside of the place plus they also have lift cameras at each floor inside the flats. I searched various time frames between the twenty-eighth of July when we know Samia was abducted from Meadowhall right through to the first of August when we believe her body was dumped in the lake and I found this little lot."

Hunter watched Barry's face split with a wide grin. He knew from his time teamed up with the investigator over the years that he loved nothing more than to have centre-stage.

Barry exaggerated the starting of the play mechanism firing the remote at the DVD player as if he was shooting a gun. A grainy image fluttered onto the forty-eight inch screen.

"This was captured at nine-thirty-six pm on the first of August. This camera is looking down on a grassed area in front of one of the buildings."

Suddenly in the right hand corner of the TV two men in dark hooded tops are seen stumbling into view and appear to be struggling with a rolled-up bundle. Barry zoomed in on the hazy images.

One of the men had his back to the camera and was bent over almost dragging along the ground what appeared to be a large rolled up rug.

Although the hoods were up on both men, hiding their faces, Hunter could clearly make out the white lettering on the back of one of the designer hooded tops. The words SEMTEX was clearly visible. He felt a surge of excitement run through him.

The team watched in silence their eyes fixed to the set. The play continued until the two men disappeared off camera with their bundle.

"I also found this footage," continued Barry.

Another image flashed onto the screen. The pan of the camera focus was a lot wider and covered a larger portion of the complex. Into view came a section of road below a grassy knoll. Along the bottom of the screen was a line of parked cars.

"This is one of the slip roads just below the flats."

From the top of the screen the camera picked up two fuzzy images, silhouettes at first, but their movement was clearly evident and no one could mistake it was the same two characters, from their attire, struggling with the rolled up carpet. The one at the back suddenly slipped and his end of the carpet slumped to the ground.

The team watched as the person struggled to hump it back up towards his midriff and then the pair continued waddling down the slope with their bundle until they reached the road.

Barry zoomed the footage again. It was still grainy but the images could be made out, though not satisfactorily enough for facial recognition.

The pair then pulled the rug towards a white van parked amongst the row of vehicles. The one wearing the SEMTEX designer top opened its rear doors and the pair loaded in the bundle. Both then jumped into the front of the van and it pulled away and drove out of camera view.

Barry freeze-framed the shot. In the top left hand corner was the time and date sequence - 9:52pm 01:08:08.

Hunter knew this all fitted. The time to travel from Sheffield to Barnwell Lake was approximately forty minutes. That meant that their witness, the sex worker, Kerri Ann Bairstow had been spot-on with her timings of her sightings of the two men and the white van at the Country Park.

"And for my encore," he added with a flourish. He re-started the DVD player. "This was captured in the entranceway at one of the internal lifts."

The image, which flickered onto the screen, showed a floor area with a squashed up section of lift doors at the top quarter of the screen.

There was little doubt in Hunter's mind that from the angle of the shot this was captured by a camera at ceiling height.

Suddenly into view came the person in the SEMTEX designer hoody. He was bent double dragging the rolled up carpet. Quickly following into the frame, also doubled up, lumping the other end of the rug came another hooded figure. The clarity of these images was excellent and Hunter could see that sections of pattern on the rolled up carpet were a perfect match to those of the rug Samia's body had been found wrapped up in. He had no doubt in his mind that he was watching the first stages of her being taken away from the place where she had just been raped and butchered.

They stopped by the lift doors dropping both ends of the carpet and the character in the designer hoody straightened himself, easing out his back with his hands. Just as he pressed for the lift he flicked back his hood and stretched his neck. There was no mistaking that face – it was Ari Arshad.

Hunter wanted to punch the air.

"That lift is on the fifth floor. Now all you've got to do is some old fashioned door knocking and you should have your attack site."

Hunter studied Barry. A pneumatic drill couldn't remove that sickly contented smirk on his face he thought. He was so pleased for him and so glad he had brought him onto the team.

"Ever thought about being a detective Barry?" said Hunter straight-faced, launching himself out of his seat.

The civilian investigator scrutinised him for a second then said "Detective Sergeant Kerr if I didn't know you better I would say you're jealous because an old hand has beaten you to the end-game."

They both flashed a grin to one another.

"One up to you Barry," returned Hunter wetting a finger and striking it in the air. "Well done you old fart."

"I'll take that as a compliment shall I. By the way I will accept payment with several pints of John Smiths amber nectar," he finished, switching the TV to off.

* * * * *

"Let me have a go at Jilani," begged Grace after briefing.

Detective Superintendent Michael Robshaw had determined that now they had the CCTV evidence damming Ari there was no rush to re-interview him and that the team should focus on Samia's parents since no one had spoken with them following their re-arrest the previous afternoon.

He had allocated that task to Hunter and Grace whilst sending the remainder of the team across to Sheffield to find Ari and Pervez's place now that Barry Newstead had narrowed down the flat complex and the floor level.

Hunter looked up from the notes he had scribbled.

"Let me try the empathy approach – Mother and daughter thing again. It might work this time coming from me. I can guess she's been subservient to Mohammed for years and even afraid of him, but I can't believe deep down that she is involved in all this. My gut instinct is she's just keeping silent because she's more afraid of her husband than she is of us."

Hunter stroked his chin and mused over her comments.

"Okay let's go for it." He clicked the top back on his pen and slid the folder of evidence across the desk. "She's all yours."

* * * * *

Jilani looked haggard. Her dark hair was unkempt, her red and gold sari crumpled and black streaks stained her cheeks from her crying.

Grace guessed that more than likely she had suffered a sleepless night. She surmised that Jilani would be jaded and feeling vulnerable and that was all stacked in her favour for this interview.

An interpreter and her solicitor were present.

Hunter started the tape recording machine.

"Jilani I want to make things easy for you. Yesterday we interviewed your nephews Ari and Pervez and one of them has admitted being involved in the abduction of your daughter Samia." Grace concentrated on Jilani's face, watching her reactions as the interpreter repeated her opening lines in Urdu.

"He has also implicated your husband Mohammed in this, actually saying that your husband forced them to carry out the abduction under threat of violence." Grace deliberately held back the sighting by Doctor Woolfe which negated this story so that they could hopefully stack up the evidence against Ari and Pervez.

There was a flicker in the woman's eyes and a quick shake of the head.

"Mrs Hassan I don't want to prolong this agony for you because what happened to your daughter was horrendous. But we have a duty to investigate this thoroughly and if we find you are involved in her murder then you will suffer the consequences. Do you understand what I am saying?"

Jilani nodded even before the interpreter finished and Grace realised for the first time that the woman had a better understanding of English than she had initially made out. That was a good thing. It would be easier now for her to look for the signs in her facial expressions and body language.

"I'm going to show you some film footage now that was captured by CCTV cameras about two months ago at Meadowhall. I must warn you it is disturbing but I want you to concentrate on it."

Hunter got up, switched on the small TV, and started the DVD rolling. It re-ran the same footage they had shown to Ari Arshad the previous day.

As it ran Grace never took her eyes off Jilani. Five minutes had gone by when suddenly the woman dropped her head onto her chest and started weeping. Grace knew at that point that the tape had just ended without seeing it happen. "I'm sorry you had to sit through that Mrs Hassan but I needed to show you just how your daughter started her suffering. I also have to tell you that we now believe she was held for five days before she was finally killed and during that time she was violently raped."

Her anguish increased to a sob.

"I can tell you that we now have enough evidence to take this to court and prosecute for murder. Ari has implicated your husband in your daughter's murder and your prolonged silence in all this is not going to help you. If you continue to refuse to talk then we will suspect you are involved in this and you will also go to court."

Jilani looked up into Grace's eyes. Black runny kohl from around her eyes scarred her cheeks further.

"Mrs Hassan I am a Mother of two daughters and if I thought my husband had been involved in their deaths I would move heaven and earth to see him punished. As a mother yourself I do not believe for one second you would want anything different. Am I right?"

With glazed over eyes she nodded. Then she began to speak in Urdu. After about twenty seconds she stopped. "I never realised that they had done that to my Samia," she suddenly delivered in broken but understandable English.

Grace reached across and took hold of Jilani's hands and fixed her a sympathetic look. "Mrs Hassan do you want to tell us what you know?"

She hung her head and dropped her gaze to the table. "I never wanted Samia harmed. I went along with my husband and told her I would disown her after what she had done with that young doctor. She knew our values and she just went against them but I never wished any harm against her. It was Mohammed he wouldn't let it go. He arranged for her to marry a cousin of his back in Pakistan. He said it would be the best thing for her, but she flung it back in his face. Then he discovered she was planning to run away and he got even angrier."

"What did he do?" Grace still held Jilani's hands.

"I knew he was arranging things with Ari but I didn't know what he intended. I know Ari and Pervez are not good people – that they have been in trouble, but I do not know what for. I pleaded with Mohammed to let things be, just disown her as our daughter, but he wanted to punish her he said for bringing dishonour to him." She lifted her head and broke into a fresh sobbing fit.

Grace let her hands go and fished a paper handkerchief from her jacket pocket and handed it over.

Jilani dried her eyes. The kohl smudged.

"Please go on Mrs Hassan."

"I never knew it was going to go this far. Mohammed told me Ari and Pervez were going to force her to go to Pakistan and everything would be sorted. When you came to the shop and I heard you say you were investigating her murder I was shocked. It was only then that I realised what Mohammed had done to Samia. Believe me I did not know this. What you have shown me on the TV, the thing that has happened to Samia – it is evil."

"Are you willing to give a statement?"

Jilani wiped her eyes again. Then she nodded.

For evidential purposes the first statement was written in English followed by a second in Urdu, by the interpreter. The evidence against Ari and Pervez Arshad and also Mohammed Hassan was damming and Hunter couldn't wait for that evening's briefing. He was also eager to get back into the incident room to find out if the flat had been located.

Hunter followed Grace out into the custody suite corridor closing the interview room door behind him. He could still hear Jilani Hassan's cries of pain. He turned to meet Grace and with sparkling eyes gave her a 'you did it' look and then pulled her head forward and planted a kiss on her forehead.

"You little beaut," he said before strolling away back to the incident room.

* * * * *

Sheffield:

Hunter and Grace rode the clanking lift to the fifth floor; they were looking for flat 508.

Just over an hour earlier they had returned to an empty incident room and learned from Isabel Stevens, the HOLMES supervisor that the whole team were over in Sheffield – the Arshad's flat had been found and they were now doing house-to-house enquiries. Upon hearing this they had immediately exchanged excited looks and decided they wanted to be in on the action.

Pervez and Mohammed could sweat in the cells a little bit longer, Hunter had determined as he scooped up a set of car keys.

They had lodged the statements made by Jilani Hassan with Isobel. Then with Hunter aggressively worming and forcing his way through heavy traffic, had quickly journeyed to the Parkhill Flats.

The instant the metal doors screeched open Hunter was greeted by a strong smell of pine disinfectant and he could hear lots of activity somewhere out along the corridor.

As he stepped out of the lift he immediately recognised the location from the CCTV footage he had seen earlier that morning. He glanced up at the ceiling at the small black domed fitment, which held the camera, and suddenly wondered how on earth the pair had been so stupid. He pointed it out to Grace and then made his way to number 508.

Blue and white police crime scene tape was draped across the dim corridor and a uniformed officer barred their way. Hunter ducked under the tape flashing his warrant card before slotting it into the top pocket of his jacket leaving the shiny silver and blue South Yorkshire Police crest showing.

The door to flat 508 was ajar and he rapped loudly on the boxwood panel and pushed it gently. It opened into a small shadowy corridor but a warm light coming from the partially open door at the other end greeted them. He and Grace stepped through and Hunter pushed open the second door, which from its furnishings Hunter clocked was the lounge. Duncan Wroe was the first person he spotted, crouching back on his haunches carrying out a careful examination of the carpet. Two other protectively clothed females were also in the room working on the spraying and swabbing of a wall opposite. A bare bulb in the centre of the ceiling gave off the only light. Heavy draped curtains covered one wall and were thick enough to keep out most of the daylight. They hadn't been pulled back yet.

The room was sparsely furnished with a flimsy two-seater sofa and a single armchair of cheap quality and yet fastened at chest height on a wall above the fireplace was a huge plasma flat screen TV.

"They've obviously got their priorities right," Hunter said wryly, glancing at Grace and pointing at the TV.

Duncan looked over his shoulder. "I wondered how long it would be before you two arrived," he said and then returned to his task.

"You know us, Duncan can't keep our noses out," Hunter quipped. "Anyway I thought you'd have finished with the scene by now. Are you holding out for overtime?"

"Very funny Hunter, very funny," he riposted without turning around.

"Seriously Duncan, is this the place where Samia was killed?"

"Oh this is it all right." Supporting his knees with his hands, he slowly eased himself up.

"I'm getting too old for this, roll on my pension." He sauntered towards the far wall where the white suited women were working. "Attempts have been made to clean down the walls but we're already picking up blood spatter patterns low down close to the skirting."

"Blood spatter?"

"Yes a spouting or squirting effect when a blow has been delivered - but by the looks of this lot I would say this is from a cut – a slashing effect. Didn't she have her throat cut if I remember rightly?"

Grace nodded.

"And there is also a pooling effect soaked into the carpet down to the floorboards." He lifted an edge of the cheap nylon carpet to reveal a dark stain ingrained in the lightwood flooring beneath. "She'd obviously lost a substantial amount of blood."

He moved back into the centre of the room. "Finally I have this for you. Switch off the light behind you."

Hunter reached behind him to the light switch and pitched the room into semi darkness. Just a little daylight poked between the gaps in the heavy drapes.

"Remember when I showed you how fibres could be lit up by a light source when I examined the white Renault."

Hunter and Grace nodded.

"As you know fragments of fibres are transferred when they come into contact with another surface and as I mentioned different fibres can give off different wavelengths which can be picked up by fluorescent lights. I already told you that we had the wavelengths of the fibres from the Asian rug because of its unique make-up."

Hunter acknowledged again with a nod.

"Well this is what I've found."

Duncan switched on a low voltage, hand-held fluorescent light and began scanning the carpet. As if by magic a line of bright blue fibres became distinguishable from the remainder of the room carpet. As he swept an area an oblong outline began to appear over the surface. "What would you say if I told you the perimeter of this is the exact same size as the rug Samia's body was found in. In other words she was wrapped up in the rug, which once fitted in this exact spot."

"You're a genius Duncan."

"Science actually Hunter but I will accept that accolade." He turned off the lamp plunging them back into darkness.

Hunter switched the room light back on.

"Another four or five hours and I'll have this room telling me what exactly went on but at least for now I've given you something which will help hold them in custody."

Hunter and Grace thanked him and made their way back to the car.

* * * * *

Barnwell:

It was just after four pm when they got back. The team were still out on enquiries and Hunter had gathered from Isobel that she expected them all back within the hour. They had gathered enough statements and material evidence to place Ari and Pervez in flat 508.

Armed with this information Hunter and Grace made their way back to the custody suite to re-interview Pervez.

Pervez was already waiting in the sticky warm soundproof interview room with his solicitor. He didn't have that air of cockiness like his brother yet nevertheless he fixed them with a penetrating glare.

As they sat down Pervez folded his arms in defensive posture and met them with a smug grin.

Hunter liked nothing more than a challenge.

Grace switched on the tape recording machine and turned around to switch on the TV/DVD player.

"Mr Arshad during your last interview you chose to make no comment throughout and as you know that is your prerogative. However it is only fair to tell you that since that last interview things have moved on considerably. We have interviewed your brother Ari and I have to tell you that he has implicated you in the abduction of Samia. We have a statement from a witness placing you at the scene where Samia's body was dumped and I must also tell you that Jilani Hassan, Samia's mother and your aunt has also made a statement implicating you and Ari."

Suddenly his eyes were restless. He searched out his solicitor who had his head down making legal notes. He returned his gaze back across the table.

"You're bullshitting."

"Mr Arshad would I be telling you this in the presence of your solicitor and on tape if it wasn't true?"

Hunter watched him roll his eyes up towards the ceiling.

Pervez unfolded his arms and wiped the palms of his hands down the thighs of his trousers.

"Now I know you have been shown the CCTV evidence of you following Samia in Meadowhall and then your involvement in her attack down in the car park and that you chose not to respond when that evidence was presented, well now I want to show you some more footage we have recently acquired, which you might find interesting."

Grace switched on the DVD player and let the footage play out which Barry had shown to the team that morning.

Hunter watched the sweat trickle down the sides of Pervez's forehead. He brushed away the trickles just before they rolled onto his neck.

Hunter heard Grace switch off the machine. He leant across the table and locked together his fingers. "We have now found yours and Ari's flat. As we speak forensics are going through the house with a fine tooth comb. We already know this was where Samia was held and where she was killed and you have seen from that CCTV footage that we now have you on camera taking out her body to dump in the lake. Now as I say you have every right not to say anything, but I hope your brother will be as loyal when he sees this."

Hunter watched Pervez's face change. He was rigid with fear.

"Ari raped and killed Samia," he suddenly barked out. "I thought we were only going to kidnap Samia and force her to go to Pakistan. That's what Ari told me. He said Uncle Mohammed wanted to teach his daughter a lesson because she had brought shame on the family and that we were to take her to our place and hold her there."

"Is that what happened then after you put her in the back of the van at Meadowhall?"

He nodded feverishly. "Yes, yes. We took her back to our flat and Ari tied her up in the bedroom. He phoned Uncle Mohammed and told him we had her and asked us what he wanted to do with her."

"What did your uncle say?"

"I don't know. Ari was always the one who talked to Uncle Mohammed, though he did come to the flat next day and started hitting Samia. Swearing at her and saying she had brought dishonour to him and she didn't deserve to live."

"Is that when she was killed?"

"No, no, he busted her mouth and nose and I cleaned her up with a towel from the bathroom. She was still alive. She begged me to let her go and then Ari came into the bedroom and dragged me away. Uncle Mohammed left and I could hear him and Ari talking in the hallway."

"What were they saying?"

"I don't know I couldn't hear. They were sort of whispering together."

"What happened then?"

Pervez's eyes started to glass over. He dabbed at them with the back of his hand. "Nothing that night, but the next day Ari told me to go out and get some food for us. I went to the local Spar and when I came back Samia was dead. Ari had killed her." Tears welled up in the corner of his eyes. "That's the truth. I swear on the Prophet Mohammed."

"When you say she was dead. Describe what you saw."

"There was blood everywhere. Up the walls and a huge puddle around her head. She was lying on the carpet in the lounge near the armchair. When I left her she was tied up in the bedroom. When I got back he was pacing up and down and he had that knife-thing in his hand. He'd cut her throat with it."

"Was she still tied up?"

"Her hands were behind her back but he'd untied her feet." Pervez gulped and look down towards the table. "She wasn't wearing her jeans or her knickers. I knew what he had done."

"When you say she was dead did you check at all to see if she was still alive?"

"I looked at her but you could tell. There was a big pool of blood. Her eyes were wide open. She wasn't breathing."

"What did you do?"

I freaked out. I couldn't believe he had done that. We argued and I asked him why. He said Uncle Mohammed wanted him to do it. I didn't know whether to believe him or not."

"What happened then?"

"Ari said we had to get rid of the body. He wrapped Samia in the carpet, wiped the knife-thing and put it in with her and then he asked me to help bind her up. After that he rang Uncle Mohammed."

"Did Ari tell your uncle what he had done?"

"Yes he told her he had slit her throat. But I don't know what my uncle was saying. I couldn't hear that part of the conversation."

"Is that when you brought Samia across to Barnwell and dumped her in the lake?"

"No we kept her body in the flat a couple of days. We put the rug in the bath so no more blood seeped out. Ari said Uncle Mohammed was going to ring him and tell him where to take the body. Then that Friday evening Ari took a call from Uncle Mohammed and said he had found a place to hide Samia where no one would find it. That's when we drove to the lake and dumped her." His voice started to quaver. "That is the truth. I didn't kill Samia. It was Ari. My Uncle Mohammed told him to do it."

* * * * *

It was just after six pm when Hunter and Grace finally returned to the incident room having completed a second interview with Mohammed Hassan. He had been more stubborn than his nephews. He had refused to accept the testimonies and evidence presented and had continually bleated that everyone was lying against him – including his wife. However as they had walked him back to his cell they had witnessed the first signs of him cracking. As Hunter had slammed the heavy, reinforced door into its metal frame he had inspected him through the door's hatch. Mohammed had looked up at him from the bench with glassed over eyes, quickly followed by a pained look as he had hung his head into his chest.

With a satisfied smile Hunter had slid the metal shuttered hatch shut with a resounding clang.

Feeling energised despite the long day he bounced into the MIT office. It was full; the Office Manager, Detective Inspector Gerald Scaife, and the SIO, Detective Superintendent Michael Robshaw, were amongst the team waiting.

Hunter could see them searching his face. He guessed Grace would be experiencing the same. He surveyed the room before flashing a wide grin.

"Result. Pervez has coughed. And he's given us enough to hang his brother and Mohammed."

The cheer was deafening.

* * * * *

Hunter swilled the remaining dregs of his pint around the bottom of the glass as if it was the finest brandy and then swallowed. "That never touched the sides," he said nudging Barry Newstead, "fancy another? I owe you one."

Barry drained the remaining half of his pint in one mouthful and wiped the froth from his dark, bushy moustache with the back of his hand. "I'll not refuse a free pint."

Hunter made his way to the bar weaving between members of the team. They had all congregated into their small groups as they usually did at these celebratory gatherings. A couple of his colleagues gave him a congratulatory tap on his shoulder as he squeezed past.

As he plonked the empty glasses down on the bar he cast his look around monitoring the faces of his workmates and couldn't help but bring to mind the first few words which had been instilled in him that first day in CID after Barry Newstead had taken him out and got him rolling drunk.

'The spirit and bonding of a team is created in the pub' he had said. 'Putting a frustrating, complicated and exhausting enquiry to bed with a celebratory drink is what gels everyone together.' How true those pearls of wisdom had been proved over the years.

As he waited to be served he mused over the hurried briefing Detective Superintendent Michael Robshaw had given less than a half hour ago. He had watched the SIO make energetic scribbled notes on the incident board, but out of those had come cohesive actions for tomorrow.

He and Grace had been given the specific job of charging Ari, Pervez, and Mohammed with murder, and also handed the task of putting together the remand file for court, whilst the remainder of the MIT were to tie up all the loose ends; logging evidence and collecting statements to make everything stick.

He knew that the hard work wasn't quite yet over; their aim was to stack the evidence so much in the prosecution's favour that a guilty plea was inevitable.

Hunter was just trying to grab the attention of one of the bar staff when he felt his mobile vibrate in his trouser pocket. He dragged it out and took a look at the incoming caller. He saw the word 'gym' flash onto the screen. This has to be his dad. He took the call.

For a second all he could pick up was heavy breathing then his father's voice came on the line. He sounded frantic.

"Hunter get down here quick," he heard his father say. "It's Billy and Rab they've just turned up."

Then the phone cut off.

* * * * *

Billy Wallace had spent most of the morning propped up in his hotel bed switching channels between TV shows unable to concentrate on any of them. He had gone through the final plans time and time again in his head. Then just before lunch he had shaved off the beard, which had been his temporary disguise for the past two weeks, and headed out on the road in his recently acquired Range Rover.

He had met Rab and the two hired helps at Woodall Services on the M1 and run through the scenario with them. Rab had stayed the night holed up in another motel with the men making sure they didn't contact anyone before the job was completed.

In hushed tones, over a late full English breakfast, Billy double-checked that everyone knew their part and then confident he had everything in place he handed over the remainder of the cash he owed to the two co-conspirators before piling into the 4x4 and setting off towards Barnwell.

It had been a frustrating and sometimes restless afternoon but finally they had spotted Jock Kerr emerging from the refuge of his son's house and get in his hired car. Billy checked his watch. It was just after six pm.

They had kept their distance as they followed him. From the direction Jock took Billy had guessed he was heading for the gym. And as he pulled into the car park he knew his intuition had been proved correct.

They watched Jock saunter across the tarmac occasionally looking around him before entering through the rear double doors.

Then Billy issued his instructions.

* * * * *

DS John Reed and his partner DC Craig McDonald stared out of the large plate glass window down towards the car park below them. They had been in the first floor office of the empty warehouse since seven am that day. It was their fourth stint in the observation post and they were becoming weary.

John Reed was thankful for the sunshine, which beamed in at them through the large window. There was no heating in the building and this was all they had for warmth. He would be glad when they had captured Billy Wallace and Rab Geddes so that he could get back home. He hadn't seen any of his family now for the best part of a week and the motel room he was sharing with his colleague was not exactly luxurious. To make matters worse he felt his working relationship with Dawn Leggate was becoming compromised because of her dalliances with the Detective Superintendent she had recently met. He had dropped in on her again last night and she had been with him. Instantly, he had registered the embarrassment in her face despite her telling him they were just discussing the joint operation. All in all he wasn't best pleased with how things were progressing.

The hiss of the radio crackling into life broke his thoughts. The other team were informing them that Jock had just left his son's house and was alone.

John Reed huffed in frustration. He had only just got off the phone with Jock trying to persuade him not to come to the gym. He made an entry in the log and set the video camera rolling.

Ten minutes later Jock's car cruised into the car park below them and the camera captured him making his way into his gym through the rear doors.

The screeching of tyres just two minutes later startled John Reed. He saw the green Range Rover sway to one side as it swept into the car park, slewing into a skid before rocking to a halt. The passenger door flew open and he was mesmerised for a second as the ski masked stocky built man leapt out. Then he was on his radio screaming for a back up, grabbing the sleeve of his partner and leaping towards the stairwell, which led down to the car park.

* * * * *

Scanning the street Billy Wallace watched the Range Rover tear into the car park and slide to a standstill. Opposite the entrance he pressed himself against the trunk of one of the many trees, which lined the road, the shade from the canopy of leaves masking his features. Rab was close by. As he watched one of the masked men leap from the passenger side his slate grey eyes began glancing away at tangents. He was watching and waiting.

It soon paid off. He saw the two detectives almost fall out through the doors of a derelict warehouse onto the car park.

He gave the signal and the passenger jumped back into his seat and before he even had time to close the door the back wheels were chewing up gravel as it sped away.

The two officers weren't far behind. Sprinting across the car park one of them aimed the key fob at a dark blue Vauxhall Vectra, which triggered the opening mechanism with a lighting of orange tail-lights whilst the other was shouting excitedly into his police radio as he leapt into the front passenger seat.

Less than thirty seconds later the unmarked police car's engine was being gunned and it was tearing off in hot pursuit.

Billy smiled to himself. It was just how he had hoped.

* * * **

Jock Kerr slowly looked around all four walls of his son's and daughter-in-law's lounge. Though he had the place to himself he was feeling anything other than relaxed. In fact if truth be told he was anxious and agitated. It felt as if he was being imprisoned.

This is doing my head in. I've had enough.

He picked up the car keys from the coffee table, trotted out of the house, jumped into the hire car and fired up the engine. Before pulling off the drive he phoned DS John Reed on his mobile.

"I'm coming down to the gym. I'm sorry but I can't take anymore of this. I can't keep hiding away." He listened to the detective's response, then replied, "look there are four of you nearby. If Billy and Rab turn up then you'll nick them won't you?" Then he hung up before giving the sergeant an opportunity to object.

He'd watched in his rear view mirror more than he usually did when he was driving but nothing untoward had grabbed his attention and he felt quite relaxed by the time he had reached his gym.

He found the entrance doors locked and checked his watch. He guessed that the boxing coach who had been looking after things in his absence had gone home early. He unlocked both the door's and let himself in.

The place was fairly tidy with just a few weights out of place. He took a long lingering look around. The pristine whitewashed walls gave the gymnasium a clean and bright if not clinical appearance to the place. A full size boxing ring took up half of the floor space with one side for weight training and another for bag work. This place was his pride and joy. It had taken him a long time to build it up. Most of his life was in this place.

I'm buggered if I'm going to lose all this because of those two evil shites!

As he began to reset the loose weights onto the metal racks he heard the screech of tyres on the tarmac outside. He stopped what he was doing and listened. Less than thirty seconds later there was a fresh screech of rubber, quickly followed by another. He snatched up the wall phone and punched in Hunter's mobile number. As his son answered Jock heard the back doors crash open. He had just enough time to tell his son that Billy and Rab were here before the line went dead.

* * * * *

Billy Wallace slipped into the room alone.

Jock saw that he was still wearing that signature Crombie of his.

After all these years, and he still dresses like he's the 'big I am'

Jock saw the menacing look Billy was aiming at him as he stepped slowly, deliberately, further into the room. He caught a glimpse of his eyes. Billy's pupils had become so dilated that his eyes appeared almost black. It was a look Jock had seen in those eyes once before. It was the look of cold death.

Then everything seemed to fast-forward. Jock saw a quick movement in Billy's right arm, it was a jabbing movement downwards, and then he spotted the glint of the long blade. A tremor raced through him. Then he realised he was still clutching one of the free weights and it gave him a strange reassurance.

"Don't be stupid Billy if you do anything to me you're going to go away for a very long time. You'll probably die in prison." Jock said, doing his best to sound calm. "You can walk away from this right now and no one will be any the wiser."

"I've done thirty six fucking years already because of you. It will be worth it," he growled, edging even closer.

Jock watched Billy's face change. He was met by a cold-bloodied stare as he stepped closer.

Jock took up a defensive stance, wrapping one hand even tighter around the six-kilogram barbell, whilst balling the other into a solid fist. Then a strange thought entered his head; two combatants locked in a fight to the death.

Billy suddenly catapulted himself forward swinging his right arm in a whiplash movement.

The knife slashed across Jock's forearm before he had time to react.

He bounced backwards with fighting instinct and the metal racks clattered against his legs.

Then he spotted the blood spreading through his sweat top, though surprisingly there was no pain. It bought memories flashing into his brain from his boxing days. He remembered he had not recognised pain back then.

He witnessed Billy pulling back the knife again, preparing for another attack. Suddenly every sinew felt stretched as tight as a bow ready to fire and he felt an immense power surge through his body. He dropped back on one leg and then exploded forward swinging the barbell up in an arc. It smacked against Billy's jaw and he knew instantly from the blankness in the eyes that he had done the damage. He'd seen that look as well so many times during his boxing bouts. He instantly followed up with a left hook, smacking the side of Billy's head just below the ear. He heard the knife clatter to the floor and saw Billy's legs buckle. Just before he sank, Jock caught him with the swinging barbell again. A dull thwack emanated from the back of his head.

Jock dropped on top of him, took a handful of hair and yanked Billy's head back violently. Then he slipped an arm to the front of his neck, slotted his windpipe into the crook between his muscular forearm and bicep, and began to squeeze.

* * * * *

Hunter grabbed Barry Newstead within seconds of the line going dead. "My dad's in trouble," he hissed bolting for the side door of the pub.

He could feel a rush of energy surge through him as he jumped into his car and fired it up. Slamming the gear into first, and stamping the accelerator, he revved the 1.9 litre engine of his Audi, and then tore out of the pub car park towards the gym.

Barry was making an emergency call on his mobile whilst attempting to buckle up.

Less than ten minutes later the car skidded violently sideways across the tarmac surface of the gym's car park and shuddered to a halt.

Hunter flew from the car leaving the engine running and propelled himself through the rear double doors into the gym.

Only seconds behind was Barry

Rab Geddes was waiting for them in the corridor, legs astride and holding in front of him a wooden baseball bat, which he was smacking repeatedly into his palm.

Hunter skidded on the surface as he slid to a stop only a few yards from him.

"Where's Billy Wallace?" he screamed.

"You're too late!" Rab retorted with a sneer.

For a second there was a face-to-face confrontation. Hunter eyed the baseball bat bouncing in Rab's hands and then anger took over. He flew at him aiming for his face, mauling with clawing hands, gouging at his eyes like a rugby player in a ruck. The force spiralled Rab sideways smashing him into the wall. Hunter heard the breath explode from his lungs and felt the warm breath on his cheek, and in a white heat of berserk fury, and using his arms like pistons, he pulled, punched and pummelled more.

Barry Newstead jumped into the fray forcing his way in because of his sheer bulk. Within seconds Rab was pinned against the wall. The baseball bat clattered to the floor as he tried to protect himself from the unexpected onslaught.

Hunter fell away gasping for breath, drenched in sweat, and doubled-up almost retching as he watched Barry slam in a couple more punches to the ribs before Rab collapsed into a heap.

"My dad," Hunter managed to gasp as he gulped in a lung full of air.

"You go and help him." Barry urged. "This guy's going nowhere fast."

Hunter turned on his heels hitting the double swing doors into the main training area with his shoulder. He caught his balance, re-adjusted himself and quickly scoured the room. He caught sight of his dad by the weight rack draped across a prostrate figure which he immediately realised was Billy Wallace. At first Hunter wondered what was happening then the reality hit home. His father was strangling Billy. He sprinted the ten yards across the wooden sprung floor and snapped his arms around him making every effort to drag him off, but his dad had Billy locked tight.

"Dad! Dad!" he screamed, "He's had enough, let him go. You're going to kill him."

He hooked his fingers into a gap and prised at his father's wrists. "Dad I said let him go –NOW."

Hunter saw by the reaction from that shout that it had registered. He caught his father's wild and staring eyes and then in the next moment they had softened. Hunter prised at his dad's hands again and this time they yielded to his force. Billy's head smacked the wooden floor.

Hunter pulled his father to his feet and pushed him away and went to Billy's aid. He quickly checked his airway, manoeuvred him into the recovery position and then checked him again. He stared at his chest and inwardly prayed. Suddenly a spluttering cough burst from Billy's mouth, racking his body into life.

"Thank god for that!" Hunter cried out in relief. He spun round to face his father who was ashen-faced and just staring down. "Christ dad you could have killed him."

His dad glanced at the blood pouring from the wound on his forearm, clamped a hand around it and started to shake.

* * * * *

Standing in the entranceway to his father's gym Hunter watched Billy and Rab being loaded into the back of an ambulance and then driven away with an armed police escort. They had a catalogue of bumps and bruises between them, and Billy had a deep wound to the back of his head, but neither of them was seriously hurt.

Within minutes DCI Dawn Leggate appeared with two members of her team. She informed Hunter that the hired help in the ski masks had been detained and were en route to the custody suite. She added that the pair were known back in Scotland as petty crooks but since they hadn't actually done anything except act as decoys and drive dangerously they didn't have anything to hold them, though she'd make sure they had a night in the cells whilst a check was made to see if they were wanted elsewhere.

That had been ten minutes ago. Now he, Barry, his father, and the DCI, were seated around the desk in his father's office. His dad had refused to go in the ambulance and so one of the paramedics had put a bandage on the laceration and told him that it required suturing and to get it treated before the day was out.

Jock had promised that he would. Now he sat in his chair nursing his forearm.

In a couple of week's time Hunter knew that his father would be showing off the scar, just like the one above his right eye. And he knew what he would be saying, once he had told everyone how he had got this new one, 'scars are the medals of heroes.' He wished he had a pound for every time he had heard his father say that. Hunter shook his head and smiled to himself. At least there was no lasting damage.

The DCI said she needed to question them all about what had happened. Hunter asked for a little time with his father and for it to be carried out after he'd visited the hospital. Deep down he knew he needed to check what his father was going to say in his statement and make sure he played down the strangulation; to ensure that he used the words 'trying to restrain' as his defence.

The DCI assented to the request.

Hunter could tell by her face that she knew what had really happened and suddenly his earlier opinions of her were quashed. He returned an appreciative smile.

"I could do with a stiff drink," his dad suddenly announced. His father sprang open a cupboard at one side of his desk, delved into it and pulled out a bottle of single malt. Then he shuffled earthenware mugs together from a wall unit behind him and began to pour a generous amount into each. "They say it's good for shock," he said handing Hunter, Barry and the DCI a mug each. "Slainte! Doon the hatch" he toasted, chinking each of their mugs.

Hunter glanced at his father. The colour had returned to his face.

You and I need to sit down and talk, but right now isn't that time.

- ooOoo -

CHAPTER TWENTY FOUR

DAY THIRTY FIVE: 27th September.
Barnwell:

Hunter flopped back on the small two-seater sofa in his conservatory. He had just inserted a Michael Buble' CD into his Bose music system and he closed his eyes and allowed 'Summer Wind' to sweep over him. His head was thumping. He was glad that the Detective Superintendent had given the team a lie in, allowing them all to work an afternoon shift that day. He knew that there was still a fair bit of 'mopping up to do' to close the investigation. Ari, Pervez and Mohammmed still had to be charged with Samia's murder, and a remand file had to be put together for court.

Disturbing images from the previous night suddenly flashed into his already aching head. Sometimes he wished he could turn off his brain. He quickly replaced then with more pleasant ones.

Beth and his Mother had joined them at the gym, thankfully after the melee had ended, and as his dad had poured them all another 'wee dram' Beth had given him a quick check over and saved him from going to the hospital by applying several 'Steri-strips' herself to close the wound to his forearm, before re-bandaging and giving him a clean bill of health.

Then he Barry and his dad had returned to the pub to re-join the celebrations of the Samia Hassan enquiry.

The team had quizzed him as to what had gone on but he chose to give them a potted version of the events promising to fill them in the next day. What he had really needed was a few more beers to bring him back down from the adrenalin rush, and what he also needed deep down was to be beside his dad, to let him see that he was there for him. Barry had lightened the mood in their small group but still the conversation between himself and his dad had been stilted and shallow. Despite this Hunter had the feeling that the ice had been broken between them.

Both of them had finally fallen through the doors at 1.30am that morning and now he was suffering.

"Morning son."

His father's voice brought him back. He rolled his eyes down from his eyelids.

"Feeling delicate?"

"An understatement dad. Rough as a bear's arse springs to mind."

His dad chuckled. "Here, get that down you. I've just mashed."

Hunter was handed a cup of strong tea, just how his dad drank it. "Thanks."

His dad sat himself down opposite and rested his cup on the small light oak coffee table. "Son, I need to apologise." There seemed to be pleading in his words.

"Don't dad." Hunter locked onto his father's hurt look.

"No I do, don't stop me. I know I should have told you about this but I thought I was doing the right thing. I now realise I was wrong keeping you in the dark."

"Dad -." Hunter attempted to interject.

"Let me finish son. I'm not proud of what I got myself into and with foresight I would have gone nowhere near that crew, but at the time I was a twenty-year old man with a career in tatters. I thought I was making a fast buck at the time and didn't know what I was getting myself into. Nevertheless I think I made the right decision to protect your ma and I haven't made a bad job of bringing you up. You've turned out a son I'm very proud of and I hope when things settle down you'll feel the same way about me. Just remember this Hunter, even though I changed my name you are of the Kerr clan. Your Mum's a Kerr and you have every right to wear that tartan."

He watched his dad pick up his cup and take a drink and then met his gaze again. "You know one thing has come good of all this. For years I've had to stay away from my family for fear of putting them in danger. Going back up there to meet the DCI when I did, made me realise just how much I've missed them. I've since been in touch and already fixed up a meeting. What about you, Beth and the boys coming up with your ma and me and I'll introduce you to your family?"

- ooOoo -

EPILOGUE

Hunter took a couple of steps back from his easel, angling his head, slowly scanning various sections of his latest oil painting – a seascape of Robin Hoods Bay. Every few seconds he halted his gaze to focus on a particular passage within the scene, checking that he had resolved the section before letting his artistic eye move on. Five minutes later pleased with how skilfully he had managed to capture the stormy mood in the piece he set his brushes down on his palette and then wiped his hands with a rag.

Time for a cuppa.

Just before making for the kitchen he took in another lingering look. It was a process he always went through before he put the canvas to one side. Then he would get it out again in a week's time and repeat his actions. He knew from speaking with other artists he was not alone in going through this critique period.

As he focussed on the blustery, rain leaden, clouds within the sky, the brushstrokes laid down in tones of purple, ultramarine blue and pink, it reminded him of a word he had heard his dad use – *Dreich.* That summed the spirit of the painting perfectly he thought.

Bringing that word to mind suddenly conjured up feelings from the recent turmoil within his life. For a brief few second's images carouselled inside his head.

He shook himself and they cleared. He guessed it would be some time before they left him permanently – if they ever would. The main thing was that he and his dad had since reconciled their differences. And he had discovered new members of his family. He had travelled up to Scotland with his father to support him during his visit to Glasgow High

Court for the plea and directions hearing for Billy Wallace and Rab Geddes, charged with murder-times-five, and the attempted murder of his dad.

That court visit had proven to be shorter than expected. The pair had refused to come out of their prison cells for the hearing and refused to enter a plea and in their absence the judge had set a trial date for the second week in January the following year.

Hunter mentally diaried the date, so that he could take time off to support his father again when had to return to give evidence.

He had also spotted DCI Dawn Leggate at the court and taken her to one side to check on the prosecutions' case. On this occasion she was far more amenable, telling him that the evidence against the pair was overwhelming. So much so that she was expecting the pair to enter a guilty plea at the last moment. She added that the Procurator Fiscal was requesting an indeterminate life sentence for both men: the likely hood was that they would die in prison.

After that they had gone on to Belshill, his father's old home town, where he had been introduced to his dad's cousins. It had been a weekend of celebrations resulting in very thick head's for both of them. Since then he had witnessed a whole new mood change in his father's demeanour and they had spent some very enjoyable sessions together, especially down at the gym.

The ringing telephone, back in the lounge, broke his reverie. He heard Beth answer it.

"Hunter it's for you," she shouted, walking towards him, holding out the handset. "It's work."

He held up his hands to her, indicating they were smeared with oil paint.

She switched it to speaker phone and turned it towards him.

"Hello."

"DS Kerr?"

He recognised the voice of one of the duty group Inspectors. "Speaking."

"Sorry to disturb you at home. I know it's your long weekend off, but I've been asked to call you in. Some of my officers are at the scene of a derelict pub. A couple of builder's there have found the remains of a body in the cellar."

- ooOoo -

Read the first book in the D.S. Hunter Kerr series

Heart of the Demon

Detective Sergeant Hunter Kerr and his partner DC Grace Marshall are called to the scene of a brutal slaying; the victim is a 14 year-old girl.

The killer has been disturbed but he has left behind a puzzle. What is the significance of the marks gouged into the girl's torso and why has a playing card been left with the cadaver?

As Barnwell Major Investigation Team struggle to resolve the mystery they are confronted with another gruesome discovery; the mummified remains of a teenage girl are unearthed from the slurry of a former colliery site. This corpse bears all the hallmarks of the first slaying and yet this body has been buried for well over a decade.

They soon realise that a savage killer is stalking Yorkshire, preying on young girls, and with the discovery of the bodies comes a series of revelations about the past.

For Detective Sergeant Hunter Kerr and his team the race against time to prevent further murders is complicated by the fact that several of his men have been involved on the periphery of earlier crimes, without even knowing it. And as the death toll mounts as more bodies are unearthed and new victims succumb to the murderer's sick appetites, he finds that this case comes very close to home.

Very close indeed..

ISBN: 978-1-907565-26-7

Lightning Source UK Ltd.
Milton Keynes UK
UKOW031315110113

204755UK00002B/6/P